the heart

the reluctant romantics
book three

KATE STEWART

The Heart
The Reluctant Romantics (Book 3)
Copyright © 2016 Kate Stewart

Second edition edit by *Donna Cooksley Sanderson*
Cover Design: *QDesign*
Formatting: *Champagne Book Design*

dedication

For Seth and Laura

To my wonderful and beautiful readers,
I'm so thankful for every single one of you. Thank
you for taking a chance on my books out of the
millions to choose from.

For all those who have been with me since *ROOM 212,*
we have officially come to the end of an *era* together.
We have laughed, we have cried, yelled, and grown
together. Thank you for all the support.

To the ones who have just entered my crazy world,
from the bottom to the top of my heart, I'm honored
and beyond grateful.

We have many exciting and new things to come ;)

XO Kate

Jack

For the last ten years, I've roamed the globe, captivated by the world around me. I've seen the seven wonders and admired sunsets from every continent. I'd lived and loved, and that was enough for me. It would have to be.

I was content, satisfied with my collection of experiences . . . until a phone call led me down a road less traveled.

If I'd known my fascination would pique and be forever quenched only a few hundred miles from where my curiosity had been born, I may have never set sail.

Rose

Stripped of the future I'd planned with the love of my life, my family and my career were now all that mattered. I'd lived and loved, and that was enough. It would have to be.

I struggled to move forward, to discard the part of me that held out hope for my obliterated heart. But I was bred a romantic, so it was easier said than done.

The chances of being struck by lightning are 1 in 960,000.

The odds of being struck twice are 1 in 9 million.

I risked those odds every minute, often cursing the dark sky, praying for static and a rumble of thunder, but it never came.

No, that second bolt hit me on a clear day.

Jack

AT A YOUNG AGE, I LEARNED THAT I DON'T THINK, ACT, OR react like the rest of the world. It was either a result of my unique set of parents and their constant need to tell me what's what or just the fact that I felt different about things than others. It was my curiosity and the need to figure out things on my own that kept me introverted. I had a million questions, but I never wanted to ask them. I wanted to discover the answers for myself.

In fact, I remember my aggravation at finding out about Columbus's journey and the realization that the world was round. However, as I got older, I found it ridiculous. I remembered thinking a rite of passage had been stolen from me with that little piece of information. But as soon as I got it, I became hungry for more. The mysteries of the world around me intrigued me. Aside from the need to sail my own ship and find my own answers, I was fascinated by people and their emotions. My parents worried about me constantly, always encouraging me to get out and explore. But I knew better.

I didn't look like the rest of the world, either.

Most days, I kept myself company with my thoughts and my questions. When my parents forced me out of the house, I would spend my time at the damp, hot playground, ignoring the stares of the kids around me while I asked my little black notebook question after question.

As I grew a little older, my curiosity never lessened. Tenacity and technology had ensured a wealth of knowledge at my fingertips. I studied it all—religion, philosophy, politics, and my true love, geography. By the time I'd outgrown that playground and looked up from that notebook full of questions, everything had changed, and the world around me became even more of a mystery. Everything was different, and so was I.

I started living and losing like the rest of the world, determined to do it better.

I failed.

And the questions came back.

If I had only known my fascination would reach its pique and remain quenched just a few hundred miles from where my curiosity was born, I might have never let my ship sail.

I couldn't stop it. It was a simultaneous failure of limbs and brain cells. His lips touched mine softly, and I let out an unexpected moan. He pulled back and watched me, hands still on both sides of my face. "Did you feel that?"—Rose & Grant (The Mind)

chapter
one

"If the Lord can create the world and all its inhabitants in seven days, you can get out of bed, Rose."

"CLAMPS," I BARKED AS I GRIPPED THE BILE DUCT WITH my forceps.

"I'm bored," Dr. McGuire said. My hands froze as I looked up at him. His eyes were hard to read due to his frown lines being so prominent all of the time. Between his facemask and his surgical cap, I was at a loss.

My surgical tech, Jamie, and I looked at each other in confusion before I spoke up. "I'm sorry, sir, is there something—"

"No, Rose, it's nothing you've done. It's a fact. I'm bored." He pulled off his gloves and motioned for another resident to step in. "Don't kill the patient, and don't make me regret this. Meet me in my office when you've closed up."

I nodded, both elated and terrified that I was finishing a surgery without my mentor. I just hoped it meant what I thought it did—and I was pretty sure it did. I winked at Jules, the anesthesiologist, and she took my cue as Nicki Minaj's "Moment 4 Life" started thumping through the room.

"Jamie," I piped as I carefully disposed of Mrs. Carter's useless gallbladder, "why don't you tell us how it went with… ?"

Jules let out a small snort, and I knew the beans had already been spilled to her. I lived vicariously through the two J's, and though they had dragged me out a night or two, I'd barely survived. I envied the two in that they were fearless in their pursuit of Mr. Right, or in their case, Mr. Always Something Wrong.

"I've gone on two dates with him. It's time you learned his name," Jamie shot back defensively.

"Forgive me," I said with an eye roll.

"His name is Bart." I pressed my lips into a line, though I was sure she could see my bubbling laughter.

"Parents can be so cruel," Jules said as she checked Mrs. Carter's vitals.

"Shut up," Jamie snapped in Jules' direction as she turned back to me with offended features. "Anyway, I like him for now. We're kind of testing the waters," Jamie said as she handed me the staple gun. I took my time fastening the skin as I quizzed my friend on her newest manventure.

"So, how is he?" I asked, knowing my question wouldn't offend her. She had no issue with casual sex.

"Well, if it's any indication, his name is *Bart,* and I'm giving him a third date," she said with a chuckle, holding the skin as I angled the gun.

"Yeah, I'm thinking this is a good thing since you dumped the last guy for eating SPAM." I chuckled, and Jules joined me.

"It wasn't *SPAM*. It was a pickled sausage, and his breath smelled like shit. And he left the wrapper in my car! Do you have *any* idea what that smells like after a day in the Texas heat? It took two weeks for me to get rid of it. It smelled like vinegar and soured ass. No, no way… I was justified in getting rid of that guy." She shook her head back and forth adamantly. "Nope, you just can't trust a man who eats processed meat." She puffed her cheeks out, then made a gagging noise.

Jules and I shook our heads with matching smiles on our

faces. Jamie was a single mom who had two loves in her life—her little boy, Drew, and the men she dated—which she kept completely separate. I respected her for it. She was forced to raise a man alone and did it without so much as an occasional whine session. I'd hoped for Jamie's sake that Bart might be the man capable of adding to Jamie's life in a way that he would eventually be granted the gift of meeting her son. Though she truly felt she didn't need the help, she deserved the love.

I smiled with pride as another successful surgery came to an end, then leaned in and whispered to Mrs. Carter. Once satisfied with my handiwork, I pulled my smock off and began to grow curious about McGuire's sudden mood swing.

"What do you think he wants?" Jules asked, reading my mind.

"Who knows? I'm pretty sure I'm safe, don't worry," I assured her, pulling off my mask.

"Want to meet up with us in an hour?" Jamie said, looking at me, equally concerned.

"Yeah, let's do lunch inside today. It's too damned hot." The two women nodded and went about their jobs as they always did. I was determined to take them with me to the center once I left Memorial. We worked so well together, and though they knew I was opening a center, neither of them let on that they wanted to come with me. I was hoping they were just waiting for an invitation— one I was most definitely going to give.

"Come in, Dr. Whitaker," McGuire barked as he threw a newspaper down on his desk. I took a seat opposite him. I didn't have to look at the paper to know he'd been reading the article announcing the center's opening.

"We've spent the last few years in surgery together. Should I be offended about this news not coming from the source?"

"No, sir, not at all. I just didn't feel it was appropriate."

"How would it be inappropriate? It's medical-related, and it's actually quite impressive. You're months away from being a senior resident, and I have no doubt you'll be named chief. I had plans for you." He sat back in his chair, his hands on the armrests as he scrutinized me. "You were a shoo-in for my fellowship."

I couldn't help my slight eye bulge and broad smile.

"That can't happen now, Dr. Whitaker."

"No, sir, I'm aware," I said, slightly disheartened yet elated at the same time. I sat quietly as he studied me.

"You're wasting your time here. You know the ins and outs of the basics, and right now, it's like a jail sentence to you. Aside from the limited rare cases that everyone fights for, there is nothing I can teach you that you haven't already learned.

"Sir, we've done nothing but open technique. If I can just try my hands at laparo—"

"I'm aware that we haven't operated *laparoscopic*. I'm not some dinosaur who believes I'll be replaced by machines and afraid to adapt to newer, better, and less evasive procedures. I was the first to use that technique in this hospital. It's important to learn both. I didn't feel I needed to explain myself to you."

"No, sir," I said as I sank a little into my seat.

Teacher, student, McGuire, got it.

"While I commend you on your future plans, I must say I'm a little disappointed that I have no other candidate for my fellowship as of now. I'm sure someone will come along, more in tune, more attentive, and more talented than you, but until that day comes, I'm going to govern over your surgical education with good care. You and your sister have taken on one hell of a feat, and you need to be prepared. You being my priority, until I find someone else to mentor, I will have to insist you start standing in on some surgeries more involved in your new specialty."

"Yes, sir," I said, having a ridiculously hard time hiding my excitement.

"Good," he said, standing and removing his lab coat before replacing it with a pea coat. "You're on call for the next three days. Get some R & R. Actually, my advice to you is to live a little, Dr. Whitaker. And when you return, get ready to get uncomfortable again."

I knew what that meant. I would be a bit clueless in the operating room like I was the first day of surgery and, the day after that, and the weeks and months that followed. No matter how prepared I thought I was or how confident, the skilled surgeons had made it their mission to rattle me to the core.

As I exited Dr. McGuire's office, I was thankful for that damned article. In its own way, it was just the pat on the shoulder I needed to keep going.

"You know, Rose, I know you feel it, too. It's okay to be a little afraid. But this is how the good ones start."
"The good ones?"
"The great ones. This will be a great one." – Grant

chapter
two

*"If a pilot can land a plane safely on the
Hudson and save one hundred and fifty-five
people, you can get out of bed, Rose."*

"AUNT WOSE," GRANT SAID, TUGGING AT MY SCRUBS.
"Aunt Wose!" He had been chasing the ducks for
the better part of twenty minutes while I remained
lost in thought. "Come on, Aunt Wose!" I watched Grant as he
wiggled his little body onto the passenger seat of the golf cart,
waving his arms. "Wet's go, wet's go!"

I grinned at him. "Okay, buddy." This would be our fourth
trip within the hour. I took one last look at the pond and jumped
in the seat next to Grant as he clapped with excitement. "Okay,
baby blue, let's go," I said, putting the golf cart into gear and making our way down the paved sidewalk and through the grounds.
It was a hot August day, and I was thankful for the light breeze
as we made our way from the pond back to the center. We were
building one of the largest cancer treatment centers in Texas and
had expanded it to the point of needing transportation from one
building to the next. Not to mention the one-and-a-half-mile trek
back to my house, which sat at the very back of the land. Some
days, especially on hot days like this, it was too far to walk.

"Faster, Aunt Wose." Grant giggled as we took a speed

bump, arms flailing in the air, his face animated. I pressed the gas and took another, launching us into the air a bit just to hear the giggle I loved so much. When we made it back to the main building, I parked the cart, then grabbed Grant before he could get away, pulling him into my arms as I covered him in kisses.

"Aunt Wose, no! I big boy now."

"Oh no you're not! You'll always be my baby," I said, nuzzling his neck as he squirmed in my arms. He was only twenty months old but had assumed the role of the man in my life. Grant had a head of thick black hair and clear blue dazzling eyes like his father, Dean, but when it came to attitude, he was my sister, Dallas.

"Who told you that you were a big boy?"

"Mommy towd me. I pee peed in da potty today," he said as he wiggled down onto the pavement.

"You pee peed in the potty!" I clapped excitedly, chasing him around the cart as he squealed and ran to get away from me. I caught him, then lifted him high above me. He started to protest when I again soaked him in another set of unwanted kisses. I checked for a diaper and was relieved when I could still feel the bulge of it in his pants.

I wasn't ready.

I looked up to find we had an admirer approaching us. My instinct had me pulling Grant tighter to me, but when I got a better view, I almost dropped my precious nephew. The stranger was tall and hellishly built. His short hair scattered perfectly around his crown in varying shades of blond. His eyes were somewhere between blue and gray and were outlined with the thickest lashes I had ever seen. His masculine features were in perfect symmetry. His only flaw, if you could even call it that, was a faint white scar on the top of his lip. He was the whole fucking package, the second coming of Brad Pitt from the movie *Thelma and Louise*.

His smile seemed genuine, and I couldn't help but take in the way his white dress shirt clung to his chest in the Texas heat.

"Aunt Wose, wet me go!" I snapped out of my daze, kissed Grant again, and then set him down.

"Can I help you?"

"You must be Rose."

"Yes," I said, curious as to how he knew who I was.

"You look a lot like your dad." I ran through the scenarios of who he could be, then jumped a little in recognition.

"Jack," I said with an easy smile. "My dad told me you were coming today. How was your trip? Alabama, right?"

"Louisiana, actually, New Orleans," he said with a proper Cajun accent sliding off his tongue as he took a long look around the massive complex with a whistle. "You know, when your dad told me what he was up to, I knew I had to jump on board. This is going to be exactly what you and your sister imagined it to be. I'll make sure of it." He looked back at me and gave me a wink as little hands gripped my scrubs again, and the three of us walked through the entrance.

"Aunt Wose?" Grant asked, eyeing our stranger with caution and slight disdain.

"What is it, buddy," I asked, having a horrible time ripping my eyes away from our visitor.

"Can I have an ice pop?"

"Sure, baby blue," I said, looking down at him and then back at Jack. "Will you excuse me? I need to go find his mom and get an ice pop. We can meet you back here for a tour."

"Of course." He nodded as I took Grant's hand, then went in search of Dallas. I found her in her newly finished office, roaming over paperwork with a fidgety eleven-month-old Annabelle in her lap. Much like Grant, her daughter looked nothing like her, either. I found it hilarious.

She addressed me before I had a chance to speak. "Have you seen a Spaniard around? Tall, gorgeous, and very close to being castrated?"

Before I could answer, Grant had a roundabout question of his own. "Mommy, Aunt Wose, ice pop?"

Dallas caught on, narrowing her eyes at me. She was all wrathy today, and I could feel it rolling off her.

"It's just a little fruit juice," I defended with a roll of my eyes as I walked across the hall to the half-finished break room and grabbed a pop from the freezer.

"I can't believe Dean's not here! I'm screwed. He was supposed to be here an hour ago before the subcontractor came!" she huffed in frustration.

"Jack is in the lobby waiting for us," I confirmed with a wince.

"Shit," she said, flustered as Annabelle ripped at her shirt with chubby hands. She stood and made her way to her office blinds to get a look at Jack. I saw her body stiffen before she turned to me with a slow smile spreading across her face. I hated that smile. It reminded me of the torturous antics I'd had to endure from her as a child. "Sorry, Rose, you're on your own."

"No way. Dad isn't here, either, and I can't answer all his questions! I'll watch the babies. You go."

Although I knew the basic plans for the center inside and out, I wasn't as versed in the details as my dad, who hadn't arrived yet, or Dallas, who'd been by his side handling everything while I spent the majority of my days completing my surgical residency at Dallas Memorial. I had a little less than two years to complete my residency. My days off were devoted to the center, but those days were few and far between.

"Sorry, I have the boobs this one needs, and as you can see, she's starving." I looked at a perfectly content Annabelle and narrowed my eyes at Dallas.

"He's hot."

"So what?" I said, crossing my arms over my chest.

"He's waiting, that's what." Dallas dismissed me, taking her seat behind her desk before waving me away as if that was the end of it.

I wanted to debate her on what was truly important in this situation, but I knew just how hard she was working to get the center ready. I couldn't give her hell when I'd been more absent than present.

"Fine."

Jack was in the lobby where I left him. The incessant noise of power tools kept him from hearing my approach. His back was to me, and he was peering through the glass behind what would eventually be an atrium. Instead of interrupting his assessment, I waited for him to turn around.

Okay, maybe I was staring at his ass.

After endless seconds of ogling his tall frame and sexy derrière, I finally spoke up. "How about a tour?!" I yelled over a newly running saw. When he didn't respond, I lightly tapped his shoulder and caught his reflection in the glass. He'd seen me checking him out and was grinning from ear to ear.

Way to be professional, Whitaker.

Aside from looking the last year, I had done no touching. My heart still wasn't in it, no matter who caught my eye. I was determined to get back on the horse—at least in the physical sense—but I was hesitant when it came to execution, not that I'd had many opportunities.

Jack turned to me as if I hadn't just feasted on his perfect, jean-clad ass.

"Sounds good. I've already taken a quick tour of the main

floor and can see your headache coming. Why don't we tour the grounds first?"

"I don't see how you can stand the noise," I said, making my way to the double glass doors of the entrance.

"I love the noise. It lets me know I'm building something," he replied. He started to ask questions right away, and I made notes of anything I couldn't answer. As the queries continued, I caught his gaze on my lips more than once. I had a horrible time looking away from the eyes that seemed to be saying something else entirely.

As we made our way outside, I searched the parking lot for my dad's truck but came up empty—I was completely on my own.

Jack and I made our way to the golf cart so I could show him the rest of the grounds. The tour became more intimate in our proximity, and I suddenly wished I had checked my appearance before jumping on the cart. Then again, it was so hot I couldn't afford to give a damn. I fisted my wild mane through a hair tie on top of my head for some relief, knowing I probably looked like the adult version of Pebbles from *The Flintstones.*

"As I'm sure you know by the blueprints, this will be a full-service facility. Using a holistic approach, we'll care for patients with advanced cases in-house through the course of their entire treatment. We want to do something a little different than pump them full of meds, send them home, and hope for shrinking tumors. We want to provide everything from initial diagnosis and treatment to aftercare, including diet, mental, and spiritual ways to help boost morale during recovery.

"Look at the alternative," I said, turning the key to the cart before I shifted the gear. "You get your chemo in the local hospital, go home and throw up alone at night while trying to hide it from your spouse and terrified children, then go back to work

a zombie without any strength. Dallas and I are all for the independent fighter, but we want to change the way this disease
is looked at and treated. It's strongly due to Dallas's input and
her experience as an oncologist. Ultimately, it was her idea to
approach treatment as both mental and physical, and not just
with a stick of the needle. And here we are."

He remained quiet, and I began to worry if I'd sold him on
the idea. Although his purpose was to prepare the facility, I was
curious about his opinion.

"So, we grow our own food here to serve the patients. We'll
insist on a strict diet right away—a one hundred percent organic
diet—and that's non-negotiable for all our patients for obvious
reasons. Most will feel the effects within the first few weeks."

"I wasn't aware of this," Jack said, surveying our fields.

"It wasn't in the original plans, just an afterthought. It will
all be donated from me to the center because it's technically my
farm. We'll ensure the food is tested regularly and meets USDA
standards, but it cuts costs tremendously."

"Rose, this is really incredible. What made you decide to
open a center?"

"We thought we could do better than simply opening a general practice. It was a lot of things, really. A lot of things," I said
absently. "So, we did better, I hope."

"That's a coincidence. That's my uncle's motto," he said as
he continued his perusal of the never-ending view.

"What was?" I asked as I steered us down the path toward
the rest of the facilities. I looked over at him for his response and
gave pause when he gave me a heart-stopping grin.

"Do better."

We took a speed bump at max speed due to my inability to
tear my eyes away from Jack. I hit my head hard on the top of
the cart and bit my tongue as Jack cursed and grabbed the wheel

before we had a chance to abandon the pavement. I managed to stop the cart despite the blinding pain, then jumped out in an all-out fit—including tears in my eyes. I jumped around, hysterically flailing my arms, the pain so intense I was wailing new words. "Ghardam, mupherfuter, whatdem hell, owe." Suddenly whisked into Jack's arms, he sat down on the grass with me on his lap and stilled me.

"Talk to me, Rose. Is it your head?"

I put my fingers to my lips, recognizing the metallic taste.

"Spit it out, Rose. Let me see your mouth." I spat out the contents of my mouth, then opened wide for him to see.

"Stick out your tongue," he coaxed gently. I have no idea why I did what he was asking. Maybe it was the pain. Maybe it was because the initial humiliation wasn't enough for me, and I wanted to make sure to finish myself off.

"Well, you bit the hell out of your tongue, but I think you'll survive." Noticing the pain-induced tears sliding down my cheeks, Jack whisked them away with his fingertips as we sat in the middle of my busy and budding complex. I took in his clean scent as my eyes remained blurred with the intensity of my injured tongue. When the pain began to subside, and I realized we were simply staring at each other—our posture incredibly intimate—I jerked back, then jumped from his lap, making quick work of resuming my seat in the cart. He slowly stood up, brushed the grass off his jeans, and then slid back into his seat, his lips pressed firmly together.

I took off again at a snail's pace as Jack chuckled. I couldn't bear to look at him. When I'd gathered some of my wits back, I stopped in front of a field and tried my best to speak a clear sentence.

"Obder der is the farlm."

Jack looked at me with wide eyes and declared, "I think we're done for the day." There was no masking his hysterical laughter, and after a few indignant seconds, I joined in, then winced at the pounding in my head and my throbbing tongue. When our laughter dwindled, I glanced his way as he turned to look at me to make one last joke. "Sure you can handle a scalpel?"

I gave him a warning glare. "Wabt to pway cadaver?" Another bout of laughter kept Jack occupied as I turned the cart around and hauled ass back to the main building.

When we reached the entrance, my dad was waiting in the lobby. He profusely apologized to us both, saying traffic was hell. Shortly after, the flustered and out-of-breath Spaniard, who belonged to my sister, hauled ass into the lobby and straight past us with a quick hello. His ass was grass—traffic or not—and he knew it. I grinned as I thought of that confrontation and the inevitable make up. My sister and her husband were more than entertaining to watch.

"Seth, this is incredible," Jack complimented, giving my dad a congratulatory handshake and pat on the back. It was odd seeing someone close to my age act so informally with my dad. I knew they had worked a few jobs together, but I wasn't sure how well they knew each other until now. If my dad trusted him, then I trusted him. It was a simple decision.

Excusing myself, Jack gave me a distracted "Thank you for the tour" as I stepped away in search of medical help. I found her doing inventory in the supply closet. I looked around for a scorned Dean but could not find him.

"Dabas, heeelp," I cried as she glanced at me with a look of alarm.

I stuck out my tongue, which I could tell was swelling, as she studied it with large eyes.

"What in the hell happened, Rose? So, you had *that* much

fun on your tour?" The tears fell fast as she chuckled, then com-
forted me with a "Poor baby, I've got this."

Later that night—after passing on dinner with Jack and the rest
of my family to tend to my bruised ego and swollen tongue—I
spent my time looking around my empty house.

"How much do you own?"

"All of it. As far as you can see."

"It's amazing."

*"Glad you like it because we're going to build our house today,
Rose."*

"What? I'm not qualified to do that!"

"Neither am I. We're just daydreaming here."

I had built the ranch home Grant and I dreamed up that
beautiful day on our pond—the day when my heart had found
its home. I surveyed the large kitchen and the extra living room.
I was the lone occupant of a house that deserved a family. Despite my dad's protests to build something new, something different, I had insisted on building the exact home Grant and I had
intended. And while I loved every square inch of it, it brought
me little comfort. Honestly, it made me feel more alone.

My gaze drifted through the floor-to-ceiling windows onto
the moonlit pond. I flipped the switch to the back porch, illuminating the large space with strategically placed lights. My back
porch—along with the house—was nothing short of spectacular. The stone waterfall lit up at intervals in alternating shades of
blue, the fire pit had never been used, and I couldn't ever remember abusing the deck for a day in the sun. Sighing, I returned to
my empty house, flipping the switch and ending my private party.

After draining a half bottle of white wine, I slipped into bed, thinking of Jack and his blue-gray eyes. Wincing at the twitch of my sore tongue, I remembered how quickly after I'd met him, I'd made a fool of myself. It had felt foreign, but at the same time, it was good to be in a man's arms again—even if it was only for a brief moment.

"I want you," he said as water cascaded around his perfect features. "I've had enough years of doing the wrong shit and being with the wrong women. I took one look at you, and a thousand memories we hadn't made hit me in waves. I can't explain it, and it may seem fast to you, but to me, it's as natural as taking my next breath."— Grant

chapter
three

"If a seventy-three-year-old man can swim the English Channel, you can get out of bed, Rose."

THREE DAYS AT THE CENTER. THREE FULL DAYS! I sat up in bed and stretched my arms and legs, feeling fully rested. Ready to give Dallas a much-needed break, I rushed through a shower and threw on some shorts and an old T-shirt. I raced to my cart, eager to get to the center and feel a little more involved in the goings-on and a little less guilty about my continued absence. I met Dallas at the double doors as she was walking out. She hooked her arm around mine and changed my direction as she pulled me toward the parking lot.

"Nope, not today or tomorrow. They're delivering and installing all of the medical equipment, and it's going to be way too crazy in there, even for us. Mom's got the kids, and Dean and I are headed to Shreveport."

"What?!"

"He's on his way." She clapped excitedly. "You know I've never been to a casino. I've never even been to Louisiana."

"Yeah," I said, disheartened.

Dallas looked at me, then pulled me to her in a brief hug. "It's okay, Rose. No one blames you for doing what you have to do, like at all. You can't be the surgeon we need you to be *here* if you don't put in the time *there*. We've mapped this out for years. It's all falling into place. We're all proud of you. Just take a day, live a little."

"Why does everyone keep telling me that!?"

"Because you need it!" she said, exasperated. "We all do. Even Dad is a little burned out."

"Daddy's burned out?" My shoulders slumped as I thought of how hard my dad was working on this project of ours.

"Jesus, Rose, get that guilty fornicating-nun look off your face. Dad's home with Mom, and they are probably arguing about the remote or what to feed the babies. Just go home, sit on that amazing deck, and get some sun, or invite the J's over and have a drink or six. Just do something *other* than work."

"Yeah," I agreed easily with a nod, knowing I'd do none of those things.

"Jack will need someone here or close by just in case he's got any questions. He's really got his shit together and knows what he's doing, but I told him where to find you."

"At home." I smiled ironically.

"Yeah," she said as she pulled her dark hair into a smart bun and fastened it on her head.

"That's okay, right?" She eyed me with caution, still fearing I would break down at any moment. I hated that I made her feel that way at any point. I was almost sure those days were safely behind me.

"Of course," I said as Dean pulled up and exited his sleek Jag to open the door for Dallas. Excitement danced all over his handsome features as he gave me a killer smile.

"Morning, Rose."

"Morning, Dean," I said as he pulled his wife to him for what looked like a promising kiss. I felt myself sink further into a pit of despair and rolled my eyes at my own selfishness.

Whatever, I can totally do time off.

Dallas turned back to me—a thought I was sure I didn't want to be voiced crossing her mind. "You know *Jack* is staying at a motel just down the highway. He's probably alone at night and could use a little company."

"I'm not going to bone the subcontractor, Dallas." Dean chuckled as he opened the trunk, fidgeting with their packed bags.

Dallas looked at me pointedly. "You could do worse."

"Fine, so he's hot as sin, but from what I could tell, he doesn't have much of a personality. He's all business behind that body, and I'm not into boring. I'm boring enough."

Just as the words passed my lips, we heard the rumble of a motorcycle approaching, and the three of us looked toward it in confusion. Jack pulled up on a newer model Harley, completely unaware of his audience. His eyes were hidden behind aviators, and he was jean-clad with a simple white T-shirt. He was a wet dream as he tapped out his kickstand in old dusty work boots and killed the ignition. I stood stunned for a moment before my sister cleared her throat. Hesitant to look in her direction, both Dean and Dallas stared at me with amused expressions, Dean even more so as he tapped the hood of his Jaguar with a lifted brow.

"Yeah, I can see how you wouldn't find him interesting," Dallas said with a knowing smirk. "Now look, honey," Dallas said sarcastically, "all the grown-ups are occupied this weekend. You'll just have to find a way to entertain yourself." She blew me a kiss before she joined Dean in the car. Just as she shut her door, he pushed an exaggerated foot on the gas and shot out of the parking lot like a bat out of hell, honking as they passed Jack. I laughed at them before I caught sight of Jack and fully drank him in.

I could still feel the rumble of that bike vibrate through me as he approached with a lady-killer smile. "Was that Dallas and Dean? They said they might take off. I bet they'll love Shreveport. It's no Nola, but it'll do in a pinch."

Jack stopped to stand in front of me. The bright, early morning sun made me squint as I looked at him. With his shades still on, it was hard to gauge what he was thinking, and I suddenly felt like a slob. Very aware my hair was still wet, an involuntary shiver danced through the top of my shoulders. I held my hand up to shield my eyes and tilted my head to get a better look at him.

"Ah, so it was your idea for my sister and her husband to gamble away my niece and nephew's future."

"Guilty," he admitted with a slow grin.

"Well," I said, "good for you. I guess a guilty conscience doesn't bother you."

"Not often, no." He smiled fully. "Everyone's got to roll the dice at least once." He looked toward the way of Dean's now invisible car, then back at me. "How's that tongue of yours?"

I froze, completely affected by him and his clean scent—a mix of something heavenly with a little sun and sweat. Beads of perspiration knotted on the smooth white scar above his top lip, and I was tempted to wipe them away so I could get a better look.

"It's much better. Thank you."

Live a little. Ask him over for dinner. Something simple. You can make that four-step goulash. It will be informal. It's just dinner. He's alone. You're alone—just a simple invite. You promised yourself, Rose.

Jack cleared his throat just as an eighteen-wheeler slowly climbed to the circular drive in front of the center.

"Well," Jack said as he stole a glance at the intrusive truck before he turned back to me, "that's my cue."

And I'd just missed mine.

Still standing in front of him, gathering my courage, I went to speak as he lifted his hands to his sunglasses, sliding them off slowly so our eyes met before turning them to place them on me with the same slow precision. "These look better on you. How about you hold on to them for me."

Stunned at the personal gesture and relieved at the renewed ability of sight, I drank him in one last time. "If you need me, you know where to find me."

He nodded, tucked his full bottom lip under his teeth, and then scraped it slowly before releasing it.

"You'll find my phone number on an extra set of golf cart keys in the break room," I added, throwing my shoulders back, a move I often did when I was nervous and had no need to be. Except the minute I did it, my chest bounced slightly, and he noticed.

"Sounds good," he said as the driver of the truck jumped out of the cab and walked toward us.

You're running out of time.

"Thanks for the loan," I said as I pointed to the glasses like an idiot. His full smile was my reply as I dismissed myself and made my way back to the cart on shaky legs.

Jack

Loyalty is a bitch I would love to screw.

And as I watched Rose walk away, it's what kept my feet planted and my lips off the pulse point that had jumped in her neck while she stood in front of me. Hair on fire—with help from the sun—her green eyes scoured me and made my chest raw. Her eyes weren't so innocent in their assessment of me, either. Not once had she taken them away from my scar, but I didn't hide it or shy away from it as I did years ago. I'd outgrown it. It had been a long damn time since I felt that strong of a pull for any woman. The minute I had her in my lap a few days ago, I'd wanted to close the gap, to taste and savor. Women were no easy feat for me, never had been. Looking at Rose made me want to forget that and dive in head first with no idea of how deep the water was. I'd ignored that urge and attraction enough times in my life to know I could handle it now.

But even as I thought that, I was reminded of why I was on Texas soil, sweating my ass off in the heat instead of being deeply lost in the Himalayas, a trip I'd planned six months ago.

I hid my grin as I took the clipboard from the truck driver, unable to keep from looking in the direction she left. Rose was in a league of her own. She was ambitious, determined, abso-lutely beautiful...*and Seth's daughter.*

I would be in and out in a matter of days. My suitcase was packed. I would still make my trip, even if the most beautiful thing about Texas had nothing to do with the landscape.

Rose

There are stupid things humans do and things that are the kind of stupid we convince ourselves we can't possibly do. For in-stance, my inability to put myself out of my misery for fear of imbalance and upsetting the stupid rules I'd laid down for myself when it came to mourning Grant. It was at least a hun-dred degrees outside, and I refused to jump into the pond. It was one of the Band-Aids I hadn't ripped off yet. I'd never been in there without Grant. And like many *things* that I'd decided were *our* things, that was one of them. I fell in love with him on a day just like today.

"*I'm not giving up,*" *he said, cutting his eyes at me as I remained in the water.* "*I might be a little ticked off with myself right now—bearing my soul to you like this, saying all these things I never thought I would say to a woman and making a damn fool of myself—but I'm not giving up.*"

"*I don't know what to say, Grant.*"

"*Stay with me, here, today. That's enough.*"

I looked up at our live oak tree—now encased by the deck—and glanced at the initials he'd carved in it.

"Not today," I said to myself. "Today is about Rose." I sat back and rubbed more SPF 50 all over as the sun made mincemeat out of me. Twenty minutes later, my mind racing with thoughts I didn't want to deal with, I turned on my outdoor sound system and walked over to the running waterfall. The reservoir was far too small to take a dip in, but I pushed my hands through the running stream and splashed the chemical-filled water all over my body.

"You're being ridiculous!" I said as I eyed the pond like a cartoon animal would a juicy steak. Larry, Curly, and Moe, my pet ducks, floated across the beckoning oasis in mocking as I splashed around the recycled water, desperately trying to cool off. Even the running water had no chance in this type of sun. It was lukewarm at best. I walked out to the edge of the water and dipped a toe in.

"*Rose, maybe you've convinced yourself you're incapable of love right now, or even worse, not worthy of it. Don't let one dickhead cheat you out of what every single person on earth deserves.*"

"*And what's that?*" *I whispered, completely leveled by his kiss.*

"*Love, baby, love. It's your time to be loved, and I'm the one who's going to do it.*"

When I moved in, I'd promised myself that I would ask the family over, have barbecues, and teach little Grant and Annabelle how to fish. I swore I wouldn't use the house as a museum or a shrine to the life I was supposed to live with the man who helped me dream it up. But those invitations to my family had yet to be sent. Grant and Anna's fishing poles remained in the packaging untouched because I had failed to treat the house I lived in as anything other than the boneyard of dreams it was.

It was so fucked up because, in so many ways, I wanted the carpet stained a bit. I wanted a little wear and tear to show some signs of life in a house that was built with so much love and meaning behind it. I wanted to make it a home. In my mind, I could never leave it, but in reality, I couldn't live fully in it… not yet.

I'd recently read in a book appropriately named *A Love So Tragic* that *"just because the person died doesn't mean the love does."* Those words had never been truer for me. And that's how I'd lived for the past few years—in love without the object of my affection. Death had taken him away, but what I felt for him remained. At first, it was a type of safety net for me, a way of keeping the promise to myself that I would never forget him. I made a conscious effort every day to remember every detail of our relationship. It kept Grant and I close, yet he was impossibly far away. Now, it was a ritual I cherished. The emotions that went along with remembering how it felt to be with him and surrender to that type of love came with a pain so intense that it resonated with my breaths and bliss so unique it was impossible to explain.

I'd found something so rare with Grant Foster. It could never be replicated or replaced. Our life together was small in measure, though in my lifetime, it remained the most important piece. I hadn't thrown my career or goals away when he died, and of that fact, I was proud. But as I lay on the deck, the thought occurred to me—as it did often—that I wouldn't ever be whole unless I resumed the other part of living, the part that included a personal life, and one without Grant. It seemed a daunting feat even years later.

Unable to face the truth I'd presented to myself, I gave up on my pursuit of sun and took up residence on my bed, sorting through my Kindle, looking for a distraction—medical journals, romance…erotica. I browsed through the smut-filled pages as I thought of the sex toy Jules had given me for my birthday. She'd shoved it in my locker at the hospital with a large bottle of Maker's Mark, my favorite poison. The toy was still wrapped in plastic, and for a brief moment, I entertained the idea of self-gratification. If I thought I'd had a dry spell before Grant came and went, I was in an all-out drought at this point.

My phone buzzed with a picture from Dallas—a roadside sign showing they had just reached Shreveport. I knew she'd sent it so I wouldn't worry, but I couldn't help the fact that it only made me feel a bit shittier. All thoughts of sex dissipated. Suddenly feeling more restless than ever, I made a quick decision and pulled out my tablet. I clicked the links to locate my online piggy bank. I'd been saving in the account since I was seven. My dad had started it for me and told me it was good practice for investing later on. I'd never touched it. I'd only added money as the years went by. I'd never needed it. But now, with all my earnings tied up in school, the house, and the center, I didn't have much to spare. It took me a good thirty minutes to remember the password, and when I saw the balance, I jerked back in surprise.

Live a little.

This is an emotional purchase. There isn't a damn thing wrong with your SUV, woman. Walk away, Rose.

After seeing the balance in my ancient piggy bank, I'd decided to go car shopping, and not exactly the kind of car shopping that a sensible doctor in debt for the next twenty-plus years would do.

As soon as I was behind the wheel, all I could hear were those three words.

Soft leather cradled me as I breathed in its delicious scent. I trailed my fingers along the dash with reverence as the salesperson did their best to sway me.

"I'll take it," I interrupted as the surprised rep eyed me behind the wheel with admiration. My confidence shot to new heights as I threw caution to the wind and bought my dream car. I signed on the dotted line and arranged to have my SUV delivered back to my house. And I wasn't finished.

I celebrated with a belly full of rich pasta and a glass of wine at one of the hundred new restaurants that had popped up in Dallas while I'd been in a career coma. Though I cringed the whole time, I went shopping and bought clothes that could never resemble scrubs. I threw bags of new designer jeans, two new dresses, and T-shirts that I could never afford to stain or replace in the back of my new convertible.

I stopped in a salon and got a Brazilian blowout and wax. The wax ended up being less adventure, more nightmare, especially after the lady who greeted me declared, "You're so very hairy." I twitched like I was being electrocuted as my calloused, neglected feet were scrubbed raw, and my toes were painted to match the color of my new car. Once pampered—if you could even call it that—I treated myself to a massage and facial. At twenty-eight years old, aside from the week before my wedding that never took place. I'd never given myself a day like that and instantly regretted it. I'd been a tree-climbing tomboy in my youth, an introvert in college and medical school, and at the moment, I had no idea who I was outside of being a surgeon. I knew that I'd always admired women who took pride in their appearance. Suddenly, I no longer had an excuse not to become one of them. But my newly polished outside had nothing to do with who I was now on the inside. For years, I'd felt broken to the point where who I'd become was the last of my worries. Only concentrating on getting through the day-to-day, self-discovery was the furthest thing from my mind. I loved food and rap music, but neither of those was a hobby.

I was in serious need of a life, one that existed outside of Dallas Memorial. My growing family and the center had managed to keep me busy in my off time, and though I was dedicated to them now more than ever, I was lacking. I'd often thought of leaving it all behind, exploring places I'd only seen in movies or read about in magazines. And though the idea appealed to me on some level, my feet were cemented in a dream that started long ago. Deciding that my trip to the city and a little self-indulgence was a good first step, I smiled, grateful for what I had because it was a hell of a lot.

Later that day, I pulled into the center just as the sun was setting. I sat idling in my new car as I watched the workers trickle out of the massive building and pack up. Jack's bike was still there, so I knew he must be exhausted. For some reason, instead of checking the progress of the clinic, I decided to keep the day for myself. I reached into my purse, gripped Jack's aviators, and walked over to his bike, placing his borrowed shades on his seat.

Getting back into my convertible, I reached behind the passenger seat to pull out my new sunglasses and put them on with a smile.

I pulled up to my dimly lit house and listened as the ducks greeted me and followed me into my driveway. "You guys shit on this one, and we'll be having duck for dinner tomorrow," I scolded, knowing it was useless. I put the top up and made my way inside with my bags.

After an hour of looking through everything I'd bought, I decided days like the one I had today were way too expensive. Still, I couldn't help but linger on a metallic blue bra and panty set I'd purchased on impulse. I may not be ready today or tomorrow to share myself that way, but when I was, I would look the part. I slipped on the satin and stood back, evaluating the way I looked. What curves I had were accentuated by the fabric that now felt like a second skin.

Expensive underwear is worth it.

My skin felt amazing from the massage and was glowing slightly from the small amount of sun I'd gotten. My long red hair felt like silk on my shoulders and looked polished and… beautiful. I looked down at my ruby-red toes, admiring the day's handiwork. It was the first time I'd felt beautiful in years. I was glowing, and my reflection confirmed it.

I walked over to my closet, pulled out the only pair of heels I owned, and slipped them on, feeling the burn start in my calves as I wondered how women wore them every day. I may never be one of those women, but right then, I felt sexy in my attempt.

Discarding the pumps, I pushed my shoulders back. "I can still do sexy." I beamed at my reflection, my confidence at a welcomed high.

"Jesus Christ!" I heard a voice boom behind me through my open bedroom door that led to the back patio. Jack stood with palms toward me, fingers spread. "I came to give you the cart

the *heart*   29

keys back. Fuck… I can't… when I saw you in nothing but your underwear, I didn't know if I should announce myself or turn back, but I was already halfway to the door, and if you saw me leave without saying… You do know that your house is made mostly of windows, right?"

I was slightly shocked but thankful he was so flustered at the sight of me. It felt like it had been one-sided, nervous sexual tension since he showed up. There was no way I would be able to hide the heat in my cheeks, but I didn't run for cover. I felt too good in my own skin and too high from the day's events. I grabbed a T-shirt from the bed, slipping it over my lingerie-clad body while I spoke, leaving my legs bare. "Let's just make peace with this and maybe say you should call or text before you come down to the house, okay? I'm well aware I live in a house made of windows. I designed it. I'm also aware there are almost two miles between me and anything close to resembling civilization."

Composed now, Jack moved his hands up to hold the door frame, the keys dangling from his fingers, a picture of perfect temptation standing outside my house while somehow still managing to invade my bedroom. He didn't bother to hide his roaming eyes as he took me in, a sexy smile tugging at the corners of his mouth. "I see more of Seth in you every time you open your mouth."

"But not when you take a *good* look, right?" I said coyly.

Are you flirting? You are flirting, Rose!

Walking over with new confidence, I grabbed the keys from his hand, not bothering to mention that I had several sets and a spare cart—which I was sure he saw in my driveway. "Goodnight, Jack. I'll lock up. I can handle it. I'm a big girl, I promise."

"I have no doubt about that," he said shamelessly. "Can I ask you a question?" Jack asked, placing a booted foot just inside my bedroom, teetering on the step it took to get inside.

"Sure." He was just inches away. I could see every detail of his chiseled face, his eyes, nose, lips, and chin. All of it appealed to me, all of *him*. There was an evident pull between us, and I could see just how much it was affecting him with the way he looked at me, though his demeanor reeked of confidence.

"What made you go out and buy a Tesla today?"

I peeked over his shoulder at my beautiful new car and exhaled deeply with a satisfied and equally confident smile before giving him an answer. My body rattled with awareness as he inched forward, and I made no move to encourage him or otherwise. I fed off him greedily, and I was sure I matched his heated stare. Taking great care not to touch him, I leaned in as close as possible.

"I felt like it," I said with a wink. I gripped the door handle behind him, and he stepped back so I could shut it. "Night, Jack."

"Night," he said, hesitating before he began to make his way off the porch. "Oh, and Rose?"

"Yes, Jack?"

"You fucking excel at sexy."

chapter
four

"If the Kardashians can live with the size of their asses and profit from it, you can get out of bed, Rose."

THE FIRST TIME I'D EVER BEEN KISSED WAS IN FOURTH GRADE. His name was Jason Hammond. We had dropped pencils under our desk in an attempt to steal a kiss in hopes of recreating the same kiss I'd seen the night before. It lacked every single detail and emotion that had made me suddenly curious about the act of kissing. No matter how many times I'd pressed my lips to his under that desk, it didn't feel anything like what I'd felt seeing my parents do it the night before.

It had been an accident, really. Long after they assumed I'd gone to sleep, I snuck downstairs, determined to devour the last two Twinkies I'd been denied after dinner. When I heard them whispering back and forth in the living room, I froze.

The lights were dim as they stood in each other's arms in front of a roaring fireplace. I made a beeline for the pantry and grabbed the box. Much to my dismay, I found it empty. Rolling my eyes with defeat, I began to creep back toward the stairs when I glanced at them and stood paralyzed at the sight before me.

"Love me, Seth," my mom whispered as he stared down at her with a look that made my heart ache. I was surprised by how much it hurt.

I gripped my chest as my dad continued to gaze at her with a look of pure devotion as she asked him over and over to love her. He held her face close to his and whispered something to her. She nodded as a tear slid down her cheek. He caught it with his thumb. With a gentle finger, he pushed the strap of her nightgown to the side, leaving her shoulder bare. He kissed it slowly with his eyes closed, and she tilted her neck back. I knew I should've left then but couldn't tear my eyes away. My mom never begged for anything. I'd never heard that type of desperation in her voice, and she'd never looked so... beautiful. He leaned in and took her lips gently. It was all I could do to keep from matching my mom's sigh as she clung to him and returned his kiss. I clamped my hands over my mouth, though I was barely breathing.

When he'd pulled his lips away, he kept his hands on her face and whispered words that made her smile. Awareness that I was not supposed to be there raced through me, and I snapped out of my wistful daze, ran up the stairs, and shut my door carefully so there was no way they could hear it. My breaths came out fast as fear crept through me. For a second, I was terrified they might have seen me and I wouldn't be able to explain myself. When I was sure my secret remained safe, I slumped against the door as my heart pounded and my curiosity soared.

I would never forget the way they looked at each other or the way she'd said his name as if he was the only man in the world who could save her. All I did know was that I loved the exhilaration that danced through me as I bore witness to it. It was the best I'd ever felt, a new craving.

The next day, I'd done everything I could to get Jason to kiss me the same way. At only ten years old, I was chasing that feeling. Frustrated after several attempts, no matter how hard I tried, I couldn't get it back.

I didn't realize it then, or even until years later, but that was the night the romantic version of myself was born. A strong and powerful kiss between my parents had awakened the believer in me. I'd spent my early years convinced that when I found the person who kissed me like that, I could own that feeling, and with each kiss, I would be able to summon it at will. Lying in my bed almost twenty years later, I knew the rarity of such a gift. That ten-year-old girl had been naïve, but she'd also been right. There were people out there capable of making you feel that way with a kiss, of summoning it with a look. It had never been the act of kissing but the connection between two people that caused such powerful emotion. It didn't take much to figure that out, and once I had, my search began.

That young romantic grew older and found that person who turned her world upside down with just the feel of his lips. She'd gotten to explore a few short months of free rein and contentment until the day it ended.

I stopped listening to that ten-year-old romanticist and the woman she grew in to. The romantic in me now remained buried due to years of living in realism and practicality. In my bitterness, it had become relatively easy to ignore her. Years later, she willingly lay dormant and disappointed.

At that moment, somewhere between shaking off the sleep haze and reliving that memory of my parents sharing the most romantic kiss I'd ever witnessed, I wondered if there would ever come a day when that silent part of me spoke again—and whether or not I would listen to her. I put my fingers to my bankrupt lips in an attempt to make sure they were still there and capable of receiving such a kiss, and then I remembered the only man I knew capable of giving it was long gone.

Penance, that's what this was. I was paying penance for buying that ridiculous car. I eyed it in the distance as I wiped the dirt off the budding summer squash. I'd been all but shooed away by the men I'd hired to tend to the farm, but I told them I needed the exercise and a simple task to keep myself occupied. They'd hesitantly obliged. Think of me what they would, but I *needed* to be a part of what was going on with the center in any aspect. It was my driving force.

"Mornin', Rose."

Cajun.

I loved the sound of it. It was especially sexy rolling off Jack's tongue.

I smiled into my T-shirt as I cleaned the dirt off my face before I turned to find him holding two cups of coffee, one extended out to me.

"No offense to your gesture, sir, but a bucket of ice water would have been preferred." I had been out in the fields for hours and was sure I was covered in dirt.

"It's iced. I usually have a fresh batch of beignets to go with my apologies, but you Texans know shit about that."

"I'm offended for all of us Texans," I said with a grin, "but you brought no donuts, either, and that's unheard of in these parts. And there is nothing to apologize for, Jack. We made peace with it, right? I'm not used to visitors, but I will have to be more careful once the center opens. So, in a way, you did me a favor by reminding me of that."

"Okay, just as long as you know, I don't make a habit of staring at beautiful women in their underwear through their bedroom windows."

Flattered by his comment but unwilling to acknowledge it, I gave him a simple reply. "Understood." I grabbed the coffee from his extended hand and took a sip.

He was dressed again in a solid T-shirt and jeans, and yet looking at him always felt like the first time. No woman in their right mind could deny Jack's appeal. From his blond spiky halo to his sharp, perfectly drawn brows, down to his sculpted cheekbones and strong jaw, he was truly a work of art. He'd had no shortage of female attention throughout his life, of that, I was sure.

"Seth and I have been friends for years, and I wouldn't want to ruin our good standing by being the peeping pervert outside your bedroom door." He winked before he sipped his coffee.

"No harm, no foul. I'm not traumatized, and I stopped running to my daddy about boys a long, long time ago," I insisted in an attempt to drop the subject.

I'd always had an insatiable sexual appetite since I discovered it, and though those thoughts had been the last thing on my mind for the last few years, they were at the forefront now as sex stood in front of me. Scenarios and what-ifs raced through my mind as I thought of what might have happened if he'd made an aggressive move last night.

Jack studied my face, but I kept my eyes averted—the air between us charged.

He broke the silence. "We're installing all of the equipment today and tomorrow. I thought I'd offer to lead you through some of the fun stuff if you want."

"Sounds good to me. And I really appreciate the coffee. I'm sure it was no easy feat to get it here on that Harley you ride."

"You'd be surprised how much you can do with a bike." He bit his lower lip with a quick nod of affirmation, and I found it sexy as hell.

I took another sip of my drink and set it down, then picked my work gloves back up. "I wouldn't know. I've never been on one."

Suddenly, the heat was unbearable. I had the urge to rip off everything covering my body for any kind of relief. The sun was relentless, and the top of my head was beginning to burn. I'd realized I'd been distracted by my thoughts while working the field, and now I was overheated and close to a meltdown. I was blaming it on the Texas sun but wasn't so sure at that point that was the truth of the matter.

Jack bent down next to me as I gathered my tools, his knees touching mine. "We should remedy that. How about a ride today after I set up?" He brushed a stray strand of hair away from my face and wiped a smudge of dirt off my chin, forcing my gaze to his. Knees now planted in the dirt, I resisted the urge to pull him on top of me so we could roll around in it. I began to pant as he watched me start to melt into a pile of sweat and red hair. He was too close. I couldn't think straight. And though any passerby who saw us wouldn't see our posture as threatening or intimate, I could feel the tension between us. It was becoming more overbearing than the incessant sun. Jack seemed to be enjoying the dynamic, cool, and confident as ever as he watched me squirm.

"I'm…not…"

Jack chuckled. "Surely you're not scared, considering you just bought one of the fastest sports cars out there? And by the way, when you've just gifted yourself a ride like that, you should be anywhere but digging in the dirt. That beauty needs her legs stretched." There was nothing but sex in his voice. Intentional or not, I was suffocating under the weight of his words.

"I agree," I said, throwing my tools back down in silent declaration that my punishment was over. "That sounds nice… the ride, I mean. I'll take you up on that, but please excuse me for a moment." I stood abruptly, forcing Jack up with me, and sprinted straight toward the pond. Not missing a step, I jumped high, gripped my knees, and cannonballed into the water, scaring the shit out of my ducks.

I resurfaced with an "Oh God, it's wonderful!"

Jack bellowed with laughter behind me as I pushed drenched, wayward hair out of my face before turning to look back at him with a grin. He stood where I left him, tapping his cup against his leg, an amused smirk on his face. "I'll pick you up at six."

"Okay," I said with renewed energy, loving the feel of the cold water. I watched Jack walk off and pretended not to notice the sun glinting off his gold-dipped hair. I stared in his direction for several minutes after he was out of sight. Now that I knew Jack didn't want to cross the line with me due to his concern over his relationship with my dad, I felt a bit more at ease.

My ducks bitched their protest as they moved past me as I started swimming toward my house.

Band-Aid gone. I didn't know whether or not to thank Jack or the Texas heat. Either way, it had been painless.

chapter
five

I WALKED OUT OF THE HOUSE WHEN I HEARD THE RUMBLE OF JACK'S motorcycle. I was nervous and dropped my keys twice while attempting to lock my door. I'd spent a few extra minutes knotting my hair on top of my head and a little longer than usual picking out my clothes. For the most part, it was the fact that I would be close to a man I was so strongly attracted to that was the cause of my apprehension. And the last time that happened… well, it was the last time.

Jack was freshly dressed in dark blue jeans and a chalky-white button-down rolled up to his tanned, toned forearms. His boots were shiny black, and he looked afuckingmazing still crouched on his bike, one hand on the throttle and the other resting on his thigh. When I approached, he rolled the throttle, and I jumped at the sound.

His chuckle was deep as I narrowed my eyes. "Can we please stick to back roads? I'm not a fan of Texas highways."

"Sure," he offered, along with a helmet. I took a deep breath and fastened it under my chin, regretting wearing my short linen shorts the minute his eyes roamed over my legs. My halter blouse was no less revealing, yet it suddenly felt that way. When I'd looked at myself in the bathroom, the outfit had seemed feminine. Jack was staring at me like I was still in my underwear. I watched him take in my high-top Chucks that matched my soft linen shorts and then give me a nod of approval.

He gathered a similar helmet out of the saddlebag for himself.

"Hear me?" he asked over the loud rumble of the bike. I smiled as his voice cracked over the speaker inside my helmet.

"Yep," I replied with a smile. I stood there, waiting as he stared at me expectantly.

"There's no door to open for you, Rose. You actually have to climb on." He chuckled as he scooted up a bit further in his seat.

"No highways?" At first, the ride seemed harmless—an easy way to give in and live a little—yet the man in front of me and the machine he straddled started to appear all too intimidating.

Jack's grin broadened at my hesitance before he spoke. "I don't want to scare you. I don't get my kicks out of shit like that. In fact, I want you to like it, so I'll be a good boy, I promise." I gave him a smile. He closed his eyes, then jerked his head toward the bike. "Come on, Rose, live a little."

"You too? Geesh, that seems to be the collective advice from every damn body these days," I muttered, lifting my leg over the backseat, then placing my hands at his sides. He gripped them immediately and pulled them tightly around him. All too aware of the smell of his skin—what smelled like a mix of woods and crisp apples—I gripped the front of his T-shirt, twisting it in my hands.

"Wow, you really are nervous," he said, untangling my hands and clasping them together around his waist.

"Let's just do this." I buried my helmet-covered head into his back, and as soon as he hit the throttle, I felt it.

It was instant. My body lurched forward, and I clung to his back like a fraidy-cat with its claws out.

"Whoa." Jack slowed down just as we were passing the edge of the pond. "No, I'm fine. Just go," I said breathlessly.

"I won't do anything crazy, Rose. I promise."

"Got it, Jack, go!"

He pulled at the throttle, and I jumped again, but this time, I was able to keep it mostly to myself. Jack quickly became engrossed in the ride as Bob Seger's "Night Moves" came through the speaker.

I shut my eyes tight and tried to ignore the sensation that was creeping through me. My shorts offered little to no buffer because it felt like I was riding the world's largest vibrator. I was humiliated again after only minutes with him. As long as he didn't find out why, I was safe. It had been so long that I'd almost forgotten what it felt like. I adjusted my body in every way imaginable to keep the sparks at bay. The minute Jack took off out of the parking lot and I felt the full effect of the bike between my legs—I knew it was useless.

I was screwed.

As Jack took the first turn off the frontage road—avoiding the highway as promised—I realized I was nothing but tight nerves and sensation.

"You good?" he asked as I tightened my grip around his waist.

"Good," I lied.

"This music okay? What's your taste? Are you more of a rock or country girl?"

He looked back at me through his side view, and I knew my face was crimson. He pushed the throttle slightly, and I couldn't keep my lips from parting at the feeling, my body now fully awake. Recognition covered his features as that same slow, sexy smile I saw the first day I met him crept over his now smug face.

Oh, Jesus, he knows.

"It's fine," I said through gritted teeth. "Whatever you want to listen to."

I felt his chest move with his soundless chuckle and glared at him through the mirror.

"Maybe we should turn back and take my car out? You know, stretch her legs like you said? I'll let you drive, okay?"

I will not orgasm on the back of this bike. I will not orgasm on the back of this—

Jack hit the throttle again repeatedly, and I let out an involuntary "Oh God."

I felt his chest shake again as I buried my helmet into his back. Great, we hadn't even had a real conversation, and Jack was about to give me an orgasm.

"We can't turn back now." He pointed over to the traffic on the opposing side of the road, and I nodded into his back. "Just give it a chance, okay?"

"Okay," I agreed reluctantly, knowing I didn't have a snowball's chance in hell of keeping my cool. He took off again, this time with a little more mercy than the last, but the pulse between my thighs refused to let up. I lifted my head, trying to enjoy the rustic view around us, praying it would distract me. The sun wasn't going to set for another few hours, but it was low enough in the sky to paint a colorful gold over the pastures we passed. I gripped Jack tighter as I listened to the song in an attempt to ignore my tuned-in body, but of course, the whole song was all about sating sexual desire.

In an attempt to make conversation, I admitted my preference. "Rap and R&B, but mostly rap," I said as he took a slow curve with care.

"Really?"

"Yep, I love it. My mom does, too. Well, we like vintage rap mostly. Snoop Dogg, Dr. Dre, Eminem, 50 Cent, Ice Cube, but not so much the new stuff. She got me hooked when I was a kid."

"Laura let you listen to Eminem as a kid?"

The world passed by in a blur as I stared at him in the side view. "I forget you know my parents," I said. "You can't be much older than me."

"I've been working with your dad for the better part of ten years, so I know them pretty well."

I remembered hearing his name in conversation a few times but never remembered meeting him in passing. During the majority of that decade, I'd been in college, then medical school, so it wasn't a mystery why we hadn't met.

"Well, I've heard of you," he said, reading my thoughts, seemingly unoffended by the fact that I didn't know of him.

He studied me briefly through the side view, and I answered his attentiveness with a smile. The man was good-looking, and I wondered if he knew of his effect on women. He was cocky, but not in an obnoxious way. It came out confident but not arrogant like so many other men blessed with ridiculously good looks. Or maybe he did know just how good-looking he was and didn't make it a point to let anyone else know. If that was the case, I liked him even more for it.

I'd only ever been attracted to one man in my life whose outside matched the beauty of his inside. I know that's what did me in with Grant—his heart. Looking at Jack's strong profile, I wondered if the same was true of him. Was he a good person, or did he manipulate women with his looks in a way that would make him unbearably ugly?

A real man wants to know and explore the inside of a woman before he attempts to claim her in any real way. That was the truth I knew—that was what being loved by Grant taught me. A sick feeling washed over me as I realized I'd only been alone

with Jack for a few minutes, and I was already comparing him to
Grant. I squeezed my eyes shut tight and tried to clear my head
in an attempt to give my friendship with Jack a chance.

"My mom didn't protect us from any words we would eventually hear," I said, returning to the previous subject in an attempt
to silence my inner musings. "She didn't see the point. She told
us which ones not to say even though she said them often."

Jack chuckled. "Sounds like Laura. Your sister seems to have
quite the colorful personality, too."

"You have no idea," I said as I gripped him tighter and lifted
off my seat slightly in a useless attempt to keep the throbbing
between my legs at bay. "Anyway, I get crap for it all the time.
No one I'm close to likes my music."

"I can't sympathize. I'm not a fan, myself. My uncle did
teach me everything there is to know about music, but given
the choice, it would never be rap."

"See," I said with emphasis. "I never win with the company
I keep."

"Sorry," he said unapologetically. "Tell you what, give me
a song to listen to every day… educate me. By the time I've set
up shop and am ready to leave, I can make a more informed decision."

"You're on," I said as a thousand song titles danced through
my head.

"So, you think my family is colorful?"

"Absolutely, and I can relate. I know exactly what it's like to
have a colorful family," he mused. "I was raised by five people."

"Five?" I asked, curious about the man I was holding onto
with a death grip.

"Yeah, my parents, both my aunts and my uncle. Technically, only my mom and dad are blood-related to me. My uncle
and my dad were best friends for years. They met my aunts on a

road trip before I was born and have been inseparable since. My aunt and uncle couldn't have children, so I guess they shared me in a way. And, well... my other aunt, she was just as much of a part of my life as everyone else. It's kind of a weird dynamic, I guess, but it's all I know."

"Must have been some road trip," I said, trying to imagine a younger Jack.

"I'm pretty sure it was. Nine months later, I was born."

We shared a laugh as Jack turned to the county road behind the center. I felt a rush of relief that I might just make it back without losing my cool. Yet the more I brushed against Jack's hard body and inhaled his scent, the more turned-on I became. His face in the mirror, his voice, and the hard lines of his body had all contributed to the state I was in. Anything could tip me over. I could feel the indents of Jack's six-pack underneath my thumbs and rubbed over them without thinking. He eyed me through the side view. It was a heat-filled warning, and behind that warning, a fire had been lit. Apparently, he enjoyed muscle appreciation as much as I enjoyed giving it. He rolled the throttle, making me jump in my seat. Our eyes met in challenge, and I couldn't help but rise to it.

All right, Jack, let's play.

I moved my hands as slyly as possible, caressing his midriff, and repositioned them just above his belt buckle as I stroked him subtly. I clenched my thighs around him and heard his reluctant curse as he kept his head averted so I couldn't get a good look at him. He was easy prey, and I wondered if it had anything to do with my unintentional strip tease last night. Secretly, I hoped it did. I let out a soft chuckle as Jack's head snapped to. Catching his eyes, the intent behind his gaze was all too apparent.

I'd been falsely confident in a game his eyes told me he was sure he would win.

The gentleman who seemed intent on sparing me further embarrassment had just left and was now replaced by a man hell-bent on torturous foreplay. Our eyes locked as he slowed at the entrance of the center. I let out a small breath of relief that maybe I'd misjudged his intentions, all the while becoming utterly engrossed in the feel of him. I was no longer at a friendly distance, my breasts pressed against his back, my legs all but wrapped around his waist. His entire body was stiff with the tension we'd created, and I could now feel the sweat between us as I adjusted myself on the seat. Jack idled at the entrance, his legs firmly planted on the pavement. He pulled the throttle and watched my lips part. I was on edge again, and there was no stopping it. He tugged at the handlebar again, and I dug my fingers into his flesh, gripping him to me as I panted into the speaker.

"Jack," I pushed out and heard the desperation in my voice. My whole body vibrated in warning as I clutched him tighter to me.

Eyes pleading with his, I willed him to stop our dangerous game, but with one last rev of the engine, I went over. A small cry escaped my lips as I clung to him for dear life. The orgasm washed through me, so intense that I went with it, no longer giving a damn about my audience. I tilted my helmet-clad head back slightly as it rolled through my body. Digging my nails into his stomach, I moaned out his name as the last powerful wave coursed through my limbs. Jack quickly parked the bike and then jumped off. He paced next to me, his helmet in his hand, as I slowly removed mine, embarrassed but… relaxed.

Owning my part, I made a light joke, though my body was still aching in a way it hadn't in years. Nervous laughter spewed out of my mouth as I felt the full weight of what had just happened. "Well, that's one way to get a girl to like a ride."

I braved a look in his direction. He stopped pacing and stood looking down at me with a mix of lust and confusion.

Avoiding his odd reaction, I made quick conversation. "I think we should do a rain check on the Tesla. I'm in need of a shower," I said, setting his helmet on the seat.

"Seth is a good friend of mine," he huffed in slight exasperation.

"We've established that," I said, looking up at him with a grin that faded as soon as I saw that wasn't the response he was looking for.

"And you want to pretend that didn't just happen?" he said roughly as his eyes lit every single nerve ending in my body on fire.

"I'm sure it happens a lot," I said with intended humor, still pinned to the leather seat by his stare. I felt exposed, yet as he looked at me with such intensity, I felt needed and beautiful. I remained silent until I saw him mentally make a decision.

I had an inclination that I was about to get kissed, and thoroughly.

Just as he went to reach for me, we heard Dallas call out from behind us.

"Hey, y'all," she said as if she hadn't just interrupted the best waking daydream of my life. Jack and I turned toward her as she hugged Annabelle to her hip and walked toward us, assumption written all over her face.

Clearing my throat, I stepped off the bike and ignored Jack's lingering stare as I walked toward Dallas.

"Hey, I thought you were in Shreveport."

"I was. We were there for all of four hours before I called home to check in and heard Mom going through a living hell because of this one." She lifted a tired Annabelle with her hip, and I leaned in and kissed her chubby cheek, then wiped a curly, sweat-covered piece of hair off her forehead.

"Hey, baby girl."

Annabelle reached for me, and I readily took her.

"It was a nice thought," Dallas said with a chuckle. "I did place a few bets, though."

Jack's easy smile had both Dallas and me struggling to catch our breath as he answered her. "Win anything?" he asked as he put my helmet back in his saddlebag.

"Not a thing. Hey, I saw the installs. I'm impressed. You look like you covered a lot of ground here." Nobody missed her insinuation. I glared at her openly, and Jack visibly tensed.

"That I did," Jack responded, taking a step forward and rubbing a finger over Annabelle's chin, making her smile. Her grin was infectious, and I joined in as we both looked back at Jack, a sigh on my lips and an audible "Haywo" from Annabelle.

"Hello to you too, pretty one."

"Well, I see you got my sister on a motorcycle, which is some feat considering she hates—"

"Where's Grant?" I interrupted her with a warning in my tone.

Dallas looked at me oddly before she answered. "Dean has him. They're grabbing dinner. I came to get my laptop."

I nodded and motioned toward the door. "I've got her. Go ahead." Dallas looked between Jack and me, and I narrowed my eyes at her to show I meant business, which meant shit to her.

"Okay, I'm going, though if you ask me—"

"I never do," I said without an ounce of politeness in my tone. Dallas chuckled and reached for Annabelle. "I've got her," I snapped.

"Right," Dallas said as she turned toward the building, but not before a quick verbal jab. "Thanks, Rosie, you're the best."

Seventeen choice words I couldn't say circled my head as I watched her retreating form with a glare. I absolutely hated that nickname, and she knew that without a shadow of a doubt.

All too aware Jack was still standing there, I turned to him as I clutched Annabelle to me.

"Thank you for the ride. I'm sure you have stuff you need to do."

He looked past me toward Dallas with a nod in her direction. "Are you dismissing me, Rose?"

"Of course not," I said, a little too hastily.

"Well, just so we're clear, you owe me a ride."

"Of course." My eyes remained trained on Annabelle, though my thoughts were still on the possibility of a kiss. "Thanks again, Jack."

Jack leaned in slowly just as the streetlamp clicked on above us, illuminating his face in soft white light. "Anytime," Jack whispered in my ear, sending chills down my spine.

"Eye!" Annabelle exclaimed, sticking her tiny finger directly into Jack's eye as he pulled away. I let out a roar of laughter as Jack bit back his curse, holding his damaged eye with the butt of his palm.

"Are you okay?" I asked as he peeked at us with his good eye.

"You Whitaker women… colorful," he said with a smile and incredulous head shake.

"Technically, she's half Martin, but we'll take that compliment," I said as I leaned into Annabelle to nuzzle her neck. "Won't we, baby?"

Jack looked at me with evident regret. "See you tomorrow, Rose."

"Thanks again, Jack. It was… stimulating." Without waiting for his reaction, I turned to walk back into the building to join my sister. I watched her as she finished typing an email and then closed her laptop to look over at me.

"Seriously, could you have made that any more awkward? You're such an ass!"

She blew me off the way she always did when I called her out on her behavior. "I can't believe you got on the back of a motorcycle when you bought and tested four different car seats for the kids!"

"I bought a damned sports car, too, got my first bikini wax, and spent a fortune on girl crap I didn't need. Do you think I'm having a mid-life crisis at twenty-eight?"

Dallas's jaw dropped as she studied me. "You got some sun, too. I was only gone a day. What in the *hell* happened?"

"I broke into my piggy bank, and I lived a little," I said, letting Annabelle down to Godzilla around the office.

"Good for you!" she said with a smile. "And Jack?"

"He's not boring, but we still really haven't had much of a conversation."

Though he did just give me my first orgasm in years, and he's practically seen me naked.

"I wasn't really interested in knowing if you'd talked about the weather."

"I'm well aware of that, dear sister," I quipped with distaste.

"Jesus, that man is hawwwt. If I didn't already have a perfectly good steak on my plate—"

"Don't finish that sentence, Dr. Martin," Dean said to his wife in warning as his son proceeded to fly into the room with an announcement. "We got echinni!"

"You did?" I said, just as animated.

Grant smiled up at me with a nod. "Mommy says it's sooooo fatering. But Daddy says he no care what mommy says."

No amount of restraint could keep the full belly laugh I

had to let out as Grant's parents stared each other down. I knew Dallas would burst if she didn't get her digs in, and I was just about to start the countdown when I heard her sound off to Dean. "Your daughter just pooped. I fed her broccoli and breast milk for lunch. I'll plate your food." I couldn't stop my laughter as Dean pulled his daughter into his arms. When the smell hit him, he visibly cringed.

Dallas plated Dean's fettuccine with a heaping helping of broccoli while across the hall, we heard unpleasant grunting. I looked at my sister, who was cutting Grant's noodles, and gave her a smile.

"You're totally happy with him, aren't you?"

She sighed with a smile and looked up at me with a gleam in her eye I'd only seen a few times.

"Dallas, it's okay to let it show. I want you to be happy."

She studied me for a moment and concluded I was being honest. "It's like the most fun I've ever had being an adult and the hardest at the same time. But, yeah, I'm totally happy with him and *them*," she said as she eyed Grant. "They're yours too, you know," she reminded, still cutting the noodles, afraid to make eye contact with me.

"I know," I said before standing to take my leave, suddenly exhausted from the day's events.

"Stay with us and eat," she said, stunned when I didn't move to grab a plate.

"Not tonight, but soon."

"Where're you going?" Dean asked, carrying a freshly changed Annabelle into the office. There was absolutely no doubt who fathered her when they were so close to each other.

"Home," I said confidently. "Where I live. And why are you guys eating here?"

"Used to it, I guess," Dallas said with a shrug. "Dean has got a patient in labor, and it's a quicker commute. We like it here."

"Just don't get burned out," I said, admiring the family in front of me. "You'll be here forever."

Dallas stopped her cutting and looked up at me with a grin. "So will you."

"Right," I said, matching her grin. "Night, love you guys."

"Wove you," Grant said, not looking up from his plate.

"Oou," Annabelle added. I closed the door and decided to walk back to my house. It never seemed like much of a walk on cooler nights. The paved, white walkway was softly lit on both sides by luminescent globes. Some nights, I would just walk up and down the paved street, thinking of how much had changed for me—both personally and professionally—since this land was nothing but pasture. It was a different world now, a different life.

Goose bumps covered my arms as a cool breeze lifted my hair from my shoulders. Grant wasn't here. It hadn't taken me long to figure that out. But on summer nights like this—with his memory still etched into every part of me—he wasn't far away.

"Did you feel that?"

His words were an echo now, an echo of the world we'd lived in together where our dreams were at our fingertips and our love was front and center. I paced myself on my walk home, no longer looking forward to a night alone. Stopping mid-step, I stared into the distance at the empty house. Clarity hit me as I stood in front of the past. I'd been waiting for a new life to start while staring in the rearview. If I wanted to change my life, my future required my attention.

As the next cool breeze ran its fingers through my hair, fear crept through me.

My life had started a long time ago and had begun to leave me behind.

chapter
six

Unknown: Good morning, beautiful. I'm ready for my first lesson.

Thinking on my toes, I sent my first text to Jack, then programmed his number.

Rose: Rap & R&B 101 - Changes, 2Pac

"You've had this place how long and never had us over?" Jules popped off as she jumped out of her SUV and whistled as an assessment of the house.

"I've been busy," I offered in a half-assed apology, a cold glass of sweet tea vodka extended toward her as she made her way up the steps.

She snatched it from my sweaty palm and swallowed it down while narrowing her eyes at me. Jules was a native of New Jersey and was raised by her five brothers. Though she did have the accent and a lot of the attitude, the last guy who had called her Snookie had been dismissed with a broken nose and a Louis Vuitton shoved up his ass. She believed in truth and loyalty, and with her, you always got the blunt truth. But when you were one of Jules' people, you got the best of her. I was one of the lucky ones.

She took no time setting her day's supplies down on the deck, which consisted of a neon green bottle of tanning oil, a misting spray water bottle—to cool ourselves down while we sunbathed—an additional bottle of expensive vodka, and her usual fifteen-pound purse, which I was sure was filled with the mysteries of her universe.

Jules was beautiful with olive skin, long, jet-black hair, and large, round blue eyes. She was top-heavy, and damn near every shirt she wore was accompanied by inches of deep cleavage. She pulled off her T-shirt, revealing a banana-yellow bikini, then made herself at home in one of my deck chairs.

"Seriously, I can't believe you've been holding out on us like this." She pulled her black sunglasses over her eyes and stretched her back like a lazy cat in the afternoon sun.

"If it makes you feel any better, aside from my family, you're my first house guest," I said as I took residence beside her in a matching chair. She looked at me sideways before giving me a quick nod.

I'd bared all to Jules one night after a long day at work and a few shots of tequila, which she insisted on and I hated. I'd told her everything I wanted her to know, including the details of my relationship with Grant. Unlike Dallas, she hadn't pushed me for anything since. Though blunt and honest, she was still the type of woman who knew her place, and if I had to guess, she masked her own pains as well.

Who didn't?

I spent an hour filling her in on my activities of the days before, leaving out mine and Jack's motorcycle ride. I'd have to have more than one drink to admit what had happened. I knew our chemistry was on dangerous grounds, but I also knew he was fighting some moral issue because of my dad and their friendship. I was sure he would've kissed me last night if it weren't for Dallas. Would I have kissed him back? Did I want him to? I thought of his slow smile when he'd figured out I was turned on to the brink. Then I realized he'd probably be packing up in the next few weeks to head back to New Orleans. For a brief moment, I wondered if he had someone to return to.

"So, you go out and get dolled up, buy a sports car, and decide to have a party? What's gotten into you?"

I shrugged in reply.

"Well, good on ya," she said before draining her spiked tea. "This is pretty good."

"It is, and I'm not having a party. Jamie is coming in a few hours after her shift. Just us girls today."

I settled in my deck chair, already feeling the burn on my shoulders. Reaching for my sunblock, I gave my body a quick rubdown. For someone so sensitive to the sun, it was a damn shame I loved it so much.

"I called TJ last night," Jules confessed after an hour of alcohol and sun-worshiping.

I looked over at her with wary eyes.

"Don't look at me like that. I can't shake him."

"I know," I said as she unfastened her top and flipped on her stomach.

"He's my kryptonite. I mean, how in the hell am I supposed to resist a man like that?"

"No one can. That's the point. He's not conservative in the monogamy department, and you—"

"I'm no saint, so save your breath…I know," she cut me off and gave me a pointed look. "I know."

TJ was everything I thought Jules *wouldn't* want in a man. Her weakness was cowboys, the kind that rope and ride. She liked them as southern and as rugged as possible. She was crazy about them, which made her personal life seem almost comical. It was like watching a mafia and a Western movie collide. For some reason, they couldn't get enough of her, either. TJ was her ultimate catch—or so she thought—until he'd decided he wanted to date around.

"Did you sleep with him?" I asked, knowing the answer.

"Yep," she said, her lips popping. "Don't tell Jamie. Don't give her any ammo. She's still pissed about the last time."

"It's because she cares." I decided to give her some of her own hard truth. "You're only hurting yourself."

"Yeah," she said with a sigh. "Fuck him."

"No," I said with a chuckle. "*Stop* fucking him." I was rewarded with a spray in the face from her water bottle. I closed my eyes, loving the feel of the lukewarm water.

"Rose?"

"Yes, Jersey?"

"I know you're scared. I like our talks the way they are, with neither of us really prying too much and all that, but can I just say something?"

I let out a sigh and gave her my full attention.

"I know TJ is going to hurt me. You know it, too, and we both know I'm going to keep on doing what I'm doing until he does. I'm not naïve enough to think I can change him or that he wants to change at all. I think it goes with being in your thirties. The optimist in me is slowly dying, anyway. I'm stuck in this pattern because I want to be—because I want *him*."

I nodded, unsure where she was going with the conversation but certain it was hard for her to admit what she just had.

"You have no idea what's going to happen next. I mean… that's something to be excited about, you know? It's not over for you, Rose, no matter how much you think of it that way. There is no way you're living the rest of your life alone." She gave me a knowing smile. "Not you. I just want you to keep an open mind, okay? Half of the fun is figuring out who it is. I think you forgot that."

"Kind of an optimistic way of thinking for a girl who's condemned herself to a lot less."

Jules looked over at me with a level of seriousness I'd never seen. "Then you get out there and give me a reason to want different."

"Afternoon, ladies."

Cajun.

"Fuckello," Jules said, pulling a T-shirt to her bare chest and giving me wide eyes.

"Jack," I said with a grin, water dripping from my chin as our eyes met. His gaze unabashedly raked my bikini-clad body. A halo of sunshine surrounded his rugged features as I got lost in them. He looked like the devilishly handsome southern gentleman he was. I couldn't help but note how well he filled out his jeans. Out of the corner of my eye, I saw Jules size him up and devour him with her wide eyes.

"I was coming by to grab you to test the new equipment, but I can see you're busy."

"I totally forgot," I replied. It wasn't like me at all to forget something like that, especially when it came to the center. Jules looked between Jack and me, then narrowed her eyes at me. I could feel the interrogation coming.

"It can wait," Jack offered, utterly oblivious to Jules' reaction. After three liquor-filled teas, I suddenly found it all hilarious. Jack eyed me with curiosity as I chuckled at my own thoughts. His eyes were zeroed in on me, and suddenly, his invitation seemed more than appealing. "I can be there in an hour or so—"

"Hellooooo," Jamie called out as she walked up the steps with her own crazy brand of commentary. Jack and I stared at one another with amused grins.

"Up on the deck," Jules called out as she pulled her hair into a tight, neat bun.

"Jesus, what a day. I swear to God, Dr. Nichols is going deaf, and if All-Hands Fischer accidentally grabs my ass one more time…anyway, damn, this place was hard to find, Rose. You've been holding out on us." I knew the minute she saw Jack because she made it fairly obvious. "Where *are* you bitches hiding—holy fuckello," Jamie sputtered out as she set down her bag and sauntered her way over to Jack without so much as a glance in Jules and my direction. "My name's Jamie."

"Jack," he said politely with a nod and the smile of all smiles.

"You don't eat processed meat, do you?"

Jules and I burst into laughter as Jack raised a brow at her and took her offered hand with a chuckle.

"Not recently, no."

"Perfect," she said, shaking his hand slightly longer than necessary.

I held out my hand with a snap toward Jules, and she gave me a wicked smirk as she handed me the water bottle. I shot a few sprays on the back of Jamie's thighs, and she jumped to attention.

"Jamie, drink mixes are on the kitchen counter," I said, trying my best to divert her attention from the golden god consuming all of the intelligence out of the three of us. We were adults, yet with Jack around, we showed no signs of being mature women. Jack had that effect. Even as I scorned Jamie internally for making a fool out of herself, I was just as enamored by his perfection. I almost groaned as I thought of how close he'd been to kissing me the night before.

"I'm obviously interrupting your plans, ladies. I'll make myself scarce," Jack mused at Jamie, who was blocking his path to freedom. Jamie, seeming to snap out of her daze, gave Jack a huge, tooth-filled smile as she did what she could to keep him from leaving.

"Would you like a drink?"

"No, thank you. I'm working today." He turned to me, his blue-gray eyes swallowing me whole in my bikini. "How about that ride... later?"

"Okay," I said without hesitation. "Thanks for coming by, Jack."

He gave me a knowing grin. "Nice to meet you, ladies," he offered, making a quick move to get out of the den full of hungry women, myself included.

After Jack disappeared from sight, Jamie turned to me expectantly at the exact moment as Jules. I shrugged, grabbed our empty glasses, and walked into my kitchen as they followed close on my heels.

"You two just made total asses of yourselves," I scorned as I replenished the glasses with ice.

"I don't think I've ever seen a man that fucking hot in my life," Jamie said, looking back in the direction Jack left. "Seriously, you guys could have warned me... you know, given a bird call... something!"

I shook the bottle of mix as I scorned her. "Uh huh, well, your flirting was shameless. What about Bart?"

"Oh God," she said animatedly as she braced herself on the counter. "He works out naked."

I rolled my eyes as she continued. "Just hear me out. I was fine with it at first... but... okay, but... have you ever seen a man do naked jumping jacks? Things were just flying everywhere! Seriously, ladies, no... just no."

"You could ask him to cover up," I said through a laugh.

"I will never get that picture out of my head," she groaned. "It's like there are no normal men out there anymore. Why do the ones I pick have to have the strangest habits? I'm on hiatus as of this moment. One month."

Jules remained quiet but entertained as she looked at Jamie and then me for an explanation, her olive skin darkened by the second from our short time in the sun.

Before she could give me any verbal grief, I came clean. "He's a contractor, lives in New Orleans, and he's installing all the medical equipment for the center."

"You didn't say a word," Jules said, sizing me up as I poured our drinks.

"Because there's nothing to tell. He took me for a ride last night on his motorcycle. It stayed PG." I was lying, but I didn't know any woman who would openly admit she was so hard up she'd had an orgasm on the back of a Harley. I looked between them. "Look, make your play if you want. We're just friends."

"No, you aren't," Jules said, taking her drink. "At least he's not interested in just friendship with you."

"I hate to admit it," Jamie said, tapping a manicured nail against the side of her glass, "but she's right. He was looking at you like he wanted to tear your ass apart." A small amount of pride swelled within me. I knew my attraction to Jack was sexual because, honestly, I had nothing to go on other than small conversation, but I loved that the girls picked up on it.

Jamie took a long drink of her spiked tea and gave me a wink. "I'm seriously depressed that I can't have him."

Jamie wasn't far away from Jules in the looks department. She was also a dark-haired beauty but with soft brown eyes and was much taller. She looked like a million bucks in her flowered swimsuit cover-up. As I noted her shiny, raven hair and curvy figure, I had to admit that it impressed me that other than friendly pleasantries, Jack hadn't paid any of my beautiful friends any attention. The pride within me swelled a little as I became more excited about our ride later. I knew without a doubt that I wanted Jack to kiss me and let my thoughts wander for a brief moment as a smile crept across my face.

"Good lord, he's going to break the seal," Jamie said, grinning at me after she read my thoughts.

"Finally," they both said in unison, chuckling at each other.

"I don't know. Maybe? I'm not in the business of denying the obvious. He is good-looking," I said, leading them back to the deck, fresh drinks in hand. "But I still don't know if I'm ready to take *that* leap."

We lay side-by-side, sipping our drinks as the girls grilled me more on Jack.

"I just met him. Seriously, I don't know much."

"Well, I say give in to him, and I mean take it *all* out on him, girl. He's hot, short-term, and seems nice enough. There's never been a more perfect time for you," Jamie said, giving me a wink.

"She's right," Jules said, looking at me with concern. "You can keep waiting, but for what?"

I nodded, taking another small sip of my drink, not agreeing or disagreeing with either of them, but at the same time, I was glad I'd invited them over because I knew I needed the confidence they were giving me. Whether I admitted it to myself or not, I was suddenly aware it was a big deal that I was considering being intimate with a man again. It was the last hurdle, so to speak, the biggest Band-Aid.

The truth was, I had spent a fair amount of time thinking about Jack in a sexual sense. I hadn't worried about the lasting effect it might have on me if we were intimate or if either of us wanted more. The girls seemed to assume he wouldn't be anything other than a conquest for me, and for some reason, that bothered me. Maybe because he was a nice guy, and objectifying him felt wrong, or maybe because he was the first man I'd really been attracted to since Grant.

"I've been doing some things on impulse lately," I said, nodding toward my new car parked in the driveway. "I may need to reel it in a bit."

"Holy shit, I didn't even notice it," Jamie noted as she studied my car then turned to me. "You are in the mood for change. Don't let it freak you out, Rose. Seriously, you need it." She looked back at my car. "I'm officially jealous."

"Don't be. You have no idea what I'm paying for it," I said, wiping my hand down my face. "I don't know what the hell I'm doing right now."

"Rose, you can either live with it or you can't. Whatever you choose, we've got your back," Jules said before sliding her sunglasses back on and resuming her sunbathing.

"Agreed," Jamie said as she rubbed oil over her legs. "But if you pass on him—"

"You'll be the first to know," I said with a chuckle.

After two hours of sobering up, the girls packed up right after sunset and made their way home. I sat on my deck in a comfortable lounger as I waited for Jack, staring at the initials carved in Grant's tree. Tiny branches were making their way out of the etched writing, and I wondered if I should pluck them out or if the new growth was somehow telling me what everyone else was—that it was time to move on. I was ready, but at the same time, in no way prepared to be let down. A majority of my grieving had to do with the fact that I'd known a love so incredible, so unique, I was sure I'd never be given the same gift twice.

"You're every dream I've ever had."

I shot awake in the deck chair as Grant's voice echoed through my thoughts, then shivered as I let out a pained cry. I'd just seen him. He'd just been there. Grant was just in front of me.

It had been so real.

I burst into tears and hugged myself, gripping the top of my shoulders as I began to sob. I barely heard Jack's faint "Rose?" and was unable to respond, paralyzed in my state. Suddenly, I felt his strong arms encase me and didn't think as I clung to him, greedy for the comfort. I cried into Jack's shoulder as jagged pain coursed through my every limb.

The pain was so intense. I couldn't believe how close it was to the same unforgiving heartache I'd felt the hours, days, and endless weeks after his death. It had been months since I'd dreamed of him so vividly. It haunted me as I shook in a stranger's arms.

I couldn't understand it. Why did this hurt so much more? Everything I loved about him had been thrust in front of me so clearly. I could still feel him all around me. I held on to it as long as I could as I allowed the tears to fall freely and let the hurt of abandonment have its way with me. I knew the pain, the god-awful pain so well. It had become second nature in the year that followed Grant's sudden death, yet it had felt like forever since it had consumed me. I'd been a fool to think I was free.

Suddenly aware I was crying, and Jack was the one consoling me, I pulled away and wiped my face. "God, I'm sorry. I must've had a dream."

Jack looked down at me, concern written all over his features. "I don't know much about you, Rose Whitaker, but I do know, without a doubt, I *hate* seeing you cry."

"I don't even know where this came from," I said, trying to gather my dignity.

"Well," he said, pushing my hair behind my bare shoulder and staring at the newly unveiled skin, "Maybe you needed it. Sometimes, the body has a way of ridding itself on our behalf."

I was stunned by Jack's words and their depth. We stared at each other for a long minute, me still shaking slightly as I pulled my knees up in the chair and hugged them to me, him sitting next to me, rubbing my shoulders before he slid them down my arms in a soothing manner. I did my best to shake off my emotions and the lingering effects of my dream. Jack stayed quiet, a calming presence while I gathered myself. I found myself thankful that he was there. Something about his strength and confidence put me at ease.

"You really were raised by more women than men, huh?" I said, admiring him again. He was freshly showered in a dark blue dress shirt, jeans, and the same shiny black boots as the night before. His smell hit me next as I appreciated the mix of gold and sand in his hair. All I could think as I watched him watch me was—were the girls right?

What if?

I gave him a small grin despite the sick but dissipating feeling in my gut. "You're quite the gentleman, Jack."

He returned my grin as he removed his hands. I felt their absence immediately, their warmth gone.

"I try," he said, surveying me again with concern. "You okay?"

"Yes, I'm okay. I'm embarrassed, but okay, thank you."

"Nothing to be embarrassed about, but it must have been some dream."

"It was," I replied, not meeting his eyes. His voice soothed me as I took a deep breath, finally able to shake the rest of it off.

I looked toward the driveway, expecting to see his bike, but came up empty. "I thought we were going for a ride?"

"We are," he said, jutting his chin toward my Tesla.

"Oh," I said, a little relieved I wouldn't have to fight his Harley again for my dignity. "Okay, I'll grab the keys."

I walked inside the house, shivered from the coolness of the air conditioning, and caught my reflection in the mirror. I was flushed, and my cheeks were tear-stained, but I was smiling. I couldn't believe the sight in front of me. It was me, but not the me I was used to seeing when I looked at my reflection. This was a version of me that I hadn't seen in years. She was a little looser and carefree—even with the recent emotional outburst. I grabbed the keys and met Jack back on the porch. He was leaning against the deck railing on his forearms, his back to me.

"There's something special about this place," he said, studying the ducks as one by one they took their turn getting into, then gliding across the still water in perfect formation, leaving ripples in their wake.

"I know. It's the perfect place for the center, don't you agree?" I asked with pride.

"One hundred percent," he said, still immersed in his surroundings. I approached and stood beside him as he spent a few moments looking around. I loved that it had that effect on people—on Jack. He wasn't immune to its charm. I sent a prayer up, thanking God once again for my dad's quick work in ensuring it was mine after Grant's death. Losing it would have been my biggest mistake. And now, years later, what I'd initially thought about the land and the serenity it brought was reaffirmed over and over by the people who came to visit it. Soon, it would bring healing to hundreds—hopefully, thousands. Even though there would never be a justifiable reason in my mind for his untimely death, I knew deep down that Grant being a part of my life, sharing this place with me, was not in vain. It was always supposed to be the home where I'd leave my legacy. I knew that now, without a shadow of a doubt.

I hadn't realized Jack was watching me as I'd drifted off in thought. When I noticed, I gave him a sideways smile in question. "What?" I asked as my flesh flushed with the weight of his stare. He was so shameless when he looked at me the way he did.

"What do you think?" he said with a twinge of playful sarcasm.

"I think you're staring at me," I said as I nudged his shoulder playfully before I turned and began to walk toward my car.

"You want me to say what I was thinking?" Jack stayed where he was, stopping my footfall with a dare in his voice. A new shiver made its way up my spine. Sudden thoughts of him behind me, branding my skin, raced through my brain, and my lips moved with a soft and barely audible "yes."

I waited for him with bated breath, loving the way it felt.

"I was thinking that I've never seen a prettier mouth on a woman."

"I'm flattered," I said, keeping my back to him as I gripped the keys tightly as the evident sex in his voice sent shivers throughout my body. I welcomed them like the old friends they were.

"I was wondering what it tasted like," he said directly behind me, making me jump. He chuckled and gripped my hips, gently pushing me forward and down to take the deck stairs. He let go as soon as we reached the bottom, and I paused at the hood of my Tesla, holding my keys out toward him. He took them but walked around to the passenger side. Opening it up, I obliged, sliding into the leather seat like it was a second skin, thankful for its ability to hold me steady. We'd started a flirtation. I thought about what Jules said earlier about anticipation and decided she was right. Things had just gotten a little bit more exciting with Jack's declaration that he wanted to taste my lips.

Jack slid into the driver's seat and adjusted it to his size before turning the key and looking at me.

"Let's stretch her legs."

An uneasy feeling crept over me. "Jack, I'm not a fan of speed. Like not at all, okay?"

"I tell you what, how about I just take you to dinner," he said without protest. The rumble in my stomach reminded me I hadn't bothered to tend to my appetite all day.

"Great," I said as he slowly pulled out of the driveway at a snail's pace. I giggled and rolled my eyes at him as he cut his eyes at me with a smirk. "Smartass."

"Nothing wrong with being a little cautious," he said, putting the car into gear. I pulled my hair up and fisted it into a knot as we made our way through the grounds. When we reached the front of the main building, Jack paused as he surveyed the finished three-story center and then turned to me.

"Wait until you see what we did today." His pride-filled grin was enough to make my heart start pounding in my chest. He was so close, and all I wanted to do at that moment was pull him in. He must have sensed it because his grin slowly disappeared, and his eyes wandered to my lips—which I licked on impulse. Tension thick in the air, my eyes implored his. I wanted him to kiss me. I wanted him to know how I tasted, and I'd hoped it turned into a craving when he did. I wanted to explore our chemistry, but I didn't want to be the one to make the first move. He'd seen the permission in my eyes and apparently ignored it as he pulled the car out of the center and hit the gas.

"I've always loved this car," he said, looking around the cabin.

"Me too. I saw it in a movie once and swore one day I'd own one."

"You're a bad influence. I have half a mind to do the same," he said, giving it a little more gas than necessary.

"Don't you have enough toys?" I asked, curious.

"Never," he said with a wicked lilt. "Know anywhere we can get a good steak?"

I laughed audibly in the wind-filled cabin and gave him a sideways glance. "Jack, this is Texas. Drive, and I'll point."

"Right," he said sheepishly. I found it adorable.

Twenty minutes later, we were seated at one of my favorite steakhouses—the décor comprised of rustic metal signs hanging from every surface and exposed wood beams. Discarded peanut shells were scattered on the floors, courtesy of the small bowls on the tables set out as hors d'oeuvres. The walls were adorned with longhorn skulls and various barn tools to complete the look.

"I like it," Jack said, taking a long perusal around in appreciation and then back to me as he scoured my body and face.

Suddenly, I was nervous. Was this a date? I'd been anything but entertaining in the last few years of my life. I was sure I was relatively boring and terrified I wouldn't have one interesting thing to say. I was giving myself whiplash with the emotions I'd experienced in the last hour. I'd gone from a crying, emotional mess to a horny widow in mere minutes. Now, I was insecure about the fact that I may not be able to hold this beautiful man's attention.

Once we were seated, the server quickly approached us, and I ordered bourbon on ice.

"Bourbon?" Jack asked, amused.

"I drink bourbon and eat bloody steak, Jack." I eyed our waitress. "What are you having?"

"Make that two bourbons and two beers." He looked at me, the corners of his mouth turning up. "I might need to make sure I have more hair on my chest than you do."

"I don't like hairy chests," I said, picking up my menu with a smirk.

"Great, neither do I. Your friends seem fun."

"They are," I shot back quickly.

"You work together?"

"Yes," I answered as I eyed him above my menu.

He gave me a wink and pulled it down to get a clear look at me. "Let's not cover the view."

"For a few years," I said, finishing my answer to his earlier question and ignoring his compliment.

"Rose, you aren't going to speak in clipped sentences with me this whole dinner, are you?"

I had to steady my breath at the intensity of his eyes. Sex... this man exuded some sort of signal that had the back of my thighs sweating. All I saw when I looked at him were full lips taking my skin and sucking mercilessly.

"Rose?"

I was completely lost in thoughts of his mouth on me. I shivered in my seat, furious with my out-of-control libido. I'd gone from insecure back to horny.

Is this PMS? I quickly did a mental calculation, trying to figure out if my new insanity had anything to do with my raging hormones.

"Rose?" Jack asked again.

"No," I countered a little too harshly. "I'm good... just as long as you know I really don't date."

Jack studied me, and I avoided him by shoveling peanuts into my mouth. A long silence followed as I kicked myself mentally for throwing a bucket of cold water on us both.

"Fine with me," he said, picking up his menu without any protest. I sat stunned. There was no fight in him whatsoever. It was too easy. There was no way I'd read him all wrong. Not with the way he looked at me, not with the last few days of flirting. Did I want him to fight me?

Woman, you have lost your shit.

I took advantage of his eyes on the menu and admired his features. His hair was a perfectly tousled mess of light and dark blond. His long eyelashes curled at the ends, softening the rest of his masculine face. What fascinated me most about him was the perfect fullness of his lips. They were way too tempting. When he looked up from his menu, my eyes were fixed on them. He gave me a smirk and resumed his reading. It was everything I could do to keep from taking his bottom lip and sucking it in front of God and everyone. I felt my lower half start to tremble. I downed the first bourbon when it arrived and ordered a second. Jack nodded to me when our waitress placed my second drink in front of me. "Ready?"

"I'll have the twenty-ounce medium rare, sweet potato covered in butter and brown sugar and a large side of slaw." I looked at Jack, who seemed a little stunned.

"Twenty?"

"Yep," I said, taking a swig out of my tumbler.

"I'll have the same," he said, shaking his head at me. "That's a lot of meat, Rose."

"I can eat," I said, sipping my fresh glass of dark liquid, thankful for the burn.

He chuckled as he handed the menu to our waitress, who seemed to have an eye for him. I didn't blame her. At that point, I would have physically slid out of my seat if I hadn't had my legs planted firmly on the floor. My entire body was covered with a light veil of sweat. Jack, though pleasing to the eyes, seemed harmless at a distance. Up close, he did lethal things to me.

"So, New Orleans," I said in an attempt to make small talk.

Jack's whole face lit up when I mentioned his home. "I live

in The Quarter. You should come visit sometime. Hell of a place to grow up," he said as he took a swig of his beer.

"I wish I had time to do things like that. It's been years since I've wandered out of Texas."

"Rose, you won't do a damn bit of good for anyone by working yourself into an early grave."

"Thank you for your concern, Jack, but how would you know how often I work?" I said, sinking into the feel of the bourbon.

"I think it's a safe assumption, considering I've known your family for years and have never seen you once. Why are you so nervous?" Jack asked, catching me off guard as I took a sip of beer.

"I'm not," I said uneasily, giving myself away.

"You are, admit it," he pressed, his accent even sexier and, at the same time, infuriating.

"I will not, and you're being rude."

"Would you prefer I let you bullshit me?"

"I'm not nervous," I said, throwing back my bourbon. The liquid oozed down my throat, and I felt a little braver. Jack reached out his hand, closing the gap between us. I jumped back in surprise until it landed in the bowl, gathering some peanuts to shell them. Another ridiculously sexy twist of his lips brought my gaze to them.

"So, tell me about you, Jack."

He put both elbows on the table and leaned in. "Not much to tell. I travel *a lot*, my home is in New Orleans, and I've been married to my job lately. A lot like you."

"We're so boring."

"Speak for yourself. I've traveled all over, grabbed experiences, and with every trip, I've left my mark or a new building.

Nothing's more rewarding than that. I'll admit, I do work a lot, but I have one up on you, though."

"Oh yeah? What's that?"

"I know when to quit," he countered, finishing his beer with a wink.

"Well, sue me. I've been busy—"

"Ah… shhhh, Rose, no shop talk."

"Fine," I said, motioning to the waitress for another drink.

"Are you going to get drunk tonight, Rose?"

"Maybe." I sighed. "I can't remember the last time I was here or even out with someone else. It's kind of depressing."

"So I'm guessing you're a glass-half-empty kind of girl?"

"I'm a bit of a realist these days," I admitted truthfully.

"It's just like I thought. You need me in your life," he whispered, his elbows still on the table as he leaned in.

I lifted a brow. "For?"

"Because I'm a glass-half-full type of guy. So, let's take work off the table tonight, okay?"

I lifted my chin. "Well, we won't have much to discuss since my life is the center."

"There's more to life than what you do," he said, leaning back in his seat, peeling at the label of his beer.

"Not really. Sorry, what you see is what you get." I lifted my hands, palms up.

He leaned over again, his eyes smoldering. "But you just told me I couldn't have you."

"I… never said that."

His brows knit together in confusion. "You said you don't date." I stared at him, a little entranced. The more he spoke, the more in tune I was with just how much effect he had on me.

"I don't date," I said open-ended.

"Exactly." He froze for a solid beat as he looked at me with a slow, sexy smile. "Wait… did you just proposition me?"

You just propositioned him!

"No, I didn't, but come on, Jack. A man with your good looks? I'm sure that if I *had* propositioned you, it wouldn't be the first time."

I saw his jaw harden a bit before he spoke. "I'm looking at the only woman I'm interested in."

The air shifted dangerously around us, and every single hair on my head stood at attention. His eyes told me everything I needed to know. Jack would probably deliver on every single dirty thought I'd had about him in the last couple of days and more. I couldn't tear my eyes away from his to admire the full plates as they were set in front of us. I was hungry, but not for the beautiful cut of meat sizzling in front of me.

"Can I get you two anything else?"

Jack and I were quickly brought back from our unspoken standoff. I shook my head no as Jack thanked her. I should have been happy to feel this way. To feel the long-forgotten sparks of recognition shooting through me, to be relieved that they still existed. Instead, I was fighting fear. Could I really go through with it? Jack looked over my rapidly rising and falling chest before bringing his eyes back to mine.

"I'm attracted to you and think I've made that clear. But I can't lay a hand on you, Rose, out of respect for your dad. And from what I can tell, you aren't exactly ready to back up what's going through that beautiful head of yours."

Slight hurt and a little embarrassment stung me as I attempted to hide my disappointment. "Please don't pretend to know what's going on in my head."

Jack moved his chair audibly as he leaned in close.

"I'm betting I could manage to take those lips I've been

thinking about tasting for the last three days and put my hands all over you without your protest. But I'm going to have to stick to flirting with you on principle."

My libido took a nosedive as I looked at him in question, but I didn't trust myself enough to speak.

Jack pushed back in his seat, readjusting himself to the table. "Like I said—" he continued cutting into his steak. "—Seth is a good friend of mine, and I'm pretty sure that would no longer be the case if he had any idea of what I was thinking about doing to his daughter. Besides, I'm into dating the women I sleep with. You don't date, that's a problem."

"I'm too busy for anything personal."

"That's a shame," he said absently.

I rolled my eyes as he chewed a bite of the tender meat. He was openly toying with me now as if he'd be doing me a favor.

"Well, I'm glad you made that decision for both of us, Jack. You know, I think you're right," I said coyly. "I'm thinking letting you do what's going through that handsome head of yours could only end in disaster. And like I said earlier, I wasn't propositioning you."

"Of course you weren't," he said way too confidently.

"I wasn't. I haven't let a man touch me in years, so don't flatter yourself."

"I won't," he said, filling his mouth again with the tender meat and fueling my new distaste for his arrogance. My blood boiled as the air around him remained the same.

Ignoring the urge to cover him in bourbon, I spent the next few minutes devouring my food in an attempt to ignore his eyes that were still on me.

"That's impressive," he noted as I took my last bite of steak.

"It's my only party trick," I said with a little too much bite in my voice. Jack reached over and lifted my chin with his fingertips, commanding my attention.

"What is it, Rose?"

I really didn't have a right to be indignant about the fact that he wasn't going to make a move on me. He'd been nothing but a true gentleman to me since I'd met him, and I had no reason to hold a grudge. Although, in the last hour, he'd acted like an arrogant ass, I really didn't see the harm in his game. If he were attempting to date me, I'd shot him down the first five minutes of dinner, and the fault was mine. If anything, I was just as relieved as I was disheartened by his hesitation because I was scared. I let my irritation slide off of my shoulders. The truth was, he was right. I had no idea what I wanted from him—if anything at all—and was still too unsure to do anything about it.

"I'm just tired," I said, pulling my chin away.

"That's not it at all. I'm not a beat-around-the-bush type of guy. Talk to me."

"Nothing to say. I'm fine, really."

He took my hand in his and waited for my eyes patiently. "Then know I'm here as a friend." Realization struck, and I jerked slightly and pulled my hand away.

"He told you?"

"Who? And told me what?"

"My dad told you?"

"I'm not following," Jack said, truly confused. I couldn't help but think more of him for his genuine concern for me. I'd assumed my dad told Jack about Grant, but it seemed it wasn't the case. What I was sure about was that I didn't want Jack to know. In just those few seconds, I'd thought he'd felt pity for me. It felt like the whole dynamic had changed, and I hated it. I didn't want that, not from Jack.

"It's nothing. I have a long day tomorrow. Would you mind taking me home now? I'm just going to use the restroom."

Jack gave me a careful nod with unanswered questions in his eyes. I quickly made my way past the bar and to the bathroom. Washing my hands, I refused to face my reflection. I had let myself down in a way and refused to admit it, even to myself. With a sigh, I exited the restroom, intent on ending the night on a decent note with Jack, when I heard my name called as I passed the bar.

"Rose."

I froze, the voice alone causing dread to race through my veins. Turning to the source, I let my eyes roam over his disheveled appearance. It took me years to get over him—years I would never get back.

"David," I said as I attempted to make my way past him. Somehow, I knew he wouldn't make it easy. He stopped me with a gentle hand on my arm. I pulled my lip in with my teeth in annoyance.

"Rose, come on, give me a minute. It's been a long time." My patience drained as I stood and took in his expensive suit, which I assumed a successful attorney would wear. His dark brown hair was styled back neatly, but the circles beneath his hazel eyes and his posture gave him away. David had always been one for keeping up his appearance, and though at one time I'd thought him the sexiest man in the world, I couldn't for the life of me remember why.

"You had plenty of minutes with me, David. I'm with company. I don't want to be rude."

"Oh, yeah," he said, uninterested, "well, they can give me one more."

"It's late, David. Don't you have a family to get home to?"

"Yeah," he said as he gripped his tumbler, his wedding ring absent.

Pig.

He looked me over with appreciation I was all too familiar with. It disgusted me.

"We're not together anymore."

"That's a shame. It was a beautiful wedding," I said, surprising myself with the lack of contempt in my voice. I'd watched him marry someone only months after ending our five-year relationship. Though I remembered it as painful, the truth was, he was wasted time. I'd stopped caring about his rejection long ago and hadn't looked back.

"Are you...attached?"

"You can't be serious," I said with a laugh. "Let me buy you another drink, David. Seriously, drunk is the only time you were ever funny."

"Rose," he said low as his fingers stroked my arm.

"Get your fucking hand off me now," I said without an ounce of femininity.

"There hasn't been a day I haven't thought about you," he said as his mouth spewed pure bullshit.

"Oh lord, David, take care. You've got a lot further to fall."

"You don't have to be a bitch," he hissed. "I wanted to apologize."

"Then apologize to the lady and make it fast before I make it painful," Jack hissed behind me. I felt the heat radiate from him as I stepped back in surprise.

David chuckled with disdain, his eyes cutting to Jack as he sipped his bourbon. "Aren't you going to introduce me to your boyfriend, Rose?"

"No need," Jack said, stepping in front of me as his face

turned dark and his voice deadly. "Allow me to introduce my-self. Jack Sawyer, bred Lousian'. That makes me your neighbor."

"Nice to meet you, Jack," David spit out with absolutely no civility.

Without missing a beat, Jack continued, "Pleasures all mine, asshole. Now, about that apology, I want her to have it, and then I want to part ways."

David laughed, and I could feel the tension in Jack as he did everything he could to keep from touching him.

"David, you're out of your league here," I pleaded as I saw Jack make up his mind.

"Am I now? Well, at least you still fear for me, *darlin'*," he drawled out in an attempt to mock Jack. "I apologize."

"I'm so glad you left me. Hindsight is blinding me right now. Seriously, David, you're scum."

"Awww now, Rose, we had some good times. Remember when—"

In a flash, Jack had David's tie pulled taught around his neck, choking him as he pinned him to the bar. "Don't finish that. I'm asking you nicely. We're neighbors, and we need to behave as such. I was raised to drag the trash to the curb before I got rid of it. If that's that case here—" he eyed David with menace "—I have no problem doing that. You regret throwing her away. It's ev-ident. You're a fucking idiot for doing it. Maybe you should learn a lesson about regrets tonight. So, I'm going to ask you again not to finish that sentence so we can part ways." Jack let go of him abruptly just as the bartender came over to assess the situation. I was shaking, as well as David, who could do very little to hide it. Jack kept his eyes glued to David's in challenge as he lifted his wallet out of his pocket and threw several bills onto the bar.

"Drinks on me, neighbor," he muttered with confidence as he grabbed my hand and led me to the door. I didn't look back.

After a silent drive back to my house, Jack turned to me and started to speak. I pushed the door open and let myself out of the car. He objected profusely as he rounded the car and handed me my keys.

"I'm sorry," I said, embarrassed. I'd spent the drive home stunned by David's sudden appearance and behavior but, at the same time, completely fascinated by Jack. I'd forced myself to look anywhere but directly at him because the truth was, as terrified as I'd been for David's safety, I was a little bit turned on by the whole thing. As I looked at Jack standing in front of my car, my headlights still on, I found myself comfortable in his eyes, as if a weight had been lifted.

"Don't be sorry for someone else's behavior. It's not your cross to bear."

I nodded, too tired to decipher my current emotions.

"Night, Jack," I whispered as I quickly made my way up to my porch.

"Rose, stop," he said, his voice filled with authority. I stood with my hand on my door and waited for him to continue. The night had gone from promising to disastrously bad, and I still wasn't sure whose fault it was—aside from David's.

"Yes?" I asked, turning to look back at him, trying to seem indifferent. I was pretty sure both of us knew I wasn't. He stayed put at the foot of the deck as he watched me.

I waited, unable to look at him.

"Get some sleep. I'll see you tomorrow."

"Actually, you won't. I'm back at the hospital tomorrow, so thank you for dinner."

"Rose?" Jack started up the steps, and I cut him off with my posture, no longer willing to play games. I felt too raw, too vulnerable. My emotions were way too apparent. Maybe I wasn't ready, or maybe he was drawing them out of me.

"Night, and thank you for all you've done for the center." I closed the door behind me, walked straight over to my dresser, grabbed the vibrator that Jules had bought me, and took it to the bathroom with me. To hell with him. He was far too damned good-looking, anyway.

chapter
seven

"If Ben Affleck can outlive the embarrassment of Gigli, you can get out of bed, Rose."

"S o?" THE TWO J'S LOOKED AT ME EXPECTANTLY AS I pulled my jacket on.

"Nothing happened, and I mean nothing." Other than the fast orgasm I'd brought myself to after dismissing Jack, I was still alone in every sense of the word. I'd drawn that conclusion after a long, restless night. I'd snubbed Jack, and he'd reacted badly, but we were both guilty. Either way, it seemed over before it began.

The girls looked at me as I blew out a harsh breath. "He's a good friend of my dad and doesn't want to screw that up."

"By screwing you," Jamie added, pulling her long, silky hair into a bun.

"Exactly, and you know what?" I said, looking at Jules and slamming my locker. "About five seconds before he told me he couldn't lay a hand on me, I'd decided to do his brains out."

"Well, at least you're finally up for it," Jamie said, patting me on the shoulder as if I needed condolence. "I mean the doing part."

"I think it pissed him off that I hinted it was all I was up for."

"Let me get this straight," Jamie said, sliding her sneakers on. "He got butthurt because all you wanted to do was have casual sex?"

"I think so. It was like he was telling me that unless he could date me, he wouldn't do anything at all."

"Out of respect for your dad," Jules added.

The excuses started to pour from me before either could press me further. "I'm six months away from being a senior resident and weeks away from opening the center. That's all that matters. I mean, what could he want from me? I don't have time." I was lying, and the looks they were giving me told me they knew better.

"Exactly," Jules said, giving Jamie a look that screamed shut the hell up.

It was becoming more apparent just how sheltered I'd become. I wasn't sticking my neck out enough—therefore, I had nothing to be afraid of. I decided then that it was fine with me. The finish line was close. I may have the worst luck imaginable when it came to personal relationships, but I would be the best-damned surgeon in the state of Texas.

Jack

I listened to the jets whirl beneath me and felt absolutely nothing. Noticing the passengers around me board the plane with smiling faces, I realized I hadn't felt even a hint of the excitement or satisfaction I usually did when I was beginning a new adventure. Frustrated, I tossed back my bourbon, savoring the taste and the burn. It was no big mystery why, either. My Aunt Nadine had pinpointed it last night when we met for dinner.

"This is new," she said, staring at her menu as I sat across from her, ignoring mine.

"What?" I asked, motioning to the waitress for two more drinks.

She laid down her menu, her detective skills coming out to play. She'd been the lead investigator in the city of New Orleans for the last thirty years alongside my Uncle Spencer, who held a seat as judge. She'd been the most challenging parent to put anything over on. Well, that and the fact that she knew me better than most.

"You haven't stuck to your two-drink minimum. You're agitated and morose. You pushed your trip back by another week. My guess is you're holding out for something. Who is she?"

Throwing the rest of my drink back, I scooted back into my seat, ignoring the girl at the bar directly over my aunt's shoulder who was trying far too hard to get my attention. It happened often, and I hated it.

"It was nothing. A flirtation that didn't go well." I knew better than to dismiss my aunt. She wasn't buying it. Neither was I.

I adjusted myself again to avoid reciprocating the stares that came my way.

"Ignore them. Talk to me. Tell me."

When I'd unexpectedly gotten the first onslaught of female attention a few years after my last surgery, my Aunt Nadine had been the one to school me on how to handle it. I'd been locked inside my head for so long that I'd had no clue what to do with my new popularity. It was a nightmare for an introvert. Nadine was one of very few to have brought me out of my shell.

"I just told you," I said as my agitation grew. "Did you ever stop to think we only have these dinners once a month so you'll stop grilling me on my personal life?"

"You don't have one," she said, sitting up in her seat, her fists balled at the end of the table, a sure sign of a conversation I didn't want to have. My Uncle Spencer had loved the fire he saw in her when they met. She was nineteen and already out of college. According to him, she had been the hardest woman in the world to handle—and still was. He loved her more than life.

"I do fine," I said in another attempt to close the subject.

"Oh, I have no doubt," she said and turned to look behind her at the woman at the bar who'd put her best assets on display for me, "if you want them fast."

"I'm thirty-seven years old. Aren't I a little old for this talk?"

"Guess not," she quipped back. "You're still running around the globe like your ass is on fire."

"I like to travel. Lots of adults do."

"I said running."

"Don't," I warned. "It was always my plan."

"Fine, I'll give you that. But how many times have you been to the Himalayas?"

I leaned forward as my temper flared. "Twice, this will be the third."

"How about Australia?"

"Four."

"Africa?"

"Six."

"Greenland, Iceland, fucking Loch Ness?"

"Fine, point taken. My turn. Do you all get together on some conspiratorial level and decide what hard questions you want to ask?"

"Yes," she said with her no-bullshit tone.

"And they send you because, what, you're the meanest?"

"Ouch," she said in mock hurt. "Yes."

"That only worked until I caught on," I said, biting into the flavored ice in my drink. "I was seven."

"Jack—" she started.

"Shit," I muttered, giving her my full attention.

I looked at my aunt and gave her the ear she was asking for.

"You're like a son to me."

"I am your son," I assured her.

I saw her eyes soften before she laid into me. "Your diet is lacking substance, and it's my job to point that out to you."

"I get it."

Her voice was a whisper as she looked at me with glassy eyes. "I don't think you do."

I paused at my aunt's emotion. She'd been a pillar of strength for me my whole life. She'd been there for me on my darkest days, the days before, and every day after. I'd never known life without her—never wanted to. I swallowed hard.

"You all feel this way?"

She nodded.

I looked out the window at the bustling streets of New Orleans, thinking of Rose and the look in her eyes when I'd almost kissed her. That look alone was worth skipping my trip.

"She's off limits."

"How so?"

"She's a friend of mine's daughter. And she's scared."

"So, she's not off limits."

"If you ignore everything I just told you, then, no, she's not off limits."

Ignoring another smile from her, I grabbed her drink and took a large swallow as she sighed in distaste. Our plates were deposited, and I took a large forkful of fish, knowing that if I didn't kick the buzz, I would end up in a cab and be forced to leave my bike—something I hated to do. I finished my plate and looked up to see my aunt with a growing smile on her face. "This talk was pointless."

"I agree."

"No, Jack." This is where the point kicked in. "You've already made your decision."

"And that decision is seat 1A in about twelve hours."

My aunt looked down at her plate with another smile as my temper flared.

"I'm not hiding, and I'm not running. I hope you know that. I hope you've known that. I've been good for a very long time," I said confidently.

Ignoring my remark, she looked on at me with pride. "You were so afraid to show that beautiful face," she mused.

"Only you thought it was beautiful."

"Beauty isn't everything. It's hardly anything."

"I know."

"You more than anyone, and now you're the most beautiful man in the world."

"Again, only you'd think that."

"Not this time, my boy," she said as she glared over her shoulder. "And who said I was talking about your face?" She stood suddenly and laid her credit card on the table. I moved to stop her from paying, but she cut me off with a look of warning. I surveyed her untouched plate and looked back up to her in confusion. "You know I would never cut our time short, but I have an appointment."

I waited as I watched a rare blush coat her cheeks. With an eye roll, she admitted the truth. "With a wedding planner."

I gave her a full laugh, and she looked down at me with a scowl while she filled out the credit card slip. My aunt, though a hard-ass, looked nowhere near her actual age and was truly a beautiful woman. She'd had it on good authority to teach me about unwanted attention, having dealt with a fair amount of it herself.

"Eat my plate before you get on that damned bike," she ordered as I stood to hug her. She wrapped around me tightly for a moment, a little longer than usual.

"Don't worry," I whispered as she held me tighter at my words before she let me go.

I watched her walk away and made a move to resume my seat

when I smelled perfume. For a second, I entertained the idea of a quick fuck. It was something I wouldn't have hesitated to do months or even weeks ago. But my aunt was right. I had dined on the same type of woman who stood behind me now for almost a decade. Empty sex in an instantly empty bed after didn't have the same sating effect it used to have. My last fling had lasted only a few months. I'd been in Vietnam on another one of my endless trips and hadn't batted an eyelash when she'd informed me that she'd moved on almost a month before my return. Still, it would be a decent attempt to get the eyes and lips I'd spent the last week thinking about out of my head—though I could never erase the impression she'd made.

Rose in my thoughts again and my decision made, I quickly turned to the woman in wait and watched her eyes widen.

"I'd hoped you'd overheard our conversation and would come over."

Her eyes scanned me up and down, and I could see the excitement build on her features.

"Oh yeah?" she said suggestively.

"So then you're ready to accept Christ as your savior?!"

She froze as I barely managed to stifle my laugh. I looked down at her deep cleavage and back up at her perfectly painted face. "He loves all of his children, no matter their sins."

She blew out an audible puff of air in defeat as she approached the bar, grabbed her purse, and made her way out of the door.

I chuckled at the memory of the woman's face as I watched the last few passengers' stuff overly full luggage into the compartments. The more they worked the luggage into the limited space, the more the plane started to suffocate me. Suddenly, all I wanted to do was grab my duffle bag and go. The trip no longer appealed to me, and I knew the reason.

"Damnit," I cursed under my breath as I gifted my aunt her wish and stood just as the flight attendant moved to lock the door.

chapter

eight

THE FOLLOWING SATURDAY—AFTER MY FAILED FIRST ATTEMPT at dating—I was sitting on the newly delivered cement picnic bench just outside the main building as my dad conducted his final meeting with the crew. I wasn't needed, and it suited me just fine. I'd decided to bring my lunch outside even though it was still hot as hell. I'd been in the freezing air conditioning most of the day and could feel my skin thawing. I was lost in my thoughts, staring into the distance, when awareness and his scent hit me.

"Mmmm, that looks good."

Cajun.

I looked up with a smile just as my wrist was gripped by Jack's hand. He brought the apple I was just about to devour to his mouth and took a large bite out of it, closing his eyes with a moan. Before I could audibly protest, he wiped peanut butter off the corner of my lip and sucked it off his finger.

"It's the perfect combination, don't you think?"

My senses reeling, I nodded in agreement before it occurred to me to be offended.

Jack—still holding my wrist—took another bite of my apple and smiled around it. I smiled back, unable to fight the urge.

We stared at each other for a brief moment before he spoke up. "Did you miss me?"

"No," I lied, holding out the apple for him to take, which he pushed toward me. I'd done nothing but think about him, knowing I'd screwed up. In front of me now, he was like a breath of fresh air while he stole mine at the same time. It had only been a week since I'd seen him, but my memory of him hadn't done him justice. Not only was he beautiful to look at, but his easy smile and the crinkle around his eyes somehow put me at ease.

"What's new with you, Rose?" Jack said, looking at my parted lips with amusement. Today, he looked dead sexy in a light green cotton T-shirt that outlined the taut muscles in his chest and arms. His eyes sparkled with more blue than gray and glittered with sexy mischief.

"What are you doing here?"

"I've got a little time between jobs, so I thought I'd lend a hand until the center opens. That okay with you?" He gripped my wrist again, taking another large bite of my apple. I pulled away, digging a spare out of the small cooler next to me, then thrust the one he'd almost devoured toward him.

"No thanks, I'm not hungry," he said with a seriousness that had me chuckling with an eye roll. He was fun when he was playful.

"I have to admit something," Jack said as he took a seat next to me on the top of the cement table and leaned in.

"Oh yeah, what's that?" I asked, curious and elated that he was sitting next to me—in front of me again. My heart began to pick up its pace.

"I've done nothing but think about you since I left," he said, making me pause mid-bite. I took my mouth away from our shared apple with a sigh.

"Jack, about the way I acted," I began apologetically.

"*I* acted like a total ass," he said, matching my tone. "I have to admit," he continued, grinning at me devilishly, "getting shot down before I even had a chance to plead my case—" he shook his head with humor "—is not something I'm used to. I didn't quite know what to make of it. It's still no excuse, so I'm going to have to beg your forgiveness." He leaned in and gripped the side of my head, rubbing his thumb along my top lip. "You knocked the wind out of me."

"Jack…"

"Hear me out," he murmured as his eyes implored mine. "I'm not the kind of guy that can't take no for an answer, but I can't help but want to try again. And, well, if you shoot me down again, at least I can say I went down with my second wind."

He leaned in close, his breath hitting my skin. Everything in me peaked, and for the first time since we met, my fear dissipated, and thoughts of only him surrounded me in a cloud. I breathed in deeply, both in relief that he was there and in the fact that he wanted to try again. At that moment, I knew I wanted him and wanted him to have me the way he wanted.

"And my dad?"

"It's not like we don't like each other. Hell, for all I know, I'm just being paranoid. Either way, we don't have to say a word to anyone—for now."

"I don't know what I'm capable of," I said honestly as he captured me with his soothing hands and soft eyes. "I swear. I don't know if I'm capable of anything at all."

"Then I guess we'll see," he said as he leaned in and brushed his lips on my cheek. "You're shaking," he whispered, running his hands through my hair. "I don't want you afraid of me."

"I'm not afraid of you." I leaned into him, completely intoxicated, my picnic forgotten.

"Maybe you should be," he whispered an inch from my

lips, "because the first time I kiss you, I'm bringing everything I've got."

"Aunt Wose!"

Our cloud disbursed quickly as an excited Grant came barreling toward us as fast as his little legs would move him, his dad close behind.

"Hey, baby blue," I said as I met him halfway and scooped him up in my arms. He quickly started wiggling in protest, so I let him down with a sigh.

"Can we pway de goft tart?"

I looked at Jack in apology and noticed him eyeing Grant with fondness in his eyes. Grant had a way of doing that. Jack looked over at me and gave me a wink.

"Jack," Dean greeted him with a short but friendly handshake.

"Dean," Jack replied as they both looked at me expectantly.

"Oh, yes," I said, looking down at Grant, who was growing impatient for an answer.

"I'll go with you," Jack said, looking at Dean. "You in? I must warn you, she's a bit reckless on the cart. We might want to look for protective gear."

"Shut up and get on," I barked as I pulled my keys out of my pocket.

"And militant," Jack muttered to Dean under his breath as I cut my eyes at him.

"You should have seen her at ten years old," Dean said with a laugh as we all piled on the cart. I gave Dean a warning look, which he ignored.

"Brightest red hair in the state of Texas, and dear Lord, her mouth, a mile a minute and so full of shit."

I caught little Grant's gasp and eventual "Daddy say shit."

"Good job, Martin," I piped as Dean made a hissing sound through his teeth, followed by an "Oops. Don't tell Mommy."

I belly laughed as we took off. Grant giggled gleefully with each speed bump. After a solid half hour of 'pway', we stopped again at the main building to see a waiting Dallas walking Annabelle around in the grass. Her little fingers were fisted around her mom's.

"Hey, Daddy," Dallas called to Dean. "Watch this!"

She loosened Annabelle's death grip, and the baby took two bold and purposeful steps forward before falling back into her mom. Dean shot out of the back seat, ran to Annabelle, and picked her up, giving her encouraging words as he showered her with kisses.

"Did we just see her first steps?" Jack asked with a hopeful hint in his voice.

I tried to hide my glazing eyes as I whispered a hoarse, "Yep."

"Wow." I looked over at Jack, who was looking at my family with admiration. There was something unquestionably good about Jack, and I saw it in that moment.

"Daddy say shit!" Grant called out as he exited the cart. Dallas lifted her head skyward and shook it as if to ask 'why' while Jack and I laughed at the spectacle before us. Dean hung his head and then nuzzled Annabelle as Dallas informed Grant that no one liked a tattle. I knew that firsthand, especially since I was the one who did most of it in our youth, Dallas being the victim.

"See you tonight?" Dallas called out to me.

"Yes," Jack and I both said in unison.

"Wait," I said, looking back at Jack. "You're coming to my parents?"

"Rose, I've been to dinner every few months for the last ten years."

"How old are you?" I asked, no longer sure of our age difference.

"I'm thirty-seven," he answered, matter of fact.

He was quite a bit older than I'd originally thought, although he didn't look a day over thirty. He was blessed with good genes—the ones he filled out were even better.

"So, I guess I'll see you there?"

"Guess so," he said, taking his leave and giving the Martins a soft wave. He turned to me and winked before he walked to his bike. Dallas looked between us and gave me a full-on smile that I pretended to ignore.

One of the things I'd always loved about my family home was that it was unpredictable. On any given day, anything could happen. My parents vowed to each other long ago to never take a day for granted, and though a good number of days at the Whitaker house were relatively boring, a good many were filled with excitement. And the source of that excitement had always been the brainchild of my parents. Tonight was no exception. They'd decided to host a fiesta.

I walked into the beautiful, Spanish-style house my dad had built years before I was born and heard hysterical laughter. I noted Jack's bike in the drive as I shut the front door, and a little jolt of something raced through me. He'd threatened to kiss me and do it well. It was kind of an asinine thing to be excited about as an adult woman, yet this woman warmly welcomed it. I was in dire need of sexual attention, but I already knew Jack wanted to take things slow.

I entered the kitchen to find my mom blending margaritas while Al Green sang "Love and Happiness" in the background.

"Hello," I called out as my dad looked up at me with a grin. "Little woman!"

I hesitated only a second before I walked toward him to give him a hug. He was a little too enthusiastic.

"And how many margaritas have you had today, sir?" I asked in jest as I pretended not to look around for Jack, who was nowhere in sight.

"Your mom may have challenged me earlier, and I may have risen to it."

"And you may have lost your ass on that bet," my mom piped happily behind him as she slowed the blender. "Hey, Rose, margarita?"

"What's with the celebration?" I said, noting my mom's slow execution of pour before she thrust a huge salted glass of margarita in my face.

"Our son is pregnant with our fifth grandchild, and our daughters are about to open a clinic to save thousands of lives. What parent wouldn't be celebrating?" my dad roared as my mom started a new batch in the blender.

"Paul!" I yelled at the top of my lungs just as he poked his head in the kitchen with a smile. "Another one?"

"Yep," he said as I lunged at him and hugged him tightly to me.

My brother Paul was a replica of my dad with strawberry blond hair and green eyes. His face was filled with pride as he looked down at me. "Can you believe it?"

"Absolutely! I'm so happy for you!" I mused, then looked past him in search of his wife. "Where is she?"

"She went to pick up the twins and head home. She's having it rough this time with sickness, but she told me to tell you to come by sometime this week."

The concerned doctor in me spoke up. "Ah, that sucks. Are you giving her—"

My older brother rolled his eyes at me while he cut me off. "Yes, doc, we have it under control. You forget your *other* brother is her doctor." My brother and his wife had a horrible time trying to conceive naturally. I could honestly claim my sister's husband, Dean, was responsible for the birth of all four of my nieces and nephews. Not only had he given Dallas the gift of her children, but as a specialist, he'd helped my brother conceive his.

"Right." I smiled at him, my chest bursting with pride. "Well, I've been meaning to come by, anyway. I want some time with the twins."

"Anytime, Rosebud," he said, taking a large sip of my margarita before handing it back to me.

"Where is everybody?"

"In the living room," he said, walking past me with an empty glass, holding it out toward my mom.

She smiled at him with the same tenderness she would with Dallas or me. Though Paul had been a result of my dad's first marriage, words like half-brother or step-mom never crossed either of their lips. We were family, and there was no half to it as far as my mom was concerned. She'd accepted Paul as her own and never looked back.

Al Green grew louder as I entered the living room and took note of the full-fledged party before me. I saw my nephew first, getting down as he bounced his diaper-clad butt around the room. His chubby hands were at his sides, and he was doing the dancing-type squat thing babies often do. I was completely enamored as I looked up to Dallas—who was recording him with her cell phone—a doting smile on her face. I loved that look on her. Dallas had been such a hard-ass her whole life, and though we all loved her regardless, it was disarming to see her so in love with her family. She was a glowing mom who took pride in her children and adored them—though she often voiced otherwise. Admittedly, her babies were hard to handle, both bursting with personality and quite demanding. It would definitely take a village to raise them, and thankfully, that's what we were. I loved being a part of it all. It was, without a doubt, one of the best parts of my life.

I was more than entertained watching Grant until I saw whom he was mimicking. Jack had Annabelle in his arms and was swinging his hips to the music in perfect time. My mouth dropped as I watched him move around the living room like a trained lady-killer while he entertained the little girl in his arms. Dallas was too busy watching her son give it all he had to notice Jack. I quickly scanned the room to find Dean digging through my parent's old records. My dad had kept a good amount of them from my parents' 'rave' days, and they would break them out every once in a while. Apparently, tonight seemed like a good time, but it was the second generation hosting this party. Annabelle laughed and cooed at Jack as the wind from his movement ran through her raven hair. With each dip Jack made with his hips, she screamed out with a giggle. Dallas egged Grant on with a "Go, baby, go," laughing to herself as Grant really got into it, shaking everything he had. I laughed along with her, still a bit dazzled at Jack's ability to move the way he did. I found it sexy as hell.

A feeling of fullness I hadn't experienced in some time surfaced as a memory of the time my parents had attempted to teach us to dance flittered across my mind. I looked at Dallas with sentimental eyes.

She would do the same for her kids, and I would be right there to help her.

Dallas had no rhythm at all, and I was full of it. Not wanting to interrupt the scene unfolding before me, I danced along with them at the living room entrance. Minutes later, I found Jack looking over at me in greeting with a warm smile and a lift of his chin. He wasn't shy at all about the fact that he was dancing in my parent's living room.

"Rose, are you seeing this?!" Dallas howled as her son roared and pulled out his best dance moves. I watched him with pride as the song finally ended, or rather, Dean scratched the record to put on some old-school Michael Jackson.

No one seemed to tire as they danced through song after song. My sister and I shared a margarita on the couch while my parents howled in the kitchen with Paul. It seemed the party was in full swing at the Whitaker house. I sent up a prayer in thanks that I hadn't missed it.

"I've got two bottles ready," Dallas said in an attempt to justify her large sip of my alcohol.

"No judging," I said, cradling the bottom of the mug and lifting it to encourage her to take a bigger sip.

"Maybe I should pump again first," she said, moving to get up.

"Dallas, you've already drunk too much to try. Chill out, she'll be fine."

"Right, okay," she said uneasily, sinking back into the couch, staring at the drink in my hand with a guilty look before she scanned the living room and her eyes fell on Jack.

"He's been at it almost half an hour," Dallas noted and turned to me with big eyes as her eyebrows did a double tap on her forehead. "Stamina."

I rolled mine at her suggestion. "They're growing up too fast," I shot back, trying to change the subject. "Go make another one."

"Have your own," Dallas said in challenge. "This oven is closed."

"Bullshit."

I pushed my margarita toward her. "Nope, that's all you," she protested.

"I can't drink another sip. I'm technically on call for another thirty minutes."

"I think Mom and Dad are drunk," Dallas said with a chuckle. "We caught them doing shots when we got here. They're trying so hard to hide it. God, I love them," Dallas said with a sigh before she turned to me. "You're looking at him again."

"Annabelle's never really been fond of strangers," I said, trying to evade the subject.

"Rose, he's single."

"Thanks for the report," I snapped as I ripped the margarita from her hands before taking a mind-numbing gulp.

"He seems like good people."

"Uh huh," I agreed, watching Jack's hip sway. He was a natural, all rhythm and looked so damned good doing it. I was having a hard time taking my eyes away despite the fact that Dallas was watching me. Feminine instinct had kicked in and was taking over. Want coursed through me, and I felt the urgent need to wrap myself around him.

Dallas pulled the drink away from me as Dean eyed her across the living room, then nodded toward Grant, who was now holding himself up on the coffee table while his head began to droop with sleep. They shared a smile, and Dallas moved to get up, but I stopped her.

"Poor baby," I murmured as I shot out of my seat. Scooping Grant up, he didn't protest at all as he buried his head in my shoulder, and I rocked him back and forth. Dean changed the music to "Drive" by The Cars, one of my favorite '80s songs, and together, Jack and I rocked the babies to sleep, eyeing each other. Dallas and Dean kept themselves busy in conversation while Jack and I had a silent one of our own. Suddenly jealous of my niece, I studied the strong arms that bulged as they held her and let my eyes trail over the rest of him.

One by one, the babies fell asleep as Dean and Dallas left us to join my parents in the kitchen, who'd started to serve dinner. Jack and my eyes remained locked as we swayed in time with the music. Jack had never looked better with my beautiful niece resting against him. He was perfectly masculine as he held her. He rocked and gently stroked her back, his eyes roaming over my face and body as I held my nephew tightly, whispering the words to him in melody. Once I was sure they were both fast asleep, with a slight jerk of my head, I motioned to Jack, and he followed me into my parents' bedroom as we took turns laying the babies down and tucking them in.

"You handle her so well," I said as I pulled a blanket over the two of them and patted Grant's diaper-clad butt. He usually slept with his tail in the air, and tonight was no exception. Jack and I shared a chuckle as I turned my attention to Annabelle.

"She's easy to handle," Jack whispered back.

"Uhhh… stick around," I said, full of sarcasm. "The child is anything but."

"I love a challenge," Jack reassured as we made our way out of the bedroom into the dimly lit hall. I could hear my family talking animatedly in the distance and was surprised at how easy it felt with Jack there. He surprised me a little every day.

A compliment ready on my lips, I turned to him as we started down the hall. "You're a good dancer. Ha-oh!"

The air was knocked out of me as I was pushed against the wall. My hands were gripped by Jack's and pinned to the sides of my head. My breathing picked up as I realized his intent, and he quickly let me know with his next words that he would have his way.

"I have to fucking taste you right now. Don't say no," he said as he lingered only a beat before he leaned in slow and drew a breathless whimper from me. I waited for him, my eyes beckoning him as they had last weekend. Just as he closed the distance between us, I braced myself.

And it was pointless.

His strong, full lips took mine in a possessive kiss. My body sank against the wall as we molded together. We were fire and wind, and the intensity was enough to knock me off my feet. His tongue slid along my lower lip, and I gasped in permission as he tasted the rest of me thoroughly. His kiss was powerful, deliberate, and consuming. Everything fell away as I greedily took it and returned it with the same fervor. He pulled back briefly, pushed my hands further over my head, and then held them there as he again dipped in and stole my breath, claiming my mouth. His tongue teased and tortured before he thrust in deep, and I became aware—more than ever—of his effect on me. I matched him lick for slow, sweet lick and moaned into his mouth, starved for more.

Thoughtless and full of the need to touch him, I fought against his hands while he put more pressure on them, leaning in to cover my body with his.

I pulled back with a plea. "Let me touch you," I begged.

"Not yet, and not here," he murmured, his voice rough, his lips like silk as he brushed them lightly against mine.

A loud burst of laughter had us stilling before we looked in their direction and back at each other. I gave Jack wide eyes as he leaned in again.

"We better get back," I argued weakly, not wanting our stolen moment to end. He nodded as he held me against the wall.

My chest rose and fell, brushing against his with each breath. He looked down at my flushed and ready body with appreciation before looking back at me. I was in a simple light blue cotton sundress and wanted nothing more than to be rid of it at that moment. His eyes told me he wanted the same.

This time, I leaned in and took his lips, and he obliged as he fully tasted me again. Heart beating out of control, I sank further into him as I gave him more and more, and he took without hesitation. It was heaven and hell—a perfect mix of satisfaction and desire. He eased away from me as electricity filled the air between us, then slowly pulled my hands down, kissing each one before he let them go.

He'd made good on his promise to bring all he had, and I was overjoyed at the fact that I could handle it and so much more. That I wanted more, needed more, from Jack. Another bout of laughter from the kitchen had us looking at each other with regret.

"You go first. I'm going to need a minute," Jack said without apology as he brushed slightly against my stomach, and I felt the fullness in his jeans. I'd always loved a man who was freely sexual, and Jack seemed to fit the bill. I boldly brushed my hand against him before I began to walk in the direction of my waiting family.

"Not nice," Jack said with a groan.

"You started it," I shot back playfully. We shared an intimate smile before I made my way toward the kitchen. I paused momentarily in the doorway to collect myself and touched my lips. They were swollen, sensitive, and, in a way, felt renewed. I briefly remembered a time when I wondered if I would ever know a kiss again.

And Jack had just wrecked me with his.

My lips ached a little for him now in his absence. As I slowly came down from the high of his touch, my body reminded me

that I'd be more ready physically if we ever became truly intimate. And that was enough for now.

I walked into the kitchen and joined my family at the table,
still reeling but elated. I was capable; at least, it felt that way for
now.

"They're out cold," I assured Dallas, who looked at me with
eager eyes. Relief covered her features, and she nodded to me in
thanks before taking a large bite of her fajitas.

Jack joined us a short minute later, and I couldn't help but
smile a little at my plate, knowing what we'd just shared. We sat
at the table, Jack next to me as if by design, as everyone held separate conversations. My dad and Paul talked shop—Paul having
taken over my dad's successful architecture firm years earlier.
My mom, Dean, and Dallas wrapped up in their own conversation about the kids.

Jack doted on me without the awareness of others, handing
me a napkin before I could ask for a spare and filling my empty
margarita with the pitcher on the table as soon as I'd drained it.
I looked at him with a soft "thank you." Though he didn't look
at me often or even force conversation, I could *feel* him with me.
It was as if he was holding my hand. It sent welcomed warmth
through me.

An hour later, the entire table buzzed with shared conversation as my parents chimed in with lighthearted parenting antics.

"Rose was the hardest with her temper," my mom said with
a laugh. "She once gave her dad and me the silent treatment for a
full day because we refused to house her grass snake. She was so
sure of everything, including her opinion, which changed daily.
She was also a klutz, which terrified us to no end when she announced she wanted to be a surgeon."

"I can see that," Jack agreed next to me.

My mom looked over at Jack as she continued. "She once

saw a homeless man downtown and insisted we take him home with us because we had the room. She cried for hours when we told her no and wouldn't let up until we went back searching for him. When we found him, she forced Seth to empty his wallet and promised we'd be back every week on the same day."

"I did?"

"You were five," my dad said, looking at my mom and then back at me. "He wasn't a friendly man at all. You should've been scared of him. Instead, you surprised us. And trust me—you didn't let us forget about him. We went back for about a month, until one day, he didn't show. You were a fearless little girl."

"I don't remember," I said as I searched my bank of memories and came up empty.

"Fearless and daring," my mom agreed. "I caught you playing peekaboo with one of the neighbor's little boys in the backyard one day. After we had a little talk, you insisted for almost a week that one day you too would have a penis."

Jack spit out some of the margarita he was drinking and looked at me with soft eyes and a loud laugh.

"Okay, parents, no need for anymore recap. I get it. I was a difficult child."

"Oh, but you were so much fun," my mom said with adoration. "Paul was responsible, Dallas was a brat but easy maintenance, and you were our wild card."

"That's why I call you little woman," my dad said in agreement with my mom. "Independent from the first year you were born. I've never seen another baby so hell-bent on doing everything for herself. You even tried to change your own diapers."

"And now I'm boring," I muttered without thinking, wishing I had one-tenth of that fearless little girl inside me. No one heard me but Jack, who protested with a tender whispered comment. "Not in the slightest."

My chest stretched at his words, and I couldn't help the slow smile that crept up on my lips.

Jack was the first to leave, wishing us all a goodnight, completely respectful of our agreement to keep our new relationship private. Still, I saw him hesitate in his goodbye to me, but only briefly as he exited the house. It had been a perfect night. I no longer had to wonder if I'd ever be a kissed woman again or if I'd ever feel the desire to share myself sexually with another man and be able to feel it everywhere.

Jack had ripped off another Band-Aid. And it was painless... until I got home.

chapter

nine

I WOKE THE NEXT MORNING AND, PER OUR AGREEMENT, WENT TO
text Jack only to realize he'd beat me to it.

Jack: Good morning, beautiful.

Rose: Rap & R&B 101 LL Cool J, Mama said Knock You
Out. And no need for flattery.

Jack: It's the truth. I should have told you that last night
before I kissed your perfect mouth.

Rose: We were up to our ears in dancing babies. Kind
of busy.

Jack: I had fun. I like your family very much. They're a
lot like mine.

I laughed hard at that. There was no way it could be true.

Rose: Not possible.

Jack: You'd be surprised. What are you doing?

Rose: About to scrub in for surgery.

Jack: See you later? Dinner?

Rose: I may be in surgery for hours.

Jack: Don't run from me.

I paused, unsure if I was making excuses.

Rose: Okay.

Jack: Okay you aren't running or okay to dinner?

Rose: Both

Jack: ☺ **Eight?**
Rose: Nine ☺
Jack: Go save someone.
Rose: Go build something.

"Jamie, let's get in the zone." She nodded at me with a wink as Lauryn Hill's "That Thing" sounded throughout the room. I only had a few minutes before McGuire came in to start the appendectomy before silence accompanied me throughout the rest of the surgery. On more than one occasion, McGuire had come in with his nose turned up in complete distaste for my music selection. Jamie was more of a Southern rock type of girl, but she always humored me—the way most people did. As far as I knew, I was a dying breed in my love of rap music. And though I hoped to persuade Jack of its appeal, I knew my love for it would never fade.

Only Dallas loved it along with me until her tastes changed a little later. Still, I loved that we shared in that. It was one of our things. I found myself a little sad when I thought of Dallas lately. I missed her terribly, even though I saw her last night. She had this huge life, and though she included me in every minute she could, we weren't the ride-or-die girls we'd once been—still as close, but *never* alone together.

I didn't resent her growing family for it. I simply missed my person. The same went for my old college roommate, Jennifer. We'd been close for the entirety of our education—both university and medical school—until she moved to California months after graduation. Jen married and began to have children, and though neither of us wanted it, we'd drifted apart. She'd been my confidant for so long, and for the first year after her move, I was lost without her. I couldn't fault her, either. She was doing what she'd set out to do. Life was moving on, and those around me were building families. If things hadn't gone the way they had, I'd probably have been a new mom as well. I shook off the threat of sadness and concentrated on my kiss with Jack as I prepared to get into my zone.

It worked.

I spent my workday doing routine surgeries. The more I operated in the same set conditions, the more I was sure I was glad Dallas and I hadn't stuck to our original plan to open a general practice. I knew that, eventually, I'd become bored with the routine, just as McGuire had stated. I looked forward to being tested on tumor removal. No case would be the same. Cancer, though my greatest enemy, was still to become my life's work. It was unpredictable, and that was the challenge I had to look forward to. As a human, I loathed the idea of anyone going through something so damning and painful. As a doctor, I was intrigued and determined to find a way to conquer my enemy.

All my years of training, the hours I'd spent buried in books and journals, and the months I'd spent practicing my techniques were all for the greater good. My purpose, my reason for being, was to fight cancer along with Dallas. All our roads and hard work had led to the center. Even pieces of our personal lives had all led up to this point.

As I closed up Mrs. Mills, I whispered in her ear, the way I did all my patients, "You did really well. You can come back now."

"What do you say to them?" Jamie asked for the millionth time. I simply winked at her as I looked at McGuire, who never asked me but gave me the stern look he always did when I completed my ritual.

"Good job, Whitaker. I've taken the liberty of setting you

up with Dr. Nichols this evening. He'll be performing a cranial tumor removal."

"Thank you, sir," I said with enthusiasm, even though I felt a little piece of me sink at the thought that I would have to cancel on Jack.

True to his pleasant nature, McGuire left the OR without so much as a kiss my ass or goodbye. I vowed then and there not to treat my staff the same. What was the point of intimidating people that way? Sure, his methods had been successful for him, but it didn't earn any more respect—at least not from me. Though I'd admired his abrasive attitude at one time, it was starting to wear on me. I again thanked fate that I wouldn't be governed by him for the rest of my surgical career.

Excitement for my professional future began to race through me. I turned to Jamie as we sat in the courtyard next to the cafeteria and finally started the conversation I'd long avoided.

"We have just eleven weeks until we open the center. Weeks!"

Jamie paused, a full spoon of yogurt in front of her. "Now you want to talk about it? Now… now you want to talk about it when we've been trying to get you to open up for a solid year?!"

I chuckled as I poured almond milk into my granola. "So, I've been tight-lipped, I know, I know, but that's only because I didn't want to jinx it, you know?"

Jamie nodded as if she understood.

"For so long, I've been measuring my life in years, Jamie. I can't believe I'm saying weeks. WEEKS!"

"I've never seen you this pumped," she said with a mouthful of yogurt.

"It's a dream come true," I said, my voice quivering with emotion and pride. "What do you do when your dream comes true?"

Jamie looked down at me just as her pager went off. She smiled as she stood to leave. "I guess you dream bigger."

As I watched her walk away, I couldn't for the life of me imagine asking for anything more.

Rose: I have to cancel, Jack. I'm sorry.
Jack: ?
Rose: Late surgery.
Jack: I understand. I'll be at the center tonight. Come see me when you get off.
Rose: It may be late.
Jack: What am I, 80? I think I can handle a late night.
Rose: LOL. You are wayyyyyy older than me. Sure you can keep up?
Jack: I'll answer that question in person.

A solid blush swept through me, and I hoped he'd make good on that threat.

Rose: See you soon.
Jack: Not soon enough.

I smiled as I scrubbed in and caught my reflection in the window. I saw *her* again. She resembled a woman capable of a genuine smile—of enjoying the moment. I knew it wasn't just the sudden attention of the beautiful man bent on entertaining our new connection. It was *everything* else, too. I was the career woman I'd set out to become. An already mildly accomplished surgeon with years of life-saving surgeries ahead of me, a career I'd dreamed of and worked my ass off for. With the help of my sister and my amazing family, and though I'd become a doctor years ago, I felt the pride that went along with the title... *really* felt it for the first time since I graduated. When I'd crossed the stage to accept my doctorate after having just lost Grant, I'd been numb to the world. I'd been stuck in an unbelievable cloud filled with pain and disbelief. Everything I'd done after that day had been busy work, a way to keep myself from falling into despair and pain, but I'd still felt it. I'd pushed through each day, promising myself that I wouldn't let my personal tragedy take my whole life from me. But in a way, it had. In a way, I'd mourned to the point that being a doctor was a chore and another thing I had to get through instead of a joyful endeavor of my choosing. As I watched the patient being prepped for surgery in my new clarity, I rejoiced in the knowledge that was no longer the case. And while I assisted in an operation that would take me years to imitate and perfect, I let the swell of pride burst within me.

I am a surgeon.

Though the last few weeks had been confusing for me as far as finding my footing in my personal life, I realized the reason for that uncertainty.

I'd just woken up.

After assisting with another successful surgery, I pulled up to the center around eleven thirty and grinned at the sight of Jack's bike. I parked next to it and grabbed the bottle of Maker's Mark Jules had surprised me with on my last birthday and the bag of goodies I'd gotten from the store. I'd never really had a reason to open the bottle until today, but I was in the mood to celebrate. And though my feet were aching—and I was sure I needed a thorough shower—I looked at the center with fresh eyes.

Excitement coursed through me as I entered the double doors and shouted out to Jack.

"In here," he called out. I saw the light on in my unfinished office, walked in, and nearly dropped what was in my arms.

"Oh, Jack!" I said, taking it all in.

I saw his pride-filled smile as he bent over a saw table with a measuring tape. He let it retract back into its case and gave my reaction his full attention. "You like it?"

I stood there in disbelief for a solid minute as I took in my office. It wasn't the simple room I'd initially designed with my dad at my insistence. It was far more beautiful. This one was filled wall to wall with custom-made shelving derived from a stunning dark oak. If I'd had the time to dream it up, it would be precisely what I would have chosen. The desk looked newly finished and polished, and I had to do all I could to keep from tearing up.

"You did all of this today?"

"I'm good, but I'm not that good. I've been working on it for a few days now."

"I had no idea," I said, setting down my bags and walking toward the desk, rubbing my hands along the dark wood. It was flawless.

"You weren't supposed to," he murmured, wrapping his arms around me from behind. I reveled in the feel of them. It was such an intimate gesture since we'd only shared our first kiss the previous night, but I welcomed it.

"I'm glad you like it. The shelving is permanent. We'd have to rip the room apart to get it out. This could have really backfired."

His breath on my skin had my eyes closing briefly before I turned in his arms and kissed him soundly on the mouth. "It's absolutely beautiful. But I thought, with our budget stretched so thin… this is too much."

"This is on me."

the heart

111

"I can't ask that of you," I scorned.

"You didn't, but no good deed goes unpunished. Your sister had a damned fit when she saw this, so I've been commissioned to do the same for her."

I rolled my eyes, knowing I would have felt the same jealousy had Dallas's office been done this way.

"It's so beautiful," I whispered as we wrapped up a little tighter in our embrace. "Thank you."

"My pleasure," he whispered back. He was covered in sawdust, and I could feel the dampness of his shirt.

"You're filthy," I said, taking in his scent mixed with dry sweat and loving the feel of his hard body against mine.

"You have no idea," he said as he fisted a handful of my hair and licked my bottom lip smoothly.

"No, Jack, I mean you *are* dirty," I said, running my short nails over his T-shirt-clad back, urging him on.

"I'm not arguing," he teased just before his lips brushed mine. I pulled him in closer, and our mouths collided in a hungry kiss. His tongue moved with mine, and I sank into him. Minutes later, we pulled apart, foreheads touching as we shared a breath of recovery.

"Jack…" I said as I pulled him tighter to me, resolute to keep him there as long as he would let me.

"Feels so good," he murmured, trailing soft kisses along my jaw. I tilted my head back as his lips traced the skin of my neck and collarbone. On fire, I gripped him tight, wanting him closer. He lifted me off my feet, wrapping my legs around his waist, then sat on my new desk with me latched to him. His hands cupped my ass as he pulled me closer, his lips moving all over as he licked and sucked. It was better than I imagined it would be, and without thinking, I began to grind against him, wet and ready.

"Fuck," Jack cursed as he gripped my hips, stilled them, and brought his mouth back to mine. I was as good as gone as I began to ride the hard bulge in his pants. My center ached, pulsed, and begged for relief.

"I need you to stop that," Jack said as I clung to him for dear life, hunger out of control as need drove me to the brink.

Jack was everything I'd been missing—temptation, lust, hunger, and comfort all wrapped up in the perfect package. I felt strangely safe with him.

When he pulled away from our kiss, I saw the warning in his eyes. I was pushing his limits.

"Rose," he pleaded as he kneaded my ass with his strong hands.

"Okay," I said as I pulled away and puffed out my lip, which he took and sucked in teasing. Sharing the same smile, he gently put me on my feet, and I beamed at him.

"You hungry?"

"Starving, actually. I got super focused on finishing this and lost track of time." He eyed my bags. "You brought me food, woman?"

"I did," I said affectionately, still moved by the beauty of my new office and our kiss.

"Let me go wash up and change T-shirts?"

"K."

Cradling my face with both hands, he moved his thumb along my lower lip. I caught it and flicked my tongue against it before sucking gently. Jack's inhale was audible as he narrowed his eyes. "You're dangerous."

"I'm harmless," I murmured and pulled my mouth away.

"You feel so goddamned good," he said, making another round on my jaw with his perfect lips before he reluctantly let go of me and made his way out the door. After a moment or two of reflection, I got busy clearing the room of debris and setting up the bag full of food I'd brought from the store. French bread, a container of chicken salad, mixed fruit, soft cheese, and crackers were all set out on the shiny new wood that made up my desk. Though rectangular in shape, the outer edges were rough and left uneven by the condition of the original wood. I wondered how long it took him to work on a desk so intricately carved. He'd said days, and I appreciated his talent. We were both good with our hands, a shared commonality. Excited for a few stolen hours alone with him and a chance to explore the mystery that was Jack, I went to the break room and filled two plastic cups with ice. I was just about to break the wax seal on the bottle of booze when Jack emerged out of the hallway with damp hair. Even with a newly built room of things to admire, Jack was by far the best design to look upon.

"You up for a drink?" I asked, pouring two healthy-sized glasses of bourbon. "I feel like celebrating."

"Sure," he said as he took the glass from me and consumed a healthy sip. "What are we celebrating?"

I spent a few minutes telling Jack about my day, less the reason behind my breakthrough. I told him of my excitement about the clinic, how Dr. McGuire had moved me into a better position to help my future patients at the center, how I felt like my dream had finally come true, and my new appreciation for what I did.

"I feel like I just woke up, you know? And I'm looking around now like, *wow*. This is really happening," I said around a mouthful of French bread. "And of course, a part of me has been aware, but it's like now… I can fully embrace it. Make sense?"

"Perfect sense," he said, sitting in the chair beside me, his ankles crossed as he nibbled on my offering.

"God, I've been talking nonstop, sorry," I said sheepishly.

"Don't ever be sorry about talking to me about something

important to you. I happen to love that you're so enthusiastic. You worked hard for this. You deserve to be happy about it."

"Thank you," I said, pushing my glass against his in a toast. "I'm relieved."

"Why's that?"

Cajun.

God, I loved it.

"Because I didn't think I would feel this way again."

Jack looked slightly confused. "Again?"

I caught myself before I gave too much away. "It's just… it started to seem like an endless amount of work, and I was blind to the reward."

"Nothing worse than not loving what you do," Jack agreed. "I've fumbled in that department."

"You weren't always a contractor?"

"No, I went to Stanford and got an MBA in business. I was a suit, can you believe it?"

I opened my mouth to speak and closed it in equal parts shock and admiration. He was highly educated, and though I wasn't at all opposed to dating anyone without an education, it made Jack more intriguing.

"Guess not," he said as he poured a little more blend into our glasses.

"It's not that at all. Tell me."

"Nothing to tell, really. I graduated, got a job making a ridiculous amount of money, did my job well, and mapped out the rest of my life. Day in and day out, from the time I graduated until my twenty-seventh birthday, I had no issue with it. Then, one morning, I woke up, and my life no longer fit. So, I turned in my tie and decided to start from scratch." At that moment, I saw a flicker of something cover his features, but it disappeared just as quickly.

"Wow," I said, sitting back in my chair.

"The next week, I took a temporary job working with my hands. I had no intention of quitting work while I figured out what my next step was. So, I helped build the Skylit building in downtown New Orleans."

I nodded with a smile on my face. "My dad's design."

"Your dad took an interest in me for some reason, and I'm forever thankful. I didn't have to look around. I didn't even question it. Once I'd seen the finished building and knew I had a hand in it, I couldn't wait to finish the next. I stayed on with Seth for a full year before I went back to school and got what I needed to be a builder. And the rest is history."

"So my dad is like your sensei."

"Exactly."

"Now I understand why you don't want to piss him off."

"I had to make sure you were worth the trouble. The jury is still out."

Wrinkling my nose at him, I smacked him on the chest before closing the small space between us.

"So, you started out a suit and ended up being a roughneck."

"I started out a man with a plan and decided my plans were shit. Your dad was there for me, and I learned a lot from him. And as cheesy as this may sound, I don't want to disappoint him." Jack leaned in and took my lips gently. "He's made it abundantly clear over the years that his family is the most precious thing to him. I can see why." Another slow kiss and I was reeling. "But since the day we met, I haven't been able to think of anything else but this," he said between breath-stealing kisses, "to touch you, taste you."

"I'm glad you came back," I said softly as I held our connection.

"There's no way in hell I couldn't," he assured me, his voice low and full of heat. "And now I've got you all to myself," he murmured.

An hour later, Jack had told me of his life since that fateful day he turned in his tie. He'd traveled the world, taking on a few international projects and collecting what he called 'experiences.' I envied him in that he'd seen places I'd only heard about in books and movies. At only thirty-seven, Jack had accomplished more than most people do in a lifetime. I wondered how he was so easily entertained sitting in my office with me. He seemed to have wandered around for the last ten years without anything really to hold on to except his next job or 'experience.'

The conversation turned to me, and I studied him endlessly as I spoke, memorizing all parts of him. From his boot-clad feet to his long torso, defined arms, and perfectly broad shoulders, he was perfection right up to the flawless head that graced his shoulders. I now knew what it was like to kiss him, and very little of me wasn't aware that I was still preoccupied with that.

"Something on your mind, Rose?"

"Sex," I admitted through a long pull of drink. "I haven't had it in years. I'm wondering what it will be like with you."

Yep, I totally said that out loud.

Jack chuckled as he gripped my hand in his. We'd remained side-by-side, sizing each other up.

"What do you think it will be like?"

"Nope, I'm not taking that bait." I stood to clean up our mess.

He pulled me into his lap. I sat there wrapped in him with a dare in my eyes.

"Why so long?" Jack asked in a whisper.

"I've been busy," I said as his hands held me still while I struggled to break free.

"Bullshit, I can already tell you have a healthy appetite." He made a trail with his silky lips with a hint of his hungry tongue from my shoulder to my ear. His hands moved from around my stomach and stopped at the top of my thighs with a squeeze. He flicked his tongue at the shell of my ear, his warm breath sending my imagination into overdrive. "And I'm pretty sure I'm going to love every second of making sure I satisfy it. I'm going to taste every part of you. I'm going to love making you come."

"Jack," I rasped out as I sank impossibly further into him.

"Just like that. I'm going to draw my name out of you every chance I get."

"Oh God," I whispered as his hands moved up my body to cup my chest.

"That too," he promised as I melted in his lap—his warm, skilled touch and thick, husky voice completely seduced me.

He waited only a minute before he spoke again. "You got hurt?"

I closed my eyes tight, thankful he couldn't see me. "Yes. Can we do anything but talk about exes?"

"Agreed," he said easily.

"Are you always this easy to get along with?" I asked as I looked back at him with a grin.

"My hands are all over you now," he said heatedly. "Why in the hell would I want to ruin that?"

I lifted the bottle off the desk and took a drink. Jack leaned in and sipped it off of my lips.

"I feel good, Jack. Thank you for ending this day with me."

"It was my pleasure," he returned sincerely, keeping me snug against him.

"I should go. I have a shift tomorrow," I sighed.

He lifted us both to stand, his strength expected and, at the same time, surprising. "Come on, Rose, I'll walk you home."

"I have my car parked out front."

"Let's walk," Jack said, discarding the rest of our drinks into the trash. Though nearly a two-mile walk didn't appeal to me at the moment, being anywhere with Jack did. The highway in front of the center buzzed with a few scattered late-night cars as we made our way toward the lit path.

"You never get scared out here alone?" Jack asked as he took my hand. It felt so natural.

"Never. I know that's strange."

"Fearless," he joked, referring to my parents' conversation about me the night before.

"I really don't remember that. I don't remember being that crazy kid."

"I was a colorful asshole, according to my Aunt Rory."

"That's an unusual name," I remarked as he stroked my hand with his thumb, seducing me with the small gesture. He was extremely gentle with me, and I wondered if it had anything to do with his nature or if I was being handled with special care because of his relationship with my dad. Either way, it was endearing and didn't seem to be forced.

"She's an unusual woman. I think I've seen about a hundred different shades of hair on her. Her eclectic dress always seems to match whatever personality suits her by the day. She trades in husbands the way most people trade in cars." Jack laughed and stopped walking before he turned to me with his next statement. "She dropped me off on my first day of kindergarten in my Halloween costume."

"You're joking!" I said, both amused and sympathetic, trying to imagine a younger Jack.

"Both of my parents were down with food poisoning, and they thought her the safe alternative. I showed up on my first day of kindergarten dressed as a zombie."

"Oh shit," I gasped out with a laugh.

"It took my mom a solid year to forgive her, although my dad thought it was hilarious."

"Aww," I said as I squeezed his hand. "And it scarred you?"

"The first of many," he said as we resumed our walk. "I think she was trying to disguise my lip, you know, so it wouldn't be as hard on me."

I didn't pause my stride, but my heart skipped a beat at his admittance.

The stars were in clear view above us, and neither of us could ignore them as we paused next to the water and gazed up at them in admiration.

"It's been a long time since I've looked up," I admitted freely as I gazed over at Jack, who took in the same glittered night sky.

"It's something," Jack said of the expansive rolling black cover painted with just the right amount of twinkling overlay. He looked over at me with concern. I was sure he could see my day setting in. "Come on, Doctor. I'll get you home." We spent the last few minutes of our walk in silence. I was thinking of any explanation I could to avoid bringing him inside my house. I wasn't emotionally positioned to do so and didn't know how it would make me feel. Jack made it easy on me by whispering a kiss on my lips followed by a "Goodnight."

"Thank you," I said to him in an inaudible whisper as he walked out of sight.

chapter
ten

THE NEXT MORNING, I WOKE UP WELL-RESTED AND SAW A NEW text from Jack.

Jack: Good morning, beautiful.

Rose: Morning, handsome. Rap & R&B 101 The Notorious B.I.G, Hypnotize.

Jack: See you later?

Rose: If you're lucky.

Jack: Cocky this morning, are we?

Rose: I slept well.

Jack: Better dreams?

I paused before replying, deciding to go with honesty.

Rose: I had a good date last night.

Jack: Lucky bastard.

Rose: Go build something.

Jack: Go save a life.

I threw off my covers, scrolled through the music on my cell phone, and cranked the volume up. Biggie's deep voice filled my bathroom as I moved my hips and scrubbed myself with a ridiculously expensive body wash I'd bought on my shopping spree. I shaved my legs twice, with a *what-if* mentality behind my grooming. I knew Jack wanted to take things slow, but if our last few private moments together were any indication, we would be doing some exploring soon enough. I looked at my naked body in the mirror and made a decision.

I pulled the silk panty set I'd purchased a week ago out of the tissue paper and slid it on. When and if Jack made a move, I'd be ready. I took the golf cart to the entrance, slightly deflated that Jack's bike wasn't in sight. I'd hoped to just have a glimpse of him to start my day off right. Still, I went to work with a renewed sense of purpose. For the first time since Grant died, I was excited about the life I was living.

By the time I was done with rounds and prepping for surgery, I was fit to be tied as I waited for any word from Jack. Though I'd played coy, I wanted to push repeat on the night before and checked my phone in vain twice before I scrubbed in.

Once out of surgery, I rushed back to my locker and smiled when I saw the picture Jack had sent of Annabelle in a patch of bluebonnets on my land. I guessed he was keeping himself busy with the center and entertaining my family. A pang of jealousy struck me—but in a good way.

Rose: She's so beautiful.

Jack: She is. I have a little crush on her. So, can I see you tonight?

Rose: Sure. I'll be earlier.

Jack: It's a date, ladies' choice.

Rose: ☺

I did a little dance where I stood and felt the thud of Jules going down on her ass behind me. I turned to see her on the floor with a shit-eating grin on her face. She'd been spying on my text exchange.

"You're seeing him!"

"I'm…" I said, pulling her tiny ass off of the floor. "Shut up!"

"Rose, I won't push, but can I just say—"

"Nope."

"I hope he's hung like a horse!" Two of the hospital staff—whom I didn't know and suddenly never wanted to—burst out laughing as they left us to our conversation.

"Discretion, Jules, Jesus," I said, pushing her to sit on the cheap plastic bench in the middle of the locker room.

"Tell me something, anything," she said, exasperated, as I changed socks and tied my shoes.

"He seems to be a really good guy," I said, knowing the shit I was about to be given for being so vague.

"That is *not* what I want to hear," she said, standing to pace in front of me.

"We haven't even made it past first base, okay?"

Jules narrowed her eyes. "Is that why you're wearing sexy underwear?"

"What?"

She pulled at the strap on my hip and let it snap back. I jumped in surprise as I pulled my pants up further to cover it.

"I have nothing to tell," I said defensively. "We have surgery in twenty minutes. Stop bullshitting," I snapped.

"Fine, jeez," she said, pulling on a fresh set of scrubs over her ass. "See if I give you another play-by-play."

"I never ask for them. You overshare, and anyways, we're too old to have nothing to talk about except men."

Jamie came in just as I was ridding myself of Jules' inquisition, and her eyes widened perceptively.

"Nothing happened," I said as Jamie held up her hands in defense and looked over at Jules, who gave her a solid nod.

"But it's going to?" Jules nodded and motioned over to me. "Silk panties and matching bra."

"That's it. I'm leaving. I'll see you in surgery." It wasn't like me to clam up when they'd been so open. I'd decided—like everything else, including my pain—to keep my new relationship to myself for the moment. I was all too aware of just how easily things could change.

The awareness had me pause mid-step as I made my way toward OR 3.

Fear crept through my limbs—familiar and unwelcomed. I pushed my shoulders back and narrowed my focus. It was go time. The person on that table needed me to be the surgeon I'd trained to be and would get nothing less.

"You'll have to take your shirt off," I said to Jack, who stood at the foot of the machine. "If you don't mind."

He gave me a sexy, crooked smile, the scar above his lip highlighted by the lighting of the room. "I was kind of hoping you would be the one to do that."

I took a confident step toward him and gripped the hem of his shirt. "You were, huh?"

"Except in my scenario, we weren't in a cold, sterile room. This isn't exactly what I had in mind when I said lady's choice tonight. Dinner," he said as I brushed my lips against his, "dancing," he continued as I kissed him again. "A movie, maybe? You know, something standard."

"It's what I want," I said, leaning in to place one last kiss on his scar. He stood, expectant, a challenge in his eyes as I lifted his shirt and studied the wall of solid muscle that stood before me. He was sculpted to perfection. Jack's chest and torso were ripped with muscle, solid pecs, an eight-pack, and even the pebbled muscle that stretched from under his ribcage and trailed around to his back. He'd worked hard for that body, and I had no intention of not appreciating it. I didn't hesitate as I leaned in and kissed his chest where his heart lay. I heard him inhale as he wrapped his fists in my hair in an attempt to gently pull me away. I didn't let him deter me as I soaked up his skin, moving with precision as my hands explored him. I trailed my mouth along his chest before I covered one of his nipples and flicked my tongue.

"Rose," Jack whispered as both a prayer and a curse.

I moved my tongue along the middle of his chest, sucking and licking up to the hollow of his neck before I went in again, tasting him with greed, letting my hands roam where they wanted. His hands twisted firmly in my hair as he pulled me back to meet his eyes—which were filled with fire. Arousal soaking every inch of me, I turned my head and sank my teeth into his defined bicep as he cradled me.

"Fuck," Jack whispered.

I took a step back and pulled my shirt over my head, revealing my heaving chest and tight nipples. Jack bit his lip and jerked me to him—our mouths met needier than ever. Tongues thrashing, his groan matched the need of my moan as we collided and teased with the same hunger.

He drew back as his hand moved up my stomach to cup my breast. I pushed into his hand in want.

"Yes," I encouraged, needing him more than I'd needed anything in a very long time.

I closed my eyes, leaning into his touch as his calloused hands roamed my skin. His mouth devoured my nipple through the silky material. In protest of wanting nothing between us, I pulled down the cup, greedy for contact, and cried out as he took my peaked nipple between his lips.

Ecstasy coursed through me from that simple contact, and I didn't realize I was being lifted until I heard the door shut behind us and was laid onto the couch in the adjacent waiting room.

He hovered above me, his eyes filled with lust as his tongue roved over my chest and neck. I opened my legs, and he sank on top of me. My mind did a mental 'click' at that moment at the way we fit. This time, there was grinding between the both of us. I gasped his name over and over. I needed him more than my next breath, and he had to be the one to free me.

"Jack, please," I said as a single tear emerged and fell down my cheek. Jack lapped it up with his tongue as he hovered, patiently waiting for me to acknowledge him. I opened my eyes to see both heat and concern.

"I need you so much."

"Okay," he said as he leaned in and drew my lips in a slow, passion-filled kiss. He twisted his body to the side of me on the couch as he cradled my neck with one hand and slipped inside my panties with the other. I bucked as his fingers grazed my tender nerves, and he pushed his finger inside, releasing a groan as he massaged me with his thumb.

"So wet and ready. I want you so much," Jack said, adding more pressure. "Rose," he beckoned. Gasping and panting, he looked down at me, and I saw a flicker of desperation behind the heat. He was at his breaking point. "Fuck, I can't handle this."

He sat up and then knelt on the floor before me, making quick work of pulling down my scrubs and panties. Once naked—aside from my bra—he looked at me while I moved restlessly beneath him.

Jack's chest heaved as he watched me, still hesitant. I pulled at the back of his head and brought him down to meet my mouth with a kiss so raw, it surprised even me. It was filled with permission and longing and returned with fire and possession.

Jack tore himself away and positioned himself at the V of my legs. His eyes still glued to mine, he slid his warm hands up my thighs and pushed them further apart before he buried his head between them. I screamed out in surprise and pleasure as his velvet tongue teased me with expert skill. He tasted and sucked, making sure I saw his every move. His fingers and tongue orchestrated together perfectly as I abandoned all my senses, letting him take me where I needed to go. I watched him devour me, his hungry tongue darting in and out while he caressed me with his free hand. The look in his eyes and the movement of his tongue sent me spiraling out as I burst into his waiting mouth. Fast breaths erupted from me as I called out to him, his fingers and tongue unrelenting as it pulled out the very last of my orgasm. My head shook back and forth in disbelief. The mere strength of it had me dissolving beneath him. Aftershocks ripped through me as I came down from the highest of highs and landed comfortably back into my body. Jack continued to soothe me with his mouth as he blazed a trail over my stomach and back to my chest.

"I think I've found something I love more than building," Jack whispered as he hovered above me and drew my nipple into his hot mouth. Wrapping my arms around him, I clung to him for dear life—a new habit of mine and one I wasn't willing to let go of.

He looked down at me with reverence, and I couldn't help the tears that overtook me at that moment.

"Oh God," I said as they slid down my cheeks.

Jack frowned and covered my face with his hands, gently wiping them away.

"Do you always cry after sex, or is it me?"

"It's just you," I said with a chuckle, and he joined me. "Why did you stop?"

"I thought you'd finished?" Jack said with another chuckle.

"No, I mean—" I cupped his bulge and moved to unbutton his pants, but he pulled my hand away and gave it a tongue-filled kiss.

"I know what you meant, and if I was in this for sex, we'd

be having it." He moved to sit up, adjusting himself and pulling my pants off the floor to sort them out. He replaced my panties and slid my scrubs back up.

"Jack, I don't think that."

"I don't want you regretting anything." He looked at me with sincerity. "I want to deserve you."

I stayed silent because I didn't want to push it and seem like the easy prey that I was. He'd just captured me with his mouth, his tongue, and his words. He pulled me to his chest as we lay for several minutes, my breathing evening out as his fingers stroked my skin.

A thousand questions I didn't ask swirled around in my head. Was he this good to every woman he dated? And if so, who in their right mind would let him go? If I asked him those questions, it would give him the right to ask the same ones, and I wanted to wait a bit longer before I reluctantly gave them.

It wasn't so much pity that scared me. It was the fact that Grant had been such a definitive force in my love life. He had declared himself my end-all-be-all and made sure I felt the same way. I didn't have any clue how to get around that idea. Even lying in another man's arms, I wasn't sure that Jack wasn't the first in a series of men I would feel unsure about. I still had no idea when, if ever, I could ever fully let myself believe otherwise.

"Let's go screen you for everything," a sated me suggested minutes later, eager to test the equipment.

"Next time, I pick the place," Jack said, pulling me off the couch and letting his eyes drift over my chest. "I'd hoped I would see this again," he said as his fingers trailed over the top of the cup of my bra, making me perk up with renewed need. "What made you wear this today?"

"I'd hoped you'd see it again, too."

"Lord, woman. In a twenty-four-hour period, I saw you in

this, and you came on the back of my bike. How in the hell is a man supposed to walk away from that?"

"Both embarrassing situations for me, Jack, okay? Let's not use these stories for reference down the line."

"The hell I won't, and don't forget about your tongue," he chided as we entered the CT room again. He took his place, a shirtless wonder on the body tray.

"I love the way you're looking at me right now," he whispered as I worked above him, our intimate connection still strong as it thrummed between us.

"Oh yeah?" I leaned over him, doing a position check for his head. "How am I looking at you?"

"Like I'm the only man in the world."

I ignored his comment as a small lump formed in my throat and did my best to concentrate on getting him into position.

"Excuse me, but could you please put a shirt on? This is highly unprofessional," he said in mock annoyance.

"Oh, Mr.—"

I froze and looked down on him just as his pointer and thumb closed on my nipple. I shrieked as he twisted it painfully and then screamed out his last name. "Sawyer, it's Sawyer!"

"Hmph, best not forget it," he slapped my ass painfully before he resumed his position.

"All right, lie perfectly still, understood?"

"Yes, ma'am," he agreed easily, though his hands continued to roam over my chest and neck as he looked up at me with a sexy grin.

"I said lie still." I placed his hands in position. "Is there any chance at all you may be pregnant?"

"Slim," he said, playing along.

"Just to make sure, I'm going to place this on your chest,"

I said, picking up the magnetic pack and throwing it into position over him.

"A girl can never be too careful," he said in a pathetic attempt at a woman's voice.

"Jack," I chuckled, looking down at him as a sudden mix of emotions struck me.

"What is it, beautiful?" he asked as he reached up to push the falling hair from around my face.

I felt myself fill with gratitude. I wanted to give him a piece of what he'd given me over the last few days, but I couldn't put it into words.

"Lie still!"

"Yep," he said, placing his hands at his sides.

I walked into the adjacent room and started the machines, knowing how to use them but also with the knowledge that we would hire the best technician to utilize them. It was a critical part of the diagnosis, and we had no room for error. As I stood in the quiet room and pressed the speaker to call out instructions, a crippling fear overtook me as he lay in the body basket. For a brief moment, I panicked as the machine began to turn. A prayer went up for the first time since I could remember, and I had to take a seat as fear swept through me.

"Breathe, Rose."

It had been almost a solid year since I'd had an attack. As I studied the images flashing across the screen, I was unable to stop myself from scrutinizing them. I took a deep breath and held it before I let it go. It came out sputtering and weak, and I felt the tears start to roll down my face. Heart pounding out of control, I braced myself and felt the inevitable panic wash over me.

"Not now, not now. Chill out, Rose," I scolded myself as I began to shake. Several long breaths later, I knew it was pointless as wave after wave of fear gripped me. My forehead damp with sweat, I began to work through it as my need to see his scans became a sort of lifeline.

I studied every scan for several minutes with hyper-focused scrutiny as they appeared. Relief swept through me as I saw a perfectly healthy set of CTs. I had to give myself another moment to collect myself. A much somber version of me walked out of that room, and I knew I would do a poor job of hiding it. I was an absolute wreck.

I pushed the button and saw Jack's easy smile as he emerged in one piece while I stood in a million before him. His smile quickly turned to worry when he saw my face.

"Rose?" He shot up from the table.

"They're all clear," I said with heavy breath.

"God, you're so pale," he said, pulling his shirt from the floor and making quick use of it before gripping my arms. "Tell me what's wrong." Jack looked around to search for the person responsible for my upset, but she was standing right in front of him.

"I'm sorry. I didn't mean to worry you. Look, I can show you where the scans are clear. Come on." I gestured toward the door.

"I don't give a fuck about the scans," he barked. "Why are you shaking?"

"I'm tired," I said as I lied truthfully. For the first time since I'd met him, I wanted to be away from Jack.

"Why won't you tell me?"

"I have to go home now, okay?"

Jack's jaw tightened as he made peace with my reluctance to share.

We took turns turning off the lights, and I locked up as he turned me to him and pulled me into his arms. I pushed back my emotion and held him tightly in front of the center's double doors.

"I'm headed back to New Orleans tomorrow for a bit, but I'll be back, okay?"

I nodded, unable to voice the words I'd wanted to say earlier. "Thank you."

"For what?" he asked in a whisper.

"For being real, being something I can touch."

"Talk to me," he implored again. "It won't matter what it is."

"I just… panicked."

Jack pulled back and searched my eyes. "You were afraid my scans wouldn't come back clean?"

I nodded with a sharp laugh as my eyes filled again. "I'm stupid, right?"

"No," Jack said with no humor whatsoever, "you have a beautiful heart."

"I'm not a fan of it," I said as he wiped the tears away from my face for the third time that night.

"It's what made me a fan of you," he said in reassurance. He pulled away and tilted my chin up. "The first time I saw you, your face was full of love for the little boy you were holding. You looked so incredibly beautiful. You knocked the wind out of me." He looked back at the building and then at me. "Just look what you're doing with this place." He leaned in and took my lips in a gentle kiss. "Look at you now," he murmured. "You make it hard to breathe, Rose Whitaker."

"And you make it easier for me," I whispered back. "I'm sorry I freaked out. I best not pull that shit on any of my patients," I said dryly.

"Probably not a good idea," he agreed.

Jack insisted on driving me home on the back of his bike, but not before he had a good laugh at my expense because of my reluctance to get on. A few short minutes later, he was on my porch, kissing me with the same need he had since his lips first met mine.

"I'll see you soon," I said as he finished our kiss and left me panting.

"Not soon enough," he whispered. "Sure you're okay?"

"Yes, I'm fine. Jack, please don't hold tonight against me."

"Never. I'll call you tomorrow." Another whisper of his lips, and he was gone.

I found myself in a scalding tub that night, brainless. I'd needed to know I was capable of feeling again, but at what cost? Was I ready to feel all that a relationship entailed? My panic attack argued against it, but everything else told me I wasn't anywhere near ready to give Jack up.

And I wasn't going to.

Like everything I'd been doing since the devastation of losing Grant took over my life, I'd have to do it scared.

chapter
eleven

"If that Octomom woman can give birth to fourteen children—eight in one go—and raise them, you can get out of bed, Rose."

DAYS LATER, I SAT AT THE DINNER TABLE WITH MY FAMILY AS my mom spoke about the opening of the center and the party she was planning for later that night after the ribbon cutting.

"Which one of you wants to speak?"

I looked to Dallas, who was looking at me. "Rose should do it since we're dedicating the center to Grant." She pushed another spoon of sweet potatoes into Annabelle's reluctant mouth, and I chuckled as she spits them out. Dallas blew out a harsh breath of frustration.

"You're a mean baby," Dallas said as Annabelle smashed the discarded sweet potatoes into her highchair tray with her chubby hand, challenging her mom with a loud "No."

"Let me try. Eat something, babe," Dean said, taking the spoon from my sister. Every day, my respect and love grew for the man who worked hard to take care of his family. Dean had come back for my sister years after they'd split up and won her back through his love and devotion—which remained a staple of who he still was to this day. I looked on as he spooned another bite of sweet potatoes from the jar. Annabelle took his bite, fooling both of her doting parents and playing with it in her mouth. And just as they praised her, she spit it out. My dad laughed loudly at his granddaughter's cruelty as Dean pleaded with his daughter to cooperate.

I looked back at my mom, who was still waiting for a response to her question. "I'll speak, but I hope you all know not to say anything to anyone about Grant, especially the crew and new employees."

My dad simply nodded in understanding as he filled his plate with food.

My mom and sister looked at me, confused. "I mean, I know the name of the center will be questioned, but we can just tell them he was a dear friend of the family without going into specifics. I had to endure months of sympathy and answering questions. It wore on me, okay? It's my story to tell, and only if I choose to. I don't want you all telling it for me, to *anyone*, okay?"

I got a collective agreement from the table and sat back, hoping it remained that way. Though my reasons for asking them now were specific to Jack, I truly hated the unwanted sympathy offered whenever I shared that my fiancé had died a week before our wedding in a horrific car accident. It wasn't something I freely talked about to anyone except Dallas, and even our conversations had died in frequency. Nothing about it seemed therapeutic to me. I didn't want to relive what happened. I only wanted to remember the time I had with Grant. For now, that meant keeping my memories separate from the current life I was living. As fucked up as it might have been, I'd compartmentalized everything. And when I was struggling to breathe or simply exist as a human day-to-day, ritual seemed the only thing that kept me grounded.

I still replayed my time with Grant every day, down to the

smallest possible detail. Even considering my new situation with Jack, I remained faithful to my promise never to forget Grant. My heart remained faithful to him, yet my affection for Jack seemed to stem from somewhere similar. I silenced the judgment that brewed inside of me. I reasoned that as long as I kept Jack within the set parameters—I could keep my promise.

The next day—after a long shift at the hospital—I wanted nothing more than my drab ritual of a hot bath and a mind-numbing amount of wine. I was absolutely floored when I arrived home to see a party in full swing at the center. Two large red tents were erect at the side of the main building on the grass, and there looked to be at least forty people or more beneath it. Zydeco music wafted through the air, and I could easily detect the smell of heat-filled spices. Slightly irritated that no one had mentioned a party by so much as a text, I stomped into one of the tents, looking for a Whitaker's ass to kick.

My mom and Jack were front and center as Jack hooked opposite arms with her, and they both stomped their feet in what I could only guess was a jig. Jack was flawless in his delivery as my mom struggled but kept up nicely. Her face was lit with so much excitement that a small amount of my anger diminished. I heard my name being called but ignored it as I watched Jack in his element. His enamored look for my mom as he taught her a thing or two was enough to make me want to go to him, and yet, as I watched, he had no idea of his draw on me. I finally ripped my eyes away from them both to look around the tent and felt transported. It was humid, and though everyone around me was damp with sweat, there wasn't one person in the crowd without a smile. A small buffet table had been set out, stuffed with crawfish, jambalaya, dirty rice, and artfully arranged breads. The tents were illuminated with strings and strings of red and white lights. Beer poured freely from a few tapped kegs, and there wasn't a hand in the house without a celebratory cup. I recognized the partygoers as the building crew and a few friends of our family. Scanning the crowd, I spotted Dallas waving to me from across the dance floor, Annabelle on her hip, her hair a sweaty mess, and a refreshing smile on her face.

I raised my hands questioningly, and she rolled her eyes, waving me over to her. I cut through the crowd and out of the tent, then made my way to her. I neared Dallas in time to see her pass Annabelle off to Dean. I began to look for Grant and couldn't find him. I pinched Dallas's ass hard through her scrub pants, and she shot up with a loud yelp as she turned to me with menace.

"Where *is* my nephew?"

"He's with the Harrisons in the other tent."

"You just pass off our baby to strangers," I said, desperately looking for my nephew as Dallas lifted a red cup to her lips.

"We've known them our whole lives, idiot."

"Yes, and they are old as shit. They'll break a hip lifting him!" I said in sheer panic.

"Oh, Jesus, you really are hard up."

I narrowed my eyes at her.

"I'll gladly hand you the highly-strung trophy tomorrow, but tonight, shut up." She shoved a cup of what smelled like pure alcohol in my face, but I pushed it away. Finally spotting Grant, who was showing the Harrisons his now signature dance moves, I breathed out a sigh of relief and then turned to my sister. "Thanks for the heads-up on the party, asshole."

"Jack thought it would be a good way to show the builders we appreciate all they've done."

"Oh, *Jack* thought, huh?"

"Yeah," she said defensively, shoving the drink back into my face. "He did, and Dad and I agreed. He literally had this whole damned thing done in a matter of hours. We also agreed to give the crew the day off tomorrow, too."

"Well, that's just dandy," I said as I looked up and saw Dean pass Annabelle off to the Harrisons as well and make his way back toward us. Thirsty from the heat, I took a large sip of the cup and nearly gasped at its strength and amazing taste.

"Holy shit!"

"Yep, I strongly suggest you go try some of his cooking. He's something else in the kitchen."

"Jack made this?"

"You should've seen him ordering Pedro around in an attempt to get it ready."

Pedro was our favorite of all the crew and one of the first employees my dad hired. He was considered family.

"I miss everything," I said, defeated. The last of my anger disappeared with each long sip I took.

"No, you don't. You're here, right?" Dallas said as her eyes bulged—Dean suddenly behind her, his body language suggestive. I rolled my eyes, lifted my glass to Dean, and left to search for a refill.

"Hey, that's my drink!"

"Not anymore. Our parents are here, you two!" I yelled over the blaring music as I made my way through the crowd. I didn't see Jack as I headed over to the buffet to fill a bowl full of sumptuous jambalaya. I watched the crew step one by one into the dance circle, taking turns showing off their skills as the rest of them roared in celebration. As far as I could tell, Jack could throw one hell of a party. I caught my parents' attention and waved hello as they spoke to some of the crews' wives as I shoved another heaping mouthful of the spicy but savory food in my mouth.

I waved back in greeting as I kept my steady pace, inhaling my fill. Once finished, I refreshed my drink from a two-gallon dispenser filled with the delicious and heavily chilled liquor mix labeled Gata Juice. Stuffed and slightly alcohol-soaked, I searched the crowd for Jack and again came up empty.

A sigh of defeat passed my lips as I began to sway my hips to the music. It really was a sight to behold as I watched people I'd known through the years of my dad's projects celebrate their hard work. The more I saw, the more I knew Jack had made the right call. I'd only wished Dallas and I had come up with the idea ourselves.

"Bonjou," I heard whispered with a thick Cajun drawl. "Ju gettin' out da car?"

"What?" I said with a chuckle as Jack stayed behind me, and we remained slightly hidden in the crowd. Instantly aware of the crisp scent that was now a familiar comfort, I leaned into him.

"Ju hips, beb," Jack said as he confused the hell out of me. "Ju is gettin' out da car."

Realization struck, and though I knew nothing of Cajun, I assumed it was slang for dancing.

"Seriously, getting out of the car?"

"Dat what dis is," he said in a singsong voice as he placed his hands on my hips and pulled them back hard into him. I gasped as he held me close. "Beb got me tinkin all day, and tinkin got me hard and all needin'." I closed my eyes and moved my hips back and forth against him. Aside from one or two wives who shot daggers my way, the crowd paid us no mind. Apparently, I had robbed them of their eye candy. Not wanting attention drawn our way, I swatted Jack's hands away but remained desperate for my own look at him.

"Mais now, boo. I seed dem frissons on de skin," he whispered as I melted. He blew on the goose bumps he'd referred to as my pulse picked up, and fire rushed below. He pushed forward with his hips and brushed against me. Hot and willing, I swayed against him, desperate for his hands. "Where put dis?"

A small gasp escaped me when I felt the evident bulge brush against my back. I swallowed hard, a mix of highly amused and completely turned on. "Where exactly did you grow up again?"

"Dem swamps." He chuckled. "I've already given you over half my Cajun lexicon."

"Ah, so you *are* trying to impress me?" Suddenly jerked away from the crowd and into the night, I felt less suffocated and rejoiced in the cooler air I inhaled. Jack led me to a neighboring large oak tree next to the tent just as a slower Cajun mix burst through the two large speakers that housed the night's entertainment.

Pinned to a tree, Jack smiled down at me, and I felt my whole body shift in new awareness.

"I want to dance with you," he whispered. "Please?" Suddenly, I was in his embrace as he moved in time with the music. I fumbled with my footing as he led me easily, taking great patience until I matched him foot for foot.

Comfortable in our pattern, I looked up to Jack, his eyes crinkled in the corners, a sexy gleam and half-grin to match.

"You love to dance?"

"I do."

"What is this song?"

"It's old."

"That doesn't answer my question."

He gripped my hand tighter. "Mais time for dancin', beb. Jaw close."

"Well, I understood that," I said in exasperation as I pushed away, but he pulled us back together, chest to chest, with a chuckle.

"Just relax, beautiful. Look at me." And I did. He guided me through our not-quite-two-step effortlessly as I followed his lead, looking into his eyes. "Better," he rasped out against my throat before he pulled back to look at me. There was enough light for us to see each other's faces clearly, and I damn near broke our dance when I noticed the look on his. It was full of want, and I wondered if he could see mine. Just as I was about to nervously start spewing words, he leaned in and began to sing in my ear.

"Go roun', go roun', lil' Alice blue gown. We'll soon be together on the bayou sundown. We'll jaw jambalaya and sing all night long.

Me and my baby and a Cajun love song."

His voice was smooth and intoxicating, and I sighed as I placed my forehead on his shoulder, giving in as I let the rest of my day roll off my shoulders.

"Thank you," I said as the song ended. "This is really—" I looked back at the tent "—something."

"It's nothing."

I looked up to him with a frown. "You could have texted me about this."

"I wanted to surprise you." I thought of my initial reaction to the party and decided I had earned the trophy Dallas spoke of.

"You did, it's wonderful."

I looked back at the crowd and then at him. The party faded out as he stared at me, and I felt the ever-present need for him.

"I had a motive," he announced as he pulled me against him, his back to the tree as his arms snaked around me.

"Care to share?" I said as my heart began to hammer.

"I don't like to dance alone. I need a new partner."

"Oh," I said as I let my body relax in his hold.

"I saw this picture once," he said, his face covered in a light sheen of sweat. "It was of a little girl on her daddy's feet. She had bright red hair."

"Oh shit," I said, immediately embarrassed. That picture hung in our hall. It was one of my mom's favorites.

"I feel like I've known you for a long time, Rose, just by knowing your family."

"But you're a stranger to me," I said carefully.

"Am I?" he said as he leaned in close, drew my lips into his mouth, and sucked on them gently before he let go. "I think we've conquered that."

"We have," I agreed.

Jack slid a hand up and gripped my hair in his fist as our mouths crashed together in a kiss. His greedy tongue took as I gave. When I had been thoroughly kissed to the point of needing much more, he took his lips away.

"It's been a long time since I've held back with a woman," he said, out of breath as I pressed further into him. "I want you wrapped around me… tight." He dipped his head as he tilted mine, his fist still in control of it. I whimpered as his tongue stroked just below my ear. "I want to know what it feels like to fit inside you." He pulled away, and I drank in his effect. "But I want you to agree to be my dance partner first."

"Motive," I said breathlessly.

He nodded with eyes on fire.

"Okay."

In haste and to shake off our spell, he let go of my hair and gripped my hand as he twirled me underneath his arm and back again. I shrieked as I tripped over a piece of stump and went flying through the air toward him. He caught me easily as I landed with a thud against his chest.

"No more Gata Juice for you," he said as I stepped back

and checked myself for injury, finding none. I'd been so close to face-planting.

"No worries, it's my cat-like reflexes. I've had to put them back into action because of you, sloppy surgeon."

I curled my lip in distaste. "Don't get cocky, Jack. I may just need a better instructor."

He crossed his arms as he looked down at me with a cocked brow.

"Okay, I tripped."

"Gata Juice."

"I have an early shift. Thank you for the dance and for everything. Goodnight, Jack." I did a half-assed curtsy and began to walk toward my house. "I'll text you tomorrow," I called out as I shivered in the suddenly cool night air.

Jack

"I'll text you first," I said, making her jump as I slipped her hand in mine. Fingers laced, we walked in silence for a few minutes before she looked up at the blanket of stars above us.

"You've been all over, Jack. Tell me the best place for this kind of view."

"Well, that would be here," I said with a chuckle.

She cut her beautiful eyes at me as we paused our steps. I thought of all the types of night skies I'd seen in my travels as she waited for me to answer.

"The northern lights, they're unbeatable."

"I can only imagine."

"You don't have to. You can go see them for yourself," I said in hopes of encouraging her. Even so young and flawlessly beautiful, she was tired. I knew that tired. I'd lived it. An experience like that could be just what she needed.

"Yeah, I'll just take a week off, head up to the northern tip of the earth to admire one huge nightlight."

"If it's important enough, you'll make the time."

Offended by my bluntness, she pulled her hand away, and I shoved mine in my pockets as I rocked on my heels.

"Things like that aren't possible for me. Not now, probably not ever."

"That's complete bullshit." I could see her longing when I spoke to her about my trips. I wasn't immune to the envy she clearly conveyed—a deep need in me wanted her to have the sight of those lights.

"Okay, well, I'll send you my schedule for the next five years, and you work that out for me." Annoyed, she turned on her heel without looking to see if I followed.

Under her breath, I heard her mutter, "I can't just leave. I don't get to do things like that."

"Because you choose to be here. There's nothing wrong with that unless you say there is."

I followed her up her porch steps as she reeled on me. "Look, hippie, just because you decided to throw in your tie and live from tree to tree doesn't mean the rest of us did. I have people who are depending on me."

"It's like I said, if it's important enough to you, you'll make time. You have responsibilities. I get that, beb. We all do. But you're not entirely responsible for saving the world on your own, and I can see it on your shoulders."

"Well, I can't just walk away on a whim to take a break."

"Oh, but you want to, at least right now you do. Admit it,

you want to see those stars, and you want me to take you to them."

"You don't know squat," she snapped as I fed her the truth.

"You have one nasty temper, Rose Whitaker."

"I resent that. You can't expect me to be as agreeable as you are. *No one* is." Unable to contain my chuckle, I could physically see her anger flare again as I stepped toward her, wanting to do nothing but put that fire out. I was just about to follow through when I caught the movement beneath her and froze.

"Rose, don't move."

Still clearly irritated, her flesh flushed from the gata punch, she looked at me for argument. "I mean, sure, I'll just stop all the progress I've made in the last year and go buy a map of the stars."

"Rose," I said sharply.

"What?!" she said as she moved lightning fast, gripped the large black snake's tail, and hurled it over her porch.

I stood shocked as she glared back at me with her hands on her hips.

Completely stunned, I stated the obvious, "You just threw a six-foot snake over your porch."

"Well, you aren't the only one who grew up in the trees," she snapped as her chest heaved. Completely taken aback, I watched her, both impressed and fascinated.

If nothing scared her, what in the hell was she so afraid of?

We stood motionless, my need to have her growing beyond anything I could control as she returned my gaze with the same intensity. I knew sexual frustration when I saw it, and this beautiful woman was about to snap. A loud crash in the distance had us whipping our heads back toward the party. A loud roar of laughter followed.

With regret, I turned back to her. "I have to go check on that."

Rose nodded, disappointment evident in her features. I smiled. "We'll have to take a rain check on that hate sex you were hoping for."

"You arrogant ass!" I took two steps and nailed her to the back of her bedroom door with my hips and mouth. There wasn't an ounce of resistance in her posture as she returned my kiss and pulled me impossibly closer—the way she often did. I slid my tongue along the seam of her lips, and she moaned eagerly into my mouth. With both hands, I cupped her ass and rubbed my hard cock against her. "Feel that?"

She broke from my kiss suddenly, her eyes wide. I stood alarmed as I thought of anything that might have set her off. She wiped her face with her hands. Confused and knowing we'd gone so much further sexually—I took a step back.

"What—"

"You better go check on that party," she said, failing to hide the shakiness in her voice.

"Okay," I said as I let my patience filter throughout my body. As much as I'd tried to earn her trust, I knew it had to come from her naturally. I turned to leave and heard her faintly whisper my name as she turned off the porch light and stepped into her bedroom.

"Jack."

"Yeah?"

"Can I still be your dance partner?"

I hid my smile. "If you want to."

"I do."

"Then you are," I said, forcing my feet away because I had no choice. "Goodnight."

"Night, Jack."

I closed my eyes after her whisper because I loved the way she said my name, especially in the dark.

chapter
twelve

Jack: Good morning, beautiful.
Rose: Morning, handsome. Rap & R&B 101 Toni Braxton, You're Makin' Me High.

DAYS AFTER THE PARTY AND FULL OF JUMBLED EMOTIONS AND stress, I decided to hide from the world in my own special place. Between my late hours and Jack's busy schedule at the center, we'd been unable to connect since our parting on my porch. I'd used the time to focus all my energy on the hospital and last-minute details pertaining to the center. My to-do list was endless, and no matter how hard I tried, I couldn't keep up.

Jack had been right about my need to escape. As much as I fought him on it, our late-night talk about his endless adventures had lit a curious fire inside me. As many dreams as I'd realized in my career and as happy as I was with my progress, the idea of taking off to explore the world outside of the one I'd lived in for so long seemed like an unreachable dream. Instead of doing something rash, I settled for a different kind of escape.

A few acres from my house—behind a row of trees—lay a small creek with a tiny clearing of grass big enough for me to stretch lazy-cat style on my favorite quilt. I decided to spend the surprisingly cool day under the warm sun with a paperback, ignoring everyone. I'd left my phone at home along with an unfinished list of things I had to get done but decided to hell with it all. I was head-spent and desperately needed a break. Books did that for me. It was my favorite way of ignoring the world and living in someone else's. No movie, not even my beloved rap music, was as consuming as being locked in the pages of a good romance or thriller. I looked down at my tattered and tarnished copy of *Anne of Green Gables* and smiled at it fondly. It was my first love affair, and I'll never forget the emotions that stirred inside me during my first reading. Over the years, I'd read hundreds if not thousands of books, but that book would forever be my favorite. I must have read my paperback a hundred times, and the weathered pages proved as much. There was a jelly stain on page thirty-three, and I had accidentally torn page one hundred and ninety but had taped it back together. Some may just throw out a book as used as my copy and buy a new one, but if there was ever a possession I cherished and couldn't live without, it was the book I held. Not only was it a reminder of my youth, but a reminder of a more wistful and hopeful version of myself. I'd fallen in love within the pages of this book, and each time I closed it, I would spend hours in silence, daydreaming of a future love of my own, wondering who my Gilbert Blythe would be. I figured that if an outspoken girl with red hair and freckles could capture a man's heart, that one day, I, too, could be gifted the same thing.

I lay in the sun, the distant trees gracing me with just enough shade to comfortably see the pages. It was absolutely perfect September weather, and I couldn't imagine being anywhere else. Not even the excitement of surgery or the feel of the scalpel appealed to me as much as staying exactly where I was at that moment. I spent a few minutes staring at the faded cover, trying to remember the last time I'd read it. After a while, it finally came to me.

I was in my first year of medical school. David had just shredded my heart, and I'd just been told he was going to marry someone else. I'd picked up my book and read without stopping in full-fledged denial until page—I flipped through to see the wrinkled page where an hour or six of tears had accrued and found it—two hundred and six. On page two hundred and six, I'd mourned the five years of life I'd spent with a man I thought was my Gilbert Blythe. I spent hours in my room with the book cradled to my chest, screaming into my pillow about the injustices of love. I'd thought David was the loss of my life.

And then—figuratively and literally—I turned the page only to suffer another.

I looked up at the cloud-filled sky with my book full of memories clutched to my chest. Suddenly, I felt like I'd lived so much life, tired in young bones and wary of anything else that could taint the girl I once was.

Was she still in there? The girl full of love's ambition, full of life, and never-ending hope of a future filled with moments to latch on to and relive? I'd had those moments. I'd *had* them. I'd been so lucky.

Had she fled from me to a place where nothing else could hurt her, or was she still in there? I missed her.

"What's going on in that beautiful head of yours, woman? And why exactly are you hiding?"

I smiled at the clouds.

Cajun.

I didn't bother looking his way as he made himself comfortable on my quilt, his head next to mine.

"I was thinking about how much life I have left to live and how old I feel."

"That deep, huh?"

God, I loved the way he spoke. It was as intoxicating as his smell. Though I resisted looking at him, I saw the tip of his black boots out of the corner of my eye and assumed he was in his typical uniform of a perfectly fitted T-shirt and jeans. Though I'd come out to my spot in hopes of staying hidden, I loved the fact that he found me.

"Yeah, that deep," I whispered as I kept my eyes glued to the sky. "I can't stop thinking about how the future might swallow me if I'm not careful. I've already spent so much time on my career, my whole life, actually. I need to have days like this to remind me just to live, you know?"

"I do," he said, taking my hand in his. "And I think this might be my fault. I'm sorry."

"You are so agreeable," I said with a smile.

"I am," he said in amusement.

"It would be hell to try and start an argument with you," I noted.

"You can give it your best shot," he fired back. "But, yeah, I'd have to agree with that, too."

Finally unable to resist his pull, I turned on my side and propped myself on an elbow. He looked over at me, his smile devastating. His eyes were more blue than gray today, matching his dark blue T-shirt. I instantly wanted to press my lips to his.

"Why are you so easygoing? I mean, not that there's anything wrong with it, but is there anything that gets you riled up?"

He cocked his brow suggestively, and I rolled my eyes. "Anything other than sex?"

"I wasn't always so laid back. I've had my moments, lots of them. I used to get into a lot of fights when I was younger. I was small, so I lost a lot of them."

"Oh," I said as he grabbed my free hand and laid it on his

chest. Comfortable and moved by the gesture, I stroked him lightly over his T-shirt, and he leaned in close.

"Kids can be assholes," he said, giving me a quick smile. I walked my fingers up to his lip and stroked it gently, knowing it was the cause of a few of those fights.

"They can," I said as he lightly kissed my finger, and I continued to trace his scar.

"You'd be amazed at what they came up with," he said without prejudice. It didn't seem to bother him at all now, but I was sure at one point in time, the beautiful man lying beside me went home heartbroken because of a congenital disability he couldn't help. My heart cracked for him then, and I leaned down without thought and kissed it with reverence.

"How old were you?"

"Too old. And the cleft took too many surgeries to correct. When I was old enough, I started fighting having them, which delayed them even longer. My parents felt guilty, but I wasn't strong enough health-wise as a baby to start young. I was born premature, and they had to get other things under control before they could worry about it. It wasn't their fault. No one is to blame. It's just the way it happened."

He lay still and let me trace the faint scar with my lips, and as I pulled away, I told him what I honestly thought of it. "I think it's beautiful, though I'm sorry for the pain it's caused you."

The look in his eyes was a mix of need and gratitude as he reached up and cupped my face, keeping me from fully retreating away from him.

"Those lips and the words that come out of them," he rasped. Gently stroking my face, he pulled me close with his next confession. "I get riled up thinking about you, Rose. Wanting to be with you, waiting to see you. I get more than riled up. I get restless."

This time, I cocked a brow. "You look pretty damn calm to me."

He took my hand again, placing it over his heart, and recognition of its faster beat had a flattered smile play on my lips.

"I'm curious." He reached out and placed his large hand on my chest, confirming with a pause what I already knew. With a deep breath, my eyes wandered over his face as he gave me a wink. I knew he could feel it racing erratically. It always did when he was close.

"And then when I got a little older," he continued, tracing the line of my T-shirt collar with his finger, "and I hit a growth spurt, I put on a pair of gloves and hammered the shit out of some of them in revenge."

"Seems fair," I breathed out as my voice gave away my budding arousal. "So let me get this straight," I countered, trying my best to keep myself from ripping his shirt off. He was pure temptation for me and had been since the moment I laid eyes on him. "You're educated, you've done everything from run a business to erect a building, and you can cook, sing, and dance. You are literally *the Jack* of all trades."

He chuckled as his finger moved over my shoulder and down my arm.

"Is there anything you can't do?"

"Yes," he replied with a sudden move, pushing me on my back and pinning my wrists next to me. My chest heaved as I looked up at him in question.

"I can't stay away from you. I can't stop thinking about you. I can't stop wanting to touch you. I can't stop wondering if you're thinking about me. I can't stop needing to be around you. I can't stop wanting to be inside you, tasting you, touching you, feeling you. I can't stop waking up without you being the first thing on my mind, and I haven't even had you in one of the thousands of ways I want to."

Completely blown away by his confession, I began rambling. "I think if we try really hard, we can get at least a few hundred out of the way in, let's say… oh, a month—"

Cut off by his kiss, all thoughts vanished as I was drawn into him one delicious tongue sweep at a time. Gone, spiraling, and wholly invested, I wrapped myself inside of him as he tasted me. He wouldn't refuse me again—of this, I was sure—but I still found myself asking. "Jack, touch me," I pleaded. "You feel so good, and it's been so long."

"I never had a choice," he whispered as he slipped his aggressive tongue into my mouth again, forcing me to open and accept him. We were fluid and in perfect sync. He moved, then I moved in complement. His hands roamed my body as he filled me deep with his kiss. Breathless and suddenly aware my shirt was off, he took my breast in his ready mouth and sucked hard, drawing a gasp from me. I bucked and reacted to his gentle touch and urgent kiss. It was heaven, and I knew at that moment that there was no stopping either of us from making the connection we both so desperately wanted. My jeans now unbuttoned—his hand found its way beneath my panties.

"How could I not touch you?" he asked as his fingers found me ready. I writhed beneath him, needing him there… everywhere. His eyes closed on an exhale. When he opened them, all I saw was fire and need. I was already ashes in his hands… conquered, a casualty of his touch before he'd even decided to take me. Every breath I took, every movement I made, was only to spur him on. I wanted nothing else but to be branded by him.

With the flick of his wrist, sensation filled me as his thumb circled me and brought me to the brink. I was a slave to his stare, his hand, and anything else he brought into the mix. I was raw desire, and he was my salvation.

"Jack," I whispered as his lips slowly captured mine, wicked in his teasing.

"I need you more than wet," he whispered as he brought me to orgasm. I let out a harsh moan that he captured with his mouth. His fingers toyed with me as I held on to his wrist as he drew every ounce of pleasure out of me. Lying beside me, he watched me fall apart at his beckoning. He took his time with me, never letting me go more than a second without his touch, yet leaving me needy at the same time. At his mercy, I willingly gave him whatever he took.

"So beautiful, so perfect. I want these," he whispered as he sucked on my lips, "wrapped around me."

I moved to do just that as he pushed his fingers back inside of me and forced my whole body to obey.

Rolling over, he moved on top of me, his eyes locked with mine, and pulled my jeans from me. He appraised me in my underwear as his eyes roamed every inch. The slow smile I'd come to love made an appearance as he pulled down my panties. I sat up with his fingers still inside me, no longer a willing victim of his agonizing pace. He kneeled before me, raw, primitive, and slightly curious, as I undid the button of his jeans and pulled down his zipper. Against my better judgment, I looked up to him for permission. He simply watched me, his hand between my thighs again, his fingers moving in a pattern of the same sweet torture. I pulled out his erection and froze.

His beautiful dick was massive.

I stroked him with a mix of what I was sure was awe and a little bit of fear. I brushed the tip of him with my finger, brought the drop of salty fluid to my lips, and licked them clean. His body stiffened in reaction as he brushed the inside of me with his fingers, and I seized again in ecstasy as another orgasm hit.

"Say it," he ordered.

"Jack," I gasped willingly. His eyes hooded with satisfaction.

I gripped his heavy thickness in my hand as the jolt coursed through me, and I called out to him again.

I looked up just as he took my hand away from his hard, thick length and brought it to his lips. He kissed it with slow fervor, then gently placed it behind my head as he lay me back down. He sat back on his boot heels, his thickness making my mouth water as he reached behind him with one hand and pulled off his shirt. In the sun, Jack looked like a golden god. Every indent of his chest and torso was outlined to perfection and washed in rays of gold. My heart hammered in my chest as he continued to undress until he was bared before me.

"You're beautiful," I said, unable to contain the truth any longer. He was too far away, and I ached to touch him as he watched me, remaining silent yet saying so much. The air between us was electric and raw. I knew my heart's pace matched his, just as it had moments ago.

"If you could only see what I see," he murmured as he placed himself between my thighs, still on his knees, and planted his hands on either side of me as his mouth began to trail kisses up the inside of my leg.

His hot mouth trailed up, and I gripped his golden threads as he stopped at my center. He looked up at me as his kiss descended where I wanted it. Jack licked, sucked, and pulled while his blue eyes burned through me.

"I crave this," he said as he caressed me smoothly over and over, flattening his tongue as my toes curled. "I need this."

"Oh…oh God," I pushed out as I burst into his mouth, and he worked his fingers and tongue at a faster pace.

Not letting up, he darted in and out of me until I was nothing but a puddle. I gripped his head and pulled him to me, admiring the flex of his chest and the trim lines of his stomach. He fit perfectly between my legs as he leaned in and kissed me, tasting me, his thick head nudging my entrance.

"Are you sure?" he whispered, tracing my lips with his. "I want you so fucking much, Rose, but I want you sure."

I reached between us and positioned him at my entrance, no longer willing to wait another second. He braced himself on his forearms and brushed the hair away from my face as he leaned in one last time, eyes closed, and took my lips. When he pulled away, our eyes met. My whole body lurched as he pushed inside of me. Fast gasps left me as I looked up at him with bulging eyes, my hands on his chest.

The second he began to pull away, I stopped him.

"No! Please don't."

"I don't want to hurt you," he muffled into my chest.

"Jack, I want this," I said as I stilled completely, waiting on him while my insides quaked.

After a brief moment, I bit my lip as he pushed in, the burn of his size overpowering. Jack looked down at me, and I reached up, gripped his full ass, and pulled him closer.

"Rose," he pushed out, his voice thick, "don't. I won't be able to stop," he groaned.

"Yes," I whispered as he pressed in inch by inch as the burn fled and sensation consumed me. When he was fully seated inside me, we stared at each other, eyes glazed and mouths parted. With his first thrust, I lost myself completely.

"Jack, oh my God, Jack!"

Jack's mouth collided with mine as we expressed in a kiss what we both felt. We were lost in our connection as Jack pressed in and my eager body gripped him. Sensation overwhelmed us both as we praised each other with lips and hands.

Jack broke from me and looked down to where we connected. I followed his eyes, watching where we were merged so intimately, and was mesmerized. He gently rolled his body, and I spread my legs wider to accommodate him. I gripped his biceps and held on as pleasure filled my every limb—fire and electricity racing through every nerve. His pace still slow, he filled me as he began to bury the whole of himself to the hilt with each stroke. His head descended as he drew my breasts into his mouth for a long, leisurely kiss while I gently caressed his arms with my fingernails.

Jack shifted again, and my whole body tensed in submission to the movement of his hips.

"Hold on," he grunted as I finally became comfortable enough to wrap my legs around his body. He leaned in, sipped my lips, and pulled back only an inch from my face. Nose to nose, he stroked my cheeks with gentle hands as he slowly made love to me.

It wasn't at all how I pictured it would be. In my mind, I saw raw, sweaty, animal sex.

This was far beyond anything I'd imagined and so much fucking better.

Unable to hold on any longer—just staring at him enough to make my body buckle—I pressed a gentle kiss to his lips.

"Jack," I breathed in warning as he swiveled his hips again, sending me spiraling.

"Come on me, baby."

Everything shook from head to toe. I let the release overtake me as Jack watched me fall apart around him. Fast breaths, words that had no meaning, all escaped me in the time it lasted. I'd never been so full, so completely… full.

Jack thrust his hands into my hair and brought my neck to his lips as he bit and gently sucked. I gripped him harder than ever as I continued to break with his name on my lips.

Minutes later, he came with my name on his.

I woke up in his arms what seemed like hours later and smiled as I watched him reading my book. His chest still bare, I scanned his body and admired him in his black boxer briefs. Slightly embarrassed about being bare myself—aside from the panties I'd slipped on immediately after we'd had sex—I moved to grab my clothes.

"Don't you dare. We stay naked in the meadow," he ordered, waving his hand toward him in a come here gesture, his nose still in the book.

"Are you really reading that?" Instead of an answer, and much to my amusement, he read a line from the book.

"'For pity's sake, hold your tongue,' said Marilla.'"

"Not really your style, is it?" I said as he continued to read to me, ignoring my comment. I moved again to grab my shirt, and he snapped, pointing at me in warning. His eyes remained glued to the pages, never breaking dialogue. I slowly moved toward him, and as soon as I was close enough, he yanked me into his open arm. Bare-breasted and over it, I looked up at his face, completely enamored, and let my smile through. Feeling comfortable, I listened to Jack read me my favorite story in his deep, soothing voice laced with a hint of Cajun.

I sank into him, content until his phone buzzed minutes later, and his jaw tensed. My eyes widened as I saw the name Seth written across his screen, and I shot up to grab my jeans.

"He can't see you, beb," he tried to reassure me.

"No? Well," I mumbled through the neck of my shirt, "if he could, we'd both be running naked!"

"Hello," he answered as I slapped my hands over my mouth to keep my dad from hearing me and then fought frantically to work the dress over my ass. "Yeah, I can be there in about…" Jack's eyebrows rose to me in question as I narrowed mine at him, making a shooing motion with my hands. "Ten minutes," he said disappointedly. When the call ended, he pulled me into his lap. Jack cradled me as his breath hit my neck, and he whispered low in my ear. "Something this perfect will always be ruined by this busy, jealous world. That's why we have to make time for the things that are important. That's why we have to push back."

I nodded, loving his depth, loving the feel of him around me. "I'm going to take about two minutes away from the time I promised him to thoroughly kiss you." His hands roamed over my skin as it became hot to his touch. He tilted my head back as he leaned in. "Because it's important, and I want it bad enough." His lips took mine, gently at first, his need pressing in as the seconds passed until it turned into something else entirely. That kiss was gas to a lit fire as we both ignited like the clock wasn't ticking, like my dad wasn't waiting, like we owned ourselves, our lives, and each other.

When Jack finally pulled away, he grabbed my book.

I shook my head and said, "You can't. It's my favorite. I've never let anybody borrow it."

"So, you'll let me," he said, pulling on his T-shirt with the book in hand.

"You don't understand. It's my most prized possession."

Jack got on his knees as he saw the panic on my face. "Look at me, Rose. Do I look like I would ever want to hurt you?"

Breathless at his stare, I shook my head and snatched the

book from his hands. He leaned in and kissed me gently as he pried it from my fingers. "You won't even read it," I challenged.

"I read *Fifty Shades*," he admitted freely and without shame.

I burst out laughing as he grinned down at me. "Seriously, you think guys don't get a little curious about all the fuss? Though reading *Fifty Shades* on a plane to Iceland got me some odd looks."

I laughed again as he leaned in.

"Go build something," I said as I kissed him one last time without a care in the world.

It was only when Jack walked away that I remembered my heart already had a home.

Jack

Two days…two fucking days.

She wasn't sure.

And I was starving for more of her. Making love to that woman had shifted everything inside me. She'd needed something. I could feel it in her body, in her touch. I could clearly see it in her eyes. And I wanted to be that something. I'd wanted it so badly. Her silence was both overwhelming and deafening. It told me that what she needed hadn't been me or my touch. Fuck if I hadn't known the second I sank inside her that I'd been right to wait because I knew how much I'd feel it. And I did.

And she felt it, too.

Sex changes some things, but unbelievable sex changes every-fucking-thing. Men who deny that are either liars or cowards.

Pounding away at particleboard, I looked to the entrance doors of the center every few minutes in vain. She was hiding, and I knew that, too. Even as I fumed, nothing in me told me that what we did was a mistake. I was already on fire for her, and having her body the way I did just gave it a gust of wind. And I'd gladly stay burning in a constant inferno for just another taste of her.

I saw her signals, all of them mixed and completely fucking unreadable. She was scared, but she had nothing to fear from me. I thought I had read her well enough to take her in the way she begged me to, but if I was wrong, that made me more of an asshole than I felt.

I wasn't wrong. No fucking way was I wrong.

This woman had me twisted.

I kept busy, knowing she'd have to face me eventually and, if this was a brush-off, make the inevitable excuse. She believed what we'd done had been a mistake, and that cut deep, deeper than it should.

What the hell was I doing, anyway?

I pulled out my ear buds blaring Wu-Tang's "C.R.E.A.M.", another one of Rose's rap suggestions, and threw my mallet down with a curse.

"Jack?"

I jerked my head up, hearing Rose's voice, but saw Dallas instead. It hadn't struck me how alike they sounded.

"Hi," I said, unable to mask my temperament.

"You okay?"

"Fine," I replied with a smile as I noticed Annabelle take a step toward me. "I'm dirty, baby girl."

"So is she," Dallas encouraged as she led her daughter my way. All my anger and worry dispersed as Annabelle took an unsure step without her mom's help and landed in my waiting arms. I didn't have much experience with kids until I met Dallas's children, and yet, somehow, it felt natural as Anna looked up at me with a one-toothed smile. She was the most beautiful little girl I'd ever seen. My chest squeezed as she began to talk to me brokenly.

"It's unreal. She's been through four sitters and came close to hating her grandparents, and with you, it's just so natural," Dallas said, amazed.

"Maybe she's just opening up a bit?" I said, bouncing her in my lap.

"Sometimes a girl just needs the right guy to get her to do it." I froze with Annabelle in my lap, knowing our conversation had moved into dangerous territory.

Dallas sensed my hesitation and reached for Anna. I kissed her cheek and breathed in her scent before I let her go. Anna protested and held her arms back out for me as I started to put my tools back into my box. I had finished the details of the lobby. I only had a few more projects left before I ran out of excuses to stay.

"I'm leaving soon."

Dallas simply nodded as she held her daughter close. "She's just... Rose is... Jack, if you'll be patient—"

"I don't think that's the problem," I said wearily. Unable to keep my thoughts to myself, I asked the question that had been weighing on my mind since the minute I met her.

"What's she afraid of?"

Dallas looked down at me with a mix of both sympathy and warning. "You."

chapter
thirteen

I WALKED OUT ONTO THE PORCH, MY MORNING COFFEE IN HAND, still in the yoga pants and Austin T-shirt I'd tossed on before I'd turned in the night before. My hair was disgustingly piled on top of my head, and I gave zero shits as I scanned the land in front of me. I'd hidden at my moms for the past two days, terrified to face Jack.

He'd texted me twice each morning to tell me I was beautiful and called once, to which I hadn't responded. His text hadn't come this morning, which stung in a way I wasn't prepared for. I hated myself for my behavior, but even more so, I hated the reaction I had to what we'd shared. There never would be a better man to take that Band-Aid away. Though this one hadn't been painless, at least not in the aftermath, the guilt… the guilt was too much to bear. I sipped my coffee, disgusted with myself.

Dallas had told me—when I confessed to her that I'd been intimate with Jack—that I'd created this hurdle in my mind and that only I could jump over it. I knew she was right. I knew somehow, I'd martyred my future romantic life in the ridiculous notion that I could keep Grant close by keeping a man's affections and attention at bay.

But the other half of me—the one that truly wanted to live again—knew the stupidity of it. I was in an all-out internal struggle to break free. Suddenly aware I wasn't alone, I looked to see Jack watching me closely from the foot of the porch. The only thing that startled me was just how breathtaking he was to look at.

"Hi," I offered pathetically.

He took the steps two at a time and was in front of me, evident irritation and confusion covering his face. He hadn't shaved in the days since I'd last seen him, and it was irresistibly sexy. I held my coffee out to him, but he shook his head.

"I could make you a cup," I offered, pointing my mug toward my open bedroom door.

Ignoring my offer, he reached out, and I flinched as he pulled the clip from my hair so it fell around my shoulders in a hot mess.

"You're beautiful," he said, which I assumed was in lieu of my missed text. Emotion choked me as he looked at me, puzzled but full of honesty. I set my cup down on the railing and faced him head-on as I pushed out a breath.

"What happened between us was…" I paused, unable to voice the reason for my hesitation.

"What happened between us was fucking perfect, and I dare you to say different. And don't even try to pretend with me, Rose. You want a repeat as much as I do." He moved toward me, and I felt my body open to him before my mind had a chance to catch up. I was in his arms, his mouth on mine, a moan vibrating in the back of my throat.

His tongue massaged me, coaxed me, and told me the truth. It had been perfect. What had transpired between us had been more than just sex, more than need, and was filled with a deep connection. With his arms around me and his mouth on mine, I didn't have to put any more thought into it until he tore his lips away with unsettled eyes.

"But you weren't sure," he declared with regret in his eyes.

I hated that look. I wanted it gone but was sure it was only a reaction to my hesitance. Once again, I was forced to hide the truth from him, but I wasn't sure why. I needed to come clean. He could see my guilt, but he didn't know the reason for it. I didn't want him to think that what happened meant any less to me than it did to him. I wanted nothing more than to explore our connection, but the fucking guilt was choking me.

I opened my mouth to speak just as his phone vibrated in his pocket. He reluctantly let go of me but pinned me with his eyes. I could feel the small amount of anger radiating from him. He briefly looked down at the text and cursed in aggravation.

"I have to go. One of the machines—"

"It's fine. I'll just... I have to get to work."

Jack nodded and withdrew, turning to walk away. I felt the pain of it and quickly spoke. "I don't regret it."

He stilled as if waiting for more of an explanation, and when I gave none, he stopped waiting. He moved quickly, walking in the direction of the center. Panic gripped me as the thought that I'd blown it with him began to race through me. Unsure of what to do, I watched him walk away, but more and more panic began to build, making it impossible for me to ignore it.

"Jack," I called after him. His steps didn't stop. I called his name again, sure he'd heard me the first time. When I got no reaction, my panic turned into action. I jumped on the cart, my hair whipping around me and my braless breasts bouncing with each damned bump I took. I was sure I looked as insane as I felt as I caught up with him and began yelling at a black T-shirt-clad back. "I've been... hurt, and I told you, it's been a long time for me... since..."

When I got no response, I went in again. "You were great. It was great." Jack gave me a sideways glance, letting me know what an idiotic statement that was, and at that moment, all I wanted to do was drive my cart into the pond.

"What I meant was, we… you… of course I want to do it again." Jack picked up his pace in an attempt to hide his smile, but I saw it.

"Will you just get on the damn cart and give me a second! I'm not a morning person!" I was failing miserably, and we both knew it. Yet I had no idea what words he wanted to hear.

Jack kept walking as he paid me no attention, and I quickly became irritated. The heat, my inability to express myself to Jack, and the fact that he was ignoring me had my temper flaring.

"Look, you horse's ass, I'm trying to be agreeable, okay!" I skidded to a stop and yelled at his back. When he kept walking, my temper boiled over, and I found myself blurting fluent idiot. "Ohhhhh, Jack, it was the best, most amaaaazing sex I've ever had! And I'm sure I would very much like to do it again and as soon as possible. Maybe right here, right now?" I tapped the seat next to me and gritted my teeth as he took one infuriating step after another. "No? Okay, so when you're done being a jerk and can forgive my inarticulate way of being agreeable, give me a call!"

I heard laughter beside me and jerked my head toward the farmers sitting at the field's edge eating their breakfast. Humiliated again, I narrowed my eyes at Jack as he remained steadfast and ignored me. Furious at this point, I floored the cart and sped up to him as he neared the halfway mark to the center. No longer willing to be cast aside, and with my dignity hanging by a thread, I ran him off the sidewalk and knocked him sideways on his ass. Completely unconcerned with his well-being, I jumped off the cart and stood in front of him as he looked up at me, amused and chuckling.

"I'm trying here, Jack! What do you want me to say?!"

Jack grabbed a hand off my hip and jerked me down into his lap, much the same way he did the day I met him. His lips claimed my parted ones, and he kissed me hard and thoroughly. I gripped him tight and kissed him back with everything in me. He pulled away with my favorite smile, and I returned it.

"Honestly, baby, I just want you to shut the hell up at this point. I think you've said enough." He shoved me off of his lap, and I landed on my ass with a thud. Indignant and still itching for a fight, I stood to watch him approach my cart and climb into the driver's side. Fully expecting to join him, I stood open-mouthed when he began to drive away in the direction of the clinic.

"Hey," I protested.

"Time-out, Rose."

"You ass!"

"Get some new material!" I could hear his smile as I all but growled behind him, coming up with plenty of fresh material.

I looked to the sky as more hysterical laughter bellowed out behind me. I raised my hand and gave the one-finger salute as I watched Jack drive off. Shoulders slumped, I turned to face my audience and glared in their direction, daring them to say a word. When nothing came, I stomped back home and broke down in a ball of laughter in the shower.

That night after my shift, I was disheartened to see Jack's bike gone. I was a twenty-eight-year-old woman in a time-out.

The next day, I decided to test the waters with Jack by bringing a catered lunch to the crew. Jack had a right to be pissed off, but we had to make peace at some point. I'd done nothing but battle guilt and fantasize about him. I owed him an apology, but more than that, I'd screwed up the first real chance I'd had at making progress in a new relationship.

I brought the sandwiches through the double doors, unable to keep from scanning the lobby for any sign of him. My eyes found him on a ladder in the midst of mounting one of two huge healing poles he'd crafted by hand by mimicking a design he'd seen in Africa. I admired his stunning work as I spread the food on a long plastic table and waited for any of the workers to acknowledge me. After several minutes, and my nerves fraying at the ends, I put my finger and thumb to my mouth and, with a loud whistle, made damn sure everyone heard it. Seeing a few of the workers make their way over, I made a beeline for the break room to grab the cooler full of drinks.

With a deep breath, I reemerged to a table full of the hungry crew, who thanked me through mouthfuls of food and eager sips of cold beverages. Jack stayed planted on his ladder, his earbuds in and his attention far from reach. I admired his immaculate body as he worked diligently on his task. He wore his usual jeans and black work boots but had decided to forgo his T-shirt for a black tank. He was pure strength and masculinity, and I had to bite my lip hard to stifle the moan trying to escape my throat.

His arms flexed with every strike of his hammer. I took in the broad shoulders I'd had my hands on just days before that led down to a perfectly trim waist. I gasped a little as I visualized the movement of his hips as he hovered over me and what lay beneath his jeans.

Needing to distract myself, I made small talk with Pedro as I kept busy, keeping the table full and replenishing the drinks.

Hadn't I apologized? Hadn't I chased him for over a mile trying to explain myself? I stood fuming as the workers dispersed, and Jack remained in his position, fucking beautiful and completely out of reach. I cleaned up quickly, no longer able to handle his blatant disregard for my olive branch. With each piece of trash I threw away, I mourned our late-night talks and the possibility of a new tradition of being naked in the meadow with him. I hated his absence and his silence.

He was giving me a taste of my own medicine. I got his message loud and clear.

I left a single sandwich and drink on the table for Jack. Looking up at him one last time, I found him staring right at me. His stare was curious as if he was seeing me for the very first time. I met his stare but only momentarily, afraid he would see the truth of what his rejection was doing to me. Seconds later, I walked out the doors, less the burden of food I walked in with and yet heavier with the idea that I may no longer have Jack to look forward to.

Guilt had proven to be my biggest hindrance in moving on without Grant. It wasn't just the sex with Jack. It was the feeling that went with sharing the most intimate part of me with him. I'd assumed our attraction was mostly physical, but Jack was both disarming and charming without bounds. He'd lifted his figurative finger at me in summons, and I'd walked toward him willingly. What I had not counted on was the new algorithm that danced in my heart.

After my shift—and another day of painful silence—I decided on a plan b. I walked into the center, claiming the bottle of Maker's that we'd started on. I went home to shower and jumped into my convertible before I had a chance to second-guess my actions. I pulled into Jack's motel and sat outside in my car next to his bike, working up the courage to approach as I took sip after sip of bourbon. Memories of how it felt to be filled by him trickled in and out as I took a deep breath and pushed open my car door. I stood outside his room, hesitating only briefly before knocking softly twice.

"Jack?"

I got no answer and looked back at his bike, puzzled. Sudden fear crept over me that he might not be alone. I jerked away from the door. My heart pounding as every worst-case scenario raced through my mind, I gave the door the one-finger salute.

"Temper, beb," Jack said behind me as he caught the bottle I almost dropped when he startled me. He slid his key into the door, a fresh bucket of ice cradled in his arm. "I saw you pull up about thirty minutes ago. I like my booze on ice."

Cheeks heated, I followed him into the room and blew out my embarrassment with my breath.

"You thought I wasn't alone," he said as a statement as he pulled my purse from my arm and set it down on the table next to the bed.

"Yeah," I said, refusing to play games.

"Why?" he said as he sat at the edge of the bed and placed his hands on his thighs. I wanted nothing more than to bare myself, tear off my clothes, and dive into him, knowing what he could do to me. I didn't want meaningful conversation, not tonight. I wanted to be handled—and by Jack.

"Because, Jesus, I mean, look at you."

He tucked in his lip, his face rigid with disdain. "Yeah, well, I don't think that way."

"You are totally sexual," I protested as I stepped away from the door and picked up the bottle to pour our bourbon.

"Only with the women I want to be sexual with," he said harshly.

"Why are you so defensive?" I asked as he took a mind-numbing drink out of his glass.

"Because you put me here," he said, aggravated.

"This was a bad idea," I said as I went for my purse and gripped my keys.

"Take off your clothes."

"What?"

"Take off your clothes, and we'll see just how bad of an idea it was."

His eyes never left mine as he took another sip of his bourbon and then crunched a cube in his mouth. I wanted to taste that cold mix on his tongue. We both knew why I was there, and suddenly it cheapened everything about our time in the meadow, our time together—period. Guilty, I looked at him and apologized.

"I'm sorry. Shit, Jack, I'm so sorry." I flinched as he made a sudden move to set down his drink and pulled his shirt off, tossing it to the floor between us.

"Rose, look at me. Tell me what you want."

I stared into his eyes, and they began to darken with desire as he watched me.

"I want to feel like I did on the blanket with you." I pushed out a breath. "I want you."

"I'm right here."

I took a tentative step forward and then another until I stood before him. He sat motionless as I pushed my fingers through his hair and tilted his head toward me. His eyes hooded as I leaned in and whispered a kiss on his lips. "I want you, Jack."

His hand slid up my bare thigh as I pulled him in for a deep kiss. As our slow, hungry tongues met, that same flicker turned into a flame. My moan echoed in his throat as he found me wet and ready beneath my shorts and panties. Jack pushed me to stand fully as he explored my entrance, his eyes never leaving mine. My lips parted as his eyes closed briefly. Breaths coming out fast, Jack's skilled touch tore my inhibitions to shreds as I began to shake with want.

"Jack!"

Sensing the crack in me, Jack kissed me, his arms wrapped around my back. I leaned into him with relief, no longer able to stand on my own. As if a switch had flipped, Jack turned us quickly, and I fell back on the mattress as his lips followed and crashed into mine. Hungry and willing, I reached into his jeans and stroked the velvet tip of him. He tore his mouth from mine as I moved my thumb over the soft skin and let him see the need in me. He twitched in my hand as I licked my lips.

Still fully clothed, I twisted beneath him as I freed his cock and looked up at him in a plea, stroking him more firmly.

A picture of restraint, Jack hovered above me as if he was fighting himself before he looked down at me again. As I had before, I saw the shift as he made up his mind. My eyes widened as he tore my shorts and panties away, lifted my leg, and buried his length inside me without hesitation.

A scream left my throat, and he clamped his mouth over mine, capturing it as he ravaged me. I bucked and moved with him in sync as our bodies made perfect conversation.

Jack leaned in and whispered, "Is this how you wanted to feel?"

He didn't let me answer as he shoved two fingers in my mouth and pulled me to the edge of the bed. Still inside me, he began to pump slower as my eyes slid from where we connected to his parted lips. He rolled his hips as I tore at the shirt on my chest, desperate to get it off. Jack stilled my hands and lifted the cups of my bra, freeing my chest. His hands covered each of my peaked breasts tenderly, and he began to pump harder. Breathless, gone, sex on fire, I threw my head back as my whole body began to tremble with my impending release.

"That's right, baby, let go." I looked up at Jack, and my mouth parted as I watched how much my reaction affected him.

I wanted more of that look. As of that moment, it was mine. It belonged to me.

"What took you so long?" he scorned as he picked up his pace. I managed to get my shirt off while he thrust into me—a man possessed, a man who craved the connection as much as I did. He'd been waiting on me. He was justified in doing so, and yet I felt a flare of anger burn through my chest. He'd been testing his own waters.

"And you thought this wasn't enough for me." He pulled out abruptly and turned me onto my stomach, not hesitating a second before I felt full of him again. A hard slap on the ass accompanied his swift return. I gasped as another orgasm struck, this time harder, and I screamed into the mattress.

My body still trembling, Jack continued to take me—hungry and insatiable—as I gripped the sheets and begged for more. He gave me exactly what I'd asked for.

"More?" he said. I couldn't answer as I felt every inch of his heavy cock both pleasure and punish me. He wrapped his fist in my hair and pulled hard, and I gasped in surprise as his touch turned carnal.

Our skin slick with sweat, Jack pulled away from me, turning me over again and lying next to me before he pulled me onto his lap. We stared at each other, breaths heavy, and hunger peaked to new heights. Unable to resist, I lifted my hips, and Jack gripped them, bringing me forward, my knees at his head. With the first brush of his tongue, I screamed again and braced myself on the headboard above him. He devoured me without apology, his greedy tongue worshipping me. In control, Jack gripped my hips and moved them on my behalf as he brushed my slick center over his mouth.

I completely let go as I watched him lick me until my body submitted and shuddered around him. Easing me back down on his lap, I hovered above him. Jack pushed inside me slowly as I let my weight carry me down until we felt our bodies click. Mouth parted and impossibly full, I looked down at him, helpless and in love with the feel of him. It was too much, way too much, and not enough all at once. I had no words, no thought, just his name—his name and those damned beautiful eyes that continued to pierce me. We stayed that way for endless minutes, connected in mouth and movement until we both spilled over with wordless cries.

When I finally had the strength to lift myself away from him, I heard his harsh "stay" as he left me on the mattress and returned with a cool washcloth to clean us both. Once satisfied, he laid beside me, cradling my body, and I wrapped my leg around his torso.

"We've never used a condom," he said as he looked down at me with concern.

"I have one in my purse, several actually," I said as I buried my face into his chest in shame. "I'm on birth control and have been for over half my life."

"I think we're okay," he said, staring down at me. "I don't sleep around. I don't have anything to worry about."

"I think you do," I said, jutting my eyes down to the largest soft shell I'd ever seen in my life before I gripped it tightly.

Jack pulled my hand away with a slight curl of his lips. "Did I hurt you?"

"No," I said with a light kiss to his chest. "I love the way you feel."

He gripped my hair tight and tilted my head so that his

mouth was to my ear. "Being inside you is the best I've ever felt. Don't hide from me anymore. I hated it."

I nodded into his chest. "I'm sorry. I hated it, too," I confessed.

"You have nothing to be afraid of with me. I can only prove it to you if you let me."

I pressed my lips to his in another silent apology. When I pulled back, I noticed my book on his nightstand and picked it up. "You probably haven't read a page."

"I was waiting to read it to you."

I leaned back and gave him an odd look.

"Aren't you bored here? I mean, for someone who spends fifty percent of his year traveling, aren't you losing your damned mind in nowhere Texas?"

"No, I'm pretty occupied at the moment," he said as he slid a hand over my bare ass.

"I don't understand you. You really aren't like… anyone."

"Then you understand me," he whispered before drawing my mouth into a long kiss, a kiss that lasted through two more orgasms.

Jack

I spent the night reading to her and making her come. I spent the majority of the morning watching her sleep. I'd had not a wink of it and was determined to keep it that way until she left my arms. I traced her spine with my fingertips, and she sank further into me. She'd come to me last night a woman full of desire, a woman afraid to ask for what she wanted. I didn't make it easy for her, but I'd made it up to her in multiples. I needed her in this… thing. I'd only wanted her to show me.

Her question was valid. What in the hell was I doing in no-where Texas when I could be anywhere else in the world?

But the answer had asked the question.

I couldn't tell her that. Even though I saw a new softness in her eyes when she looked at me and said my name, I knew better. She was holding out, holding back. As much as I embraced our new relationship, I knew it scared her. She'd been hurt—that much was evident—but by whom? Jealousy raced through me as I thought of who could've possibly hurt this woman. I was sure it wasn't that spineless dick in the bar. She hadn't been affected by him in the least. She was better than him.

She was incredible… and still a mystery to me. Most women who graced my bed were, and yet I never asked the questions.

"If a two-year-old can chain-smoke and run the streets of the Philippines, you can get out of bed, Rose."

I turned over to see Rose's eyes open and widen when she realized she was in bed with me. I burst out in incredulous laughter as I looked her over. She buried her head into her pillow in embarrassment. Still chuckling and more than curious, I pulled the pillow from her grip until she was forced to give it up and look my way.

"Explain, lady, or you aren't leaving this bed."

I could barely see her green eyes as she peered at me through a sea of auburn hair. She looked beautiful in the sun-kissed room.

She pushed her hair out of the way as she smiled at me fully. It stole my breath. "Okay, so I give myself a little encouragement to get out of bed in the morning."

"By talking about chain-smoking babies?"

"Before I open my eyes, I think of something to get me mo-tivated. Most of them are human feats, and some are spiritual.

It's just a thing I do," Rose admitted as she began to slip out of bed. I pulled her to me with a negative headshake.

"I have surgery in three hours," she protested, barely resisting my hold on her. She looked up at me with a curious smile, and I told her the truth. "Good morning, beautiful." She sighed as she nestled further into my arms, and I felt another switch flip. She was under my skin and beginning to filter everywhere else.

I chuckled as I thought of her telling me off as she threw that snake over the railing. I'd never in my lifetime get over that. One minute she was impossibly feminine. The next, she was shoveling a side of rare beef in her mouth and wrestling reptiles.

"What?" she muffled into my chest.

"You're the poster child of a hot mess." She stiffened in my arms as I continued. "You're all over the place. Feisty one minute and full of love the next. I have no doubt that you're the picture of control in the operating room, but out of it, well… I've never known anyone like you."

Her arms tightened around my waist as she placed a small kiss on my chest. "Then you understand me."

"I see what you want me to see, but you get no complaints here," I said as I dragged my fingertips from her knee to the top of her thigh.

She looked my way, a devastating smile on her face. "So, what happens next?"

In a sudden move, I turned her on her back and moved between her legs. I slipped an inch inside her as her breath hitched and kissed her neck as she moaned in welcome.

"I give you two more orgasms, and we have coffee," I said hoarsely as I began to push further inside her. She thrust her hips up in an effort to gain more of me, and I teased her as I circled them.

"And then," she rasped as she dragged her nails down my back.

"And then we shower together," I said as I pushed in fully and buried myself in heaven.

I remained still as she opened up to me. Every layer of space between us evaporated as I waited for her eyes to connect with mine. My arms locked next to her shoulders, and I rolled my hips and watched her catch fire.

"This is so fucking perfect," I whispered as I leaned in and kissed her before I rolled again and got impossibly deeper.

"Jack," she gasped as her body began to tremble and her tightness clenched around me.

"Here," I whispered as I placed a kiss on her forehead. "Here," I said in the same tone as I kissed her chest where her heart lay. "Here," I said as I pulled back and thrust hard, watching her fall apart beneath me. "Lots of this, that's what's next," I promised through clenched teeth as I began to frantically move. I wanted to believe it was the truth. That there would be more nights like last night and even more of these mornings. She fascinated me and would take a piece of me with her when she left, a piece I had given to her after I had realized I was in a free fall.

It felt like a risk, but a risk worth taking.

I paused above her, positive I'd aimed for something else entirely when I'd pushed inside her this morning, and it had turned into something else altogether.

"Jack, let go," she urged as I spent myself inside her. And just as her words registered, my decision was made.

I didn't want to let her go. I didn't want her out of my bed or out of my sight. But I learned a long time ago that it wasn't up to me. You can make a woman smile, crave, and come, but you could never make a woman feel.

And that was the most fascinating thing of all.

chapter
fourteen

Jack: Good morning, beautiful.
Rose: Morning, handsome. Rap & R&B 101 Hate It or
Love It, The Game ft 50 Cent.
Jack: Go save someone.
Rose: Go build something.

H E SENT A PICTURE OF A BUILDING HE HAD CO-DESIGNED, and I gasped at the progress they'd made. He was in Lubbock for a few days overseeing the breaking ground of the project so he could spend some off time with me. He was running out of projects to help the center and decided to split his time—so his reason for staying wasn't obvious. I appreciated it more than he knew. I wasn't ready to share yet, but it had been a week since I'd seen him, and I hated it. His absence tugged at me—it gnawed. I savored every minute with him. Jack had completely taken me by surprise. Though a Southern gentleman to the core—and more than proud to be from his fair city of New Orleans—he was so much more than I'd originally given him credit for. Southern-bred but worldly at the same time. I couldn't wrap my head around some of the things he'd seen and done. I was small-town Texas, and he was… everywhere. Each day we spent together, we gave a little more of ourselves, our minds, and our bodies. It felt surreal.

His presence excited me, his depth moved me, and his touch sated me.

Jack reminded me that life lay beyond my demanding career, a career I'd chosen and still loved. But my walks on the grounds became a lot less lonely with thoughts of my time with him to keep me company. My need for him grew each day. When he was in Texas, I spent all my nights with him at his hotel or the center, both of us still intent on keeping our stolen moments private—though more for me than Jack.

He refused to let our relationship be limited. Oftentimes, he would force my hand on days I wanted to relax and take me out on spontaneous trips he would plan. We'd been tubing down the Guadalupe River, attended the Bluebonnet Festival—taking Grant and Annabel—and had even gone to Billy Bob's so he could properly train me as his dance partner.

That night…that night had been both the best and the worst.

"You look beautiful," he whispered in the cabin of my car as he kept his hand on my thigh. I looked over at him, pleased that he'd noticed the extra effort I'd put in. My usually corrupt hair was tamed straight, and I'd bought new black jeans and boots that fit like a second skin. My dark blue tube top was tight and showed what little cleavage I had and came just short of showing an inch of my midriff.

"So do you," I said, moving my hand over his. I compared the size of the two and saw his was impossibly large next to mine.

"But they fit perfectly," he said as he noticed my comparison and laced them together.

"They do," I said as I looked over his dark eyes, lashes, nose, and lips.

"Think you can handle a night of country music?" he said as he parked the car in the busy station at the Fort Worth Stockyards. The

Yards were a mix of industrial and southern in feel. A stomping ground for cowboys and girls alike. It was a strip of bars, shops, and eateries. My parents had taken us here a few times to see them release the longhorns on the street—a daily tradition. It was as Texas as Texas could get.

The excitement in me had built throughout the day. Jack—without knowing it—had given me the chance to break free, get out of the norm, and blow off the steam that had been building inside of me for some time.

"I'm so ready for this," I beamed at him.

"C'mere, beb," he said in thick Cajun as he parked the car and turned to look at me. I leaned over the console, and he cupped my face and pulled me in the rest of the way. Our mouths met with tenderness as Jack kissed me with passion and need. Ache brewed inside me the way it always did when he kissed me like he meant it.

And Jack always kissed me like he meant it.

"I think I've fallen in love," Jack said slowly as my breath hitched and fear shook me, "with your mouth."

He saw the relief cover my features, and his jaw tightened. Without pause, I exited the car and felt lighter in the night air.

Jack met me at the hood of the car with a scold. "I get your doors for you."

"Sorry," I smiled ruefully. "I keep forgetting."

"So, I'll keep reminding you." His words were a little harsh, but I knew it had everything to do with my panic back in the car. I ignored his silence as we made our way inside the honky-tonk, fingers clasped. Music reverberated through my every pore as the bass pounded throughout the crowded bar. Jack never let go of my hand as he summoned the all-legs bartender in short black shorts, who noticed Jack immediately and made it her mission to get over to him.

"Two bourbons on ice, please. Maker's if you have it." He squeezed my hand as I stiffened behind him, watching the woman in front of us

shamelessly eye fuck him. Even with his reassurance, I quickly surveyed the rest of the crowd around us and saw the eyes of several women glued to him. I looked back to Jack, who was dressed in a button-down, collared, dark blue shirt, dark blue jeans, and new black boots. His hair was a lightly gelled chaos of blond. His profile alone—lit by the amber light of the bar—had my mouth watering. Possessiveness took hold as I held his hand tighter, and he looked over at me with a wink.

Jack wasn't immune to the attention he was getting by simply standing at the bar. He was well aware of it and shifted slightly on his feet. Though his demeanor screamed confidence, I could tell by the tick in his jaw that it bothered him. It made me even more curious. I leaned into him just as his hand twisted in my hair, and he pulled my lips to his for a brief but message-filled kiss. When he pulled away, I saw it. I was the only woman he wanted at that moment, and that was enough for me.

When our drinks arrived, we stood at a table nearby, admiring the people on the dance floor. I turned to Jack, who silently watched the couples.

"Who taught you to dance?"

A pained, faint smile crossed his lips briefly. "A friend. You?"

I smiled. "My parents."

"Well," he said thickly as he watched me drain my glass. "Let's see what we're working with."

He grabbed my hand, exuding confidence as he led me to the floor. Clinging to him through the dense crowd, my hand on his bicep, I followed behind, unsure if I would be able to keep up. He made space for us, then turned to face me. Jack gripped my body tightly and began to move. I looked up at him as he started to two-step me effortlessly around the floor. I fumbled slightly with my steps as he commanded my attention.

"Look at me, beb, not your feet."

I'd been out dancing once or twice in my life, but to music completely different. Yet, as I looked into his eyes, I let my body relax in *trust, and soon we were in sync. Jack never stopped his feet. Song after song, we danced, fast or slow, our eyes locked, our smiles matching. For all we knew, we were alone on that dance floor. It felt amazing. Inch by inch, the separation between us disappeared. In Jack's arms, I felt beautiful, needed, wanted, and cherished. I was high on him, and he seemed to feel the same.*

Jack had moved his hand from around my waist and kept it behind my neck, keeping our faces as close as possible. His fingers massaged my neck while his thumb moved to stroke beneath my ear.

Under his spell, I was completely lost in his eyes and what he was saying without moving his lips.

I felt it then, the unmistakable shot to the chest, and in his eyes, I saw my future. I closed them as tightly as possible as emotion overflowed, and heard the tiny sob escape my lips.

Jack stopped his feet. I stumbled forward into his chest and kept my head buried there.

"Rose?" He'd felt it. He'd seen it. He knew.

I kept my eyes tightly shut as he again addressed me with patience. "Rose."

I opened my eyes to see his wide smile, and that smile undid me.

"I have to use the restroom." I leaned in and gave him a light kiss, escaping his arm just as he reached to keep me with him. I raced through the crowd, tears coming fast and hard as I pushed past people and saw the line. Panicking, I pushed again through the same offended crowd and out the front door. "Oh shit," I said as I ran away from the never-ending crowd of people. "Oh shit," I mouthed into my palm as I found refuge between buildings shrouded in darkness and away from the noise.

I made quick work of gathering myself, knowing Jack would come looking for me sooner rather than later.

"Don't do this to me," I begged the pumping vessel that betrayed me. "I can't do this again!"

I put my hands against the brick wall and took several calming breaths. I was running out of time and was still visibly shaking. My connection with Jack was natural. It was always going to happen.

Taking one last calming breath, I wiped my face and rounded the corner to go back.

I froze when I saw Jack at the entrance of the bar. His hands were shoved in his pockets, and he was clearly looking for me. I put on my game face as I moved toward him. I stopped dead in my tracks as a beautiful brunette approached him. Not stopping my stride, I watched their exchange. Jack, clearly irritated, searched around her, looking toward the street for me.

My fear morphed into jealousy at seeing another woman so close to him. I stopped just short of him, his back angled toward me as I listened to the conversation he wasn't interested in having.

"You lose your dance partner? I'd be happy to save one for you." She really was beautiful, but by the way she looked at him, she was definitely interested in more than dancing.

"I'm all set," he said, clipped and clearly finished with her. "Have a good night."

I watched her face fall, but she remained where she was. "How about a drink, then?"

"Actually, I was hoping you would come over and give me a chance to talk to you." I reared my head back in shock, as did she. Anger coursed through my veins as his following words struck me in the chest one by one.

"I can see you've got a body full of sin."

Her eyes widened as she leaned in closer, clearly turned on by the Cajun accent. He was laying it on thick. She scanned his body, hanging on his every word as I stood motionless and furious, waiting on his next words.

"And I speak now on behalf of Jesus Christ to let you know you can be forgiven. God loves all his children no matter the number of sins. Would you care to pray for your soul right here on the street?"

I clamped a hand over my mouth for the second time but couldn't control the laughter that escaped me as she looked at Jack with confusion before stuttering her reply.

"I… I… I'm all set, thanks."

"Jesus loves you," he called out after her as she fled from him like she'd been lit on fire. Jack's hand shot out behind him, making it obvious he knew I was listening, and he pulled me into him as I laughed hysterically. After a solid minute of nonstop belly laughter, I looked up to see the same smile I'd just fled from.

"Nothing like a little religion to scare people away," he said with a chuckle as I shook my head. "Why are people so afraid of Jesus? He was the best of all humans."

"He was," I agreed as I wrapped myself tightly around him, my laughter slowly fading.

"It's not right to run from something that's good for you," he whispered as he wrapped his arms around my waist and looked down at me. I nodded without a good response.

"Beb, don't disappear from me like that, okay?"

"The line was too long. I had to find—"

Gray eyes pierced me as my lie died on my lips. "Okay."

"Let's go home." He made quick work of fusing our hands and pulled me across the street to our parked car. After he'd shut my door and joined me in the front seat, we smiled at each other.

"Do you do that often?"

"Often enough."

"You are wicked," I said with a conspiratorial smile before asking the question on the tip of my tongue. "What do you believe, Jack?"

"No, no way, not tonight," he said, cutting the air between us with his hand.

"And why is that?" I asked as I closed the space between us and planted a suggestive tongue-filled kiss on his neck. Jack let me explore him but stopped my hand just as it reached the hard bulge in his pants.

He wrapped my sweat-dampened hair in his hand and pulled it tightly, forcing my lips from his neck.

With heat in his eyes and lust in his voice, he gave me the only answer I could want. "Because you've got a body full of sin, beb, and tonight, I want to be your only redeemer."

"Earth to Rose," Jules spouted as I sat with my sneaker in my lap, replaying the marathon of breath-stealing moments that followed that night.

"I hate you." She sighed as she took a seat next to me on the bench. "But I'm happy for you."

"Me too," Jamie said as she eyed me from her open locker. "Even though *we* are the ones actively *looking* for a man while you hide in this hospital. Even though *he* practically fell in your lap while *we* suffer awkward dates. Even though *we* have to deal with the SPAM eaters of the wor—"

"Shut up, Jamie. Don't be jealous. It's bad karma," Jules snapped. "And we need good juju for tonight."

I looked between them with a smile. "What's tonight?"

"Want to come?" Jamie asked, taking the bench opposite of us. I smirked at her polka dot-covered scrubs. The girl refused to wear anything without color. "We're going to the Stockyards. Jules is ready to find a new cowboy."

My grin broadened as I declined. "No, I was just there, actually. Jack took me dancing."

Jules looked heavenward as she scrubbed her face. "Of course he did."

"Now *you* sound jealous," I said as I scowled at her while I laced my shoe.

"I am, and so in punishment, we're Ubering it to your place when we strike out tonight so you can share in our agony. So have Advil and something greasy ready for consumption. I'm exhausted from adulting and need to be free of these shackles."

"Fine," I said with a laugh, then scanned them both with hopeful eyes. "But what if you don't strike out?" I dodged Jamie's bra as she threw it at me, followed by Jules' heavy brush.

Warding off the assault of toiletries being hurled at me, I waved my white flag. "Fine, I'll be ready, but do me the honor of warning me, ladies, okay? I may not be alone."

"I thought Jack was in Lubbock?"

"He is—" I sighed, "—but he's supposed to be back tonight or tomorrow, job permitting."

"I guess," Jules said, approaching me and looking ten feet tall though she barely cleared my chin, "we should be flattered you would push him aside for a night ender with us."

"Yes, you should be," I said, recalling the nights I've missed with my sister since Dean became her priority, "but you were here first."

"See this, this right here is why I like her," Jules said pointedly at Jamie.

"I was on a date," Jamie defended as they resumed an argument I wasn't familiar with. I left them to their squawking as a text came through.

Jennifer: I'm pregnant again! I hate him!

I laughed hard as I made my way to the break room to down some last-minute coffee. I sat back in the empty room as I replied.

Rose: Congrats ☺

Jennifer: I can see your evil smile from California, jerk. Think you might find time to meet one of them before I have a litter and can't distinguish names?

I felt a wave of guilt cross over me as I thought of how much time had passed since I'd seen her. I'd almost missed her wedding several months after Grant's death in a bout of pure selfishness. I'd pushed through and was thankful for it because Jennifer had been there for me for the majority of my adult life. I doubt she would have forgiven me.

Rose: A weekend after we open the center. I promise.

Jennifer: Please. I still need to know you. I love you, bitch.

Rose: Love you too.

I held my fingers over the keys, tempted to tell her about Jack. I typed a paragraph to let her know I was doing what she'd been praying for the last few years but deleted it word by word. I ignored the opening door of the break room until I saw Dean walk in.

"Dean," I said, looking at him with a smile. He looked down at me, softness in his eyes. The same look he'd given me when I first met him almost twenty years ago. "Going into surgery?"

"Hysterectomy," he said. "You?"

"Assist on a gallbladder, and I'll need this," I said, shifting my eyes to my coffee cup as I took a sip.

"It feels totally different when you're in charge," he assured me, pouring his own cup before he sat down next to me. I sensed Dean's brief hesitation and already knew his question before he spoke. "Tell me about Jack."

"I'll kick her ass and then yours if you tell my dad," I said without hesitation. "She just can't keep anything from you, can she? God, it's like when you two got married, I lost secrecy."

"I'm persuasive," he said with a chuckle.

I rolled my eyes. "And I'm sure I'll get another niece or nephew out of it, so I'm not griping."

Dean sat back in his chair as smooth as ever as he looked at me with a devilish grin. "Tell me."

I let out a harsh breath as my brother-in-law grilled me about Jack. I trusted Dean with my life and had no issue with the truth. Dallas knew that, so I forgave her for telling Dean.

He'd always been a bit protective over me. I looked at him after a few minutes of telling him enough of what he would want to know—that Jack treated me well, that he was truly the good guy he portrayed himself to be. I leaned in, knowing my next question may tell him more than anything else.

"Dean?"

I felt my chest tighten as I walked over to the coffee pot so he couldn't read my nervous posture.

"If you hadn't come back for Dallas, or if she'd been married to Josh when you got here, and you were forced to move on—" I turned to meet his eyes, not wanting to miss a second of his reaction "—do you think you could have loved again? I mean, really loved? Like you love her?"

I saw the answer immediately and felt my lip tremble despite my best effort. Everything in me sank as he remained quiet for a long moment. My brother, whom I loved more than anything in the world, refused to lie to me, and though I respected him for it, I felt my anger flare.

"Rose—"

"Don't. Don't worry about it. I need to go scrub in."

Dean stood and blocked the door, a helpless expression on his face.

"It's a different situation," he offered in poor excuse.

"Bullshit," I said, no longer able to mask my hurt. "The only difference is mine died, and yours is alive—thank God for that—but how can you expect me to believe it, too? You two have pushed me so damned hard to move on, but how can you expect me to if you couldn't?"

"Rose," he said again, his voice pained as he let me pass to open the door. I paused with my hand on the knob, feeling guilty for making him feel like shit for simply being honest. There was no other love for him than Dallas and never would be.

"I'm sorry I asked," I said sincerely and plastered a forced smile on my face. "But you know what? You gave me the next best thing—Grant and Anna. I love them so much, Dean. You gave me that." I walked out just as the rest of the pain surfaced and burst through my chest.

Later that night, I sat on my deck, wrapped in the quilt we'd made love on, replaying my time with Jack. I pulled it firmly around me as I thought of Dean's words or lack thereof. He was convinced he could never love again the way he did Dallas. And that had been the truth for my parents as well. If this was the case, how in the hell was I expected to do it?

Was I capable? It sure had felt like love on that dance floor and every time I was in his arms. When Jack was near, I had tunnel vision. He was my sole focus and more than enough to keep me sated both in mind and body. But my heart?

My fucking heart?

Minutes later, as I pondered the ability of the muscle in my chest, it leaped as I heard the rumble of Jack's bike. I looked up to see him flying down the path. I'd been waiting for the two Js to arrive, drunk and jilted, and had a mess of food ready as promised. I just wanted a bit of girl talk, but it was getting late.

Jack took off his helmet, unaware I was watching him, and looked up to the house. The inside was lit, and I knew he was looking for movement. And though I felt my chest stretch at the sight of him, I remained quiet as he surveyed my home. He stood for several minutes just watching, the look on his face unmistakable. There was something in there he wanted, and that something was me.

There was something so enigmatic about him, yet he'd spoken so freely with me in our time together. Still, I knew there was so much about him to explore. That thought, mixed with the sight of him, had me ravenous with need—for him, his words, and his touch.

"I'm over here," I said, standing to announce myself in the blue lights next to the waterfall.

"Hiding from me, beb?" he said, taking two steps at a time and crossing the porch with authority until he reached me. Without another word, he gripped my hair and landed a consuming kiss on my mouth. I let the blanket fall off my shoulders and pulled him to me hard. I looked for and found everything in his kiss, my doubts from the day erased with just the feel of him around me. I pressed into him with every ounce of passion I possessed. He tore his lips away, and I followed, recapturing my unrelenting want of him. He obliged with a growl as he took and savored me until we were both panting.

"Not hiding," I said as he looked down at me with a mix of surprise and hunger.

The slow, sexy smile I loved so much made its presence known as he cradled me in his warmth.

"I drove almost four hundred miles to kiss you goodnight and fuck if it wasn't worth it."

My heart began to pound in Jack's rhythm as I looked into the gray-blue depths of his eyes.

"You're so good to me," I said as I pushed up on my toes and began to kiss his neck. "So damned good," I whispered as I let my hands wander from his shoulders down to his arms, licking as much of his salty skin as I could. "I want to be good to you, too." My voice was hoarse, and I made my intention clear as I started working the belt on his jeans.

Jack looked down at me as I kneeled on a cushioned patio

chair as I freed his hardness from his pants. I felt his hesitation and stifled it with the flick of my tongue across his tip. "I want this."

"Good God," he gritted out through his teeth as I looked up at him with earnest eyes. I grabbed his hand and pushed it through my hair. He took his cue and wrapped it in his fist. I wasted no time and gripped him eagerly as I licked the underside of his impossibly hard length. I was rewarded by the hiss through his teeth as his grip on my hair tightened.

"I want you in control," I rasped between leisurely licks. "Take my mouth, Jack." He peered down at me, not an ounce of hesitancy left as I took the tip of him inside and molded my lips firmly around him.

"So fucking beautiful," he grunted as he thrust inside me, slow at first, and then guided my head and lips to consume him. His other hand stroked my face tenderly as his eyes stayed glued to the lips that surrounded him. I moaned in arousal as I felt the wetness seep out of me and took him to the hilt. I heard Jack curse as I kept my eyes on his, and he struggled to keep his gentle pace.

"I'm going to lick you back until you beg me to stop. Bet on it," he pushed out as he thrust fully into me and swiveled his hips.

I gripped his sculpted ass and pulled him to me as I relaxed my throat further, taking every movement of his hips and asking for more.

"Rose… God… baby… fuck…" He was close, and I felt him twitch in my mouth. I dug in deeper, feeling his need, his desire. It spurred me on to the point of madness. I wanted to taste him on my tongue. He gripped me harder as his body tensed and began to pull me away by my hair. I shook my head and gripped the sides of his jeans in protest as I inhaled his long, thick cock, coating every inch of it with my tongue.

I took Jack's orgasm and his moans in sweet victory as his

body trembled and he sang my praises. I continued to suck until there was nothing left of him and licked my lips with satisfaction as he looked down at me.

"I couldn't have dreamed that better," he said as his fingers trailed down my throat and stroked the cleavage my low tank top revealed. Jack moved quickly and threw me on my back on the lounger, his eyes liquid black and full of desire. His hungry mouth teased and lit every surface his fingers had just whispered across.

"Ready to beg, beb?" he said in a growl just as he reached the button on my shorts.

"Ca-caw! Ca-caw!" I heard in the distance as Jack looked in the direction of the intrusion, and I groaned in frustration.

Jack looked down at me as I heard a second shriek sound through the air.

"I must apologize for them in advance," I said, pushing back to my knees as Jack buckled his pants. Mourning the loss of him and what I was sure would have been mind-blowing retaliation, I surveyed my state of dress and refastened my hair. I was about to pass Jack on the porch when he pulled me back to his chest, and his arm wrapped possessively around my neck.

"Not so fast," he said as he pushed his hand into my shorts and beneath my panties, running a single finger through my folds. Still overheated from moments before, I almost hit my knees at his welcomed touch.

"Your mouth on me turned you on this much?" he said with a hint of awe as he flicked his wrist, and I whimpered in his arms.

I turned my face to him as he slipped his finger through one more time and brought it to his lips.

"You turn me on that much," I said as he took my mouth with desperate hunger. He pulled away as the next shriek hit the otherwise silent night air.

"Ca-caw, ca-caw," Jamie belted out as she approached at full speed in one of the center's golf carts. Jules burst out laughing before she added her own birdcall, and they came to a screeching stop just before hitting my new car in the driveway.

"Ca-caw, ca-caw," Jamie sounded out again as Jack studied them in amusement before looking back to me with a Cheshire grin.

"They truly are smart humans. Really, Jamie doesn't get out much, and well, Jules is from New Jersey."

"And that's an excuse?"

"I'm just going to go with yes." I pressed my lips together as the cawing continued. The girls ran into my yard with bottles in hand and sauced looks on their faces. Clearly, they had struck out, and now, because of them, so had I.

"I'm sorry, Jack. Maybe tomorrow?"

"Don't worry about it, beb," he said as he leaned in and gave me a promising kiss before an even more promising whisper. "You better believe I'm going to make that up to you."

"Ca-caw!"

Jules was feet away now, and Jack and I both jumped in surprise.

"Jules, we can see you." Jules stood there with a shit-eating grin on her face. Her hair was a rat's nest, which I was sure was a result of driving around on the cart, and her dress was situated in a way that barely kept her valuables covered.

"Hey, you two," she said as she stood and pointed between us. "I have a very important question… for Rose." Jack looked at me with brows raised as she turned to me with a sudden, serious expression. "If you both end up on a sinking ship in icy waters, will you move your big ass over so he can fit on the floating headboard?"

Jack laughed hysterically as I blew out a breath of dread. It was going to be a long night. Looking for Jamie, I spotted her over the railing as she chased my traumatized ducks.

"Ca-caw!" she shrieked at them as they ran for their lives.

"I'm going to get dumb and dumber into a cold shower and make some strong coffee," I said as I gripped Jules by the strap of her dress and pushed her through my bedroom door.

"Good idea." He winked as he made his way down the porch steps, and Jamie made her way up.

"Hey, you!"

"Hey back at you," Jack said without stopping.

Smart man.

Jamie paused at the top step and bent halfway over, examining Jack's ass closely as I cleared my throat.

"That," she whispered, "is a work of art, I say!"

I crossed my arms as she approached me with pouty lips, equally as drunk as her predecessor. "In my deflense, I don't drink shots, and Jules made me have sleven."

"And that's why you sound like Daffy Duck?" I gripped her purse strap, pulled her inside, and caught Jack's laugh as he turned back in our direction to let out his own "ca-caw!"

Jamie quickly answered back enthusiastically as she blew out my eardrum.

"Thanks a lot, buddy, really. You'll pay for that!" I called after him. I looked to my bedroom, where the girls stripped themselves of heels, chunky jewelry, and half of their attire before raiding my kitchen. I sat with them at my counter as they devoured a large pizza and started on cheese and crackers.

"I'm too old for this shit," Jules said as her glossy eyes began to close while she preached. "I am! I'm in my thirties. I shouldn't be going to bars chasing cowboys and raising hell."

"I'm with you," Jamie said as they fist-bumped. "Tomorrow will be hell. I can't handle my liquor anymore."

Jules downed her water bottle as she eyed me. "And just what exactly were you up to when we got here?"

"He'd just got back from Lubbock and stopped by," I said sternly in an attempt to ward off the confession of the insatiable minx I'd behaved like with my lips around him minutes before they arrived.

"Sorry," Jamie said as she looked at me with regret.

"This is punishment, right?" I said with a shrug.

"No," Jules answered sharply. "We just want you around, and if you won't come out, we'll come to you, babe."

"I'm flattered," I said dryly but with a wink.

"You should be," Jamie said, "not many people get to experience all this awesomeness."

I raised a brow as I herded them out of my kitchen, and we made our way to the couch. The girls spent half an hour telling me about their night out and how cool their Uber driver was before they passed out face first, Jules in my bed and Jamie on my couch. Instead of being turned off by their behavior, I decided to join them the next time they went. Maybe I wasn't ready for it when they'd initially taken me out, but I was now. I wanted to experience more now that I was coming out of my numb state. I sat up alone, drinking a glass of wine and ignoring Netflix as I thought of what Jack had said to me.

"Everyone has to roll the dice at least once in their life."

Hadn't I done that with Grant? And hadn't I watched those dice circle the drain, helpless to stop them from going down?

Though I was still knee-deep in an identity crisis, I was positive I was finally getting rid of the bitter and jaded version of myself—the one who blamed loss and declared her life over.

Life was a bitch, but I had to forgive her. It was time.

chapter
sixteen

Jack

I'D ALREADY DRIVEN OVER FOUR HUNDRED MILES ON MY BIKE, AND though I was exhausted, I'd purposely missed my motel exit as my mind reeled. I rode on through the dark night on the surprisingly empty Texas highway, reveling in what had just happened and, at the same time, hungrier than I'd ever been in my life. I'd never had a wife to come home to, a woman to call home. I'd made it that way. I was okay with it. The woman who had come before her had no expectations. I was always on my way out. Tonight, when I'd stared into Rose's home, I'd expected to meet her at her door. I wanted inside that house—to feel the warmth of the woman who owned it. Just kiss her lips, look into her eyes, and wish her better dreams. That would have been enough for me.

What I got, I would fantasize about for the rest of my living years. Jesus, those eyes, those lips, her need to please me, to take possession of her, I could never get enough. If heaven were a sexual act, I'd just visited.

The French call the orgasm la petite mort (the little death), and I'd gladly die a little every day to keep that feeling alive inside me. But the comfort of her had been a far sweeter reward. At thirty-seven, I'd never had that, never felt that, and never wanted anything more than to feel it again. I pulled the throttle as the world passed me by in a blur of lights. Another shift had hit me tonight. All my years of traveling, I'd felt slightly privileged over the majority. My decision to turn in my tie and put on my captain's hat had given me an edge on the masses and the never-ending rat race. I felt justified as the tortoise that had stopped to appreciate the beauty of the world.

Hindsight was a bitch, especially when she told me I might have been the one who'd been missing something. Either way, I was too fucking far gone to look back. I zipped through the summer night with a new craving. A need I'd never known had now become my new obsession. I wanted a new kind of home. I wanted to belong, but I wanted to belong to her. She was that home—she had the heart I needed, and I wanted in.

Rose
One Month Later

"Now, this is the tricky part. We have to temporarily clip the blood source, which is where Dr. Whitaker?"

I moved instead of responding, as I often did with McGuire, and was scolded. "I didn't tell you to do it. I asked you to tell me the location. Do not ever make a move again without my say-so, understood?"

"Yes, sir."

"McGuire said you were the best of his residents. The best he's had in years."

"That's flattering, sir," I said dryly as I waited for the punch line.

"I have half a mind to tell him what an ass he is with the move you just pulled."

"Understood, sir, it won't happen again."

I stood for what felt like the millionth hour while Dr. Hanson berated me in front of the rest of the surgical staff. I was stiff and aching from endless hours at the table. Hanson was the biggest dick on the surgical staff. While McGuire was militant, Hanson was everything else—arrogant, rude, condescending.

"Marks," Hanson barked at the other surgical resident assisting in today's surgery. "Replace Whitaker at the table. She's got an attitude problem."

I didn't bother with any defense. He was determined to do as much damage to my ego as possible and was getting no satisfaction. I'd already been hazed my first two years as a resident. There was very little I now took offense to.

"Whitaker, you're dismissed," he barked as he robbed me of my new number of finished surgeries. I took a step back and snapped off my gloves. "Let the record show that Whitaker left the OR at noon."

I looked at the clock and kept my mouth closed. He'd not only robbed me of a completed surgery but an additional hour, too. I decided to choose my battles and left the OR without a word. I hastily passed McGuire, who looked at me oddly but didn't ask any questions. I was completely over it. I went to the bathroom to calm myself, took up the accessible stall, and managed deep, relaxing breaths.

After a few minutes of silence, I walked to the locker room, snagged my phone, and scrolled through, looking for some distraction or word from Jack.

Dallas: Annabelle is walking!! She's not even a year old! Don't forget we have interviews tomorrow.

I rolled my eyes at her tenth reminder. We had a day of interviews set up for our center's staff. We had handpicked a majority of people fit to work at the center, and I was excited while Dallas was nervous.

My brother was next.

Paul: Remember how you wanted to spend quality time with the twins?

Enclosed was a picture of their living room covered in what looked to be flour. I let out a hearty laugh as I scrolled through, seeing picture after picture of their twin boys, both carrot tops, grinning from ear to ear, and thoroughly covered in the thick powder. I knew my mom would get a kick out of it, so I forwarded the pictures in case my brother didn't think of it. The last text was another picture, this one from Jack. I hadn't seen him since last Friday, and though we'd had several long phone conversations, I was getting anxious.

I opened the picture and shot off the toilet. It was a selfie of Jack sitting on his bike in front of Memorial. I raced through the lobby, my ass on fire, as at least three nurses tried to stop me. I made quick excuses, passing the buck without apologizing as I went outside. Jack was nowhere to be found. I looked at the picture again and noted that the text was sent almost an hour ago.

Deflated, I walked back inside and sent him a message.

Rose: I missed you ☹

Jack: I'd hoped you would.

Rose: No, I mean, I missed you being here.

Jack: Again, the result I was hoping for.

I groaned in frustration as he toyed with me.

Rose: I mean at the hospital.

"No you didn't, beb. Look up."

Cajun.

"Bonjou," he said, knowing what his accent did to me. Six feet-three inches of gloriousness stood across from me in that hospital hall, and I didn't pause my stride for a second as I collided into him with relief.

"Hi," he whispered as I hugged him tightly to me. "Rough day?"

"The worst," I said, beaming up at him, "but it isn't now. You didn't tell me you were coming!"

"So, let's make sure I'm hearing this right. You *did*, in fact, *miss* me," he said, looking down at me with the same happy expression.

With quick thinking, I gripped his hand and led him to an empty conference room. As soon as the door shut, I was nailed to the back of it.

Lips, tongues, hands, limbs, it was all a blur as we kissed like we'd never see each other again. I was desperate for him, and it seemed him for me. After minutes of relentless assault, I pulled away with a smile.

"That smile was worth the drive."

"You're some kind of man, Jack, and yes, I missed you," I said as his comment hit me hard in the chest. "I don't want to be Dr. Whitaker anymore today."

He pressed a light kiss to my jaw and then cupped my face. "*Really* bad day."

"Just an asshole using me as a verbal punching bag," I admitted. "I don't get the ego trip of some doctors. It's like good looks and no personality, so full of potential but completely worthless in the space they're using and the air they're breathing."

Jack raised his brows. "Want to go take a few sips off our bottle and play technician?"

I nodded with a smile. "Please, get me the *hell* out of here."

"Say no more," he said with another soft kiss. "Got everything you need?"

"No, let me hit the locker room, and I'll meet you outside."

Jack nodded as I opened the door and took leave of the room before him. I was on my way to tell McGuire that my last surgery was cut short when I heard him firing off at what I'd first thought was an intern. When I stopped at his door, I quickly learned differently.

"You sabotaged my resident. Why, Hanson? Answer me."

"She's too confident and didn't take direction well."

"Bullshit," McGuire barked. "She's more capable than half of the staff and will be able to do your job better than you in half the time. I did you a favor by lending her to you for surgery, but never again. From now on, you'll get the less polished of my residents, and maybe then you'll be able to distinguish the difference."

"Take it easy, McGuire. No one is bullying your resident."

"Not from this moment forward, Hanson. I can promise you that. Your ego is unearned. You're a decent surgeon, but you aren't worth the trouble. I had to convince the board to keep you on last year. This year, I won't raise a finger."

"McGuire, calm down," Hanson said with nervousness in his voice.

"I am calm," he quipped with precision. "It is *you* who is starting to panic."

I didn't need to hear another word. I strode down the hall with a gangsta strut and met Jules in the locker room.

"Hey, baby!" I danced her around in circles with her pants halfway down as she pushed me off in irritation.

"The hell? Didn't you just get your ass handed to you in surgery?"

"Yes!" I said with wide eyes and enthusiasm. "Are you the tattle?"

"Nope, it was the surgical tech, Christine."

"Let's take her out with us next time," I said, still reeling and high.

"Yeah, sure," Jules said, pulling on a T-shirt and giving me an odd look. "Considering we go out maybe twice a year, which annual event will we invite her to? What's up with you?"

Realization crossed her features as she gave me a nod. "He's back?"

"He's outside," I said, stuffing my backpack full of dirty scrubs and ensuring I had everything I needed. "I'm on call tomorrow. Make sure they don't call me."

"And how the hell am I supposed to manage that?"

"You're Jules, do your Juju," I piped back as I headed toward the door. "I have a day full of interviews. I have to be home."

"Uh huh," she said suspiciously. "Okay, but if I don't get a play-by-play—"

"Oh, you won't," I assured.

"Then what's in it for me?"

"A job at my center making more than you ever will here, paid vacation, and holidays."

Jules sat on the bench, almost missing it in her shock.

"You knew I would offer it. No interview necessary." I winked as I walked out the door, backpack full and my feet way too heavy. "And don't tell Jamie. I'm offering her the same next shift."

I heard a hearty "I love you!" come from the locker room as I made my way down the hall and saw Dr. Hanson visibly cringe when I came into view. I gave him a Texas-sized smile as I drifted past him and out the door. At the entrance, I looked up to see Jack perched on his bike and smiling in my direction. My stomach fluttered as elation hit me at the sight of him. All that there was to feel, I felt for him—and with him. He'd become a need for me, a want, and a hope.

At that moment, I concluded that he deserved everything I had to give, and I would let him know the minute he let me.

Alive with excitement, I'd hastily agreed to ride with him, thinking I could handle the twenty minutes back to the center. My excitement turned into terror as we were narrowly missed by an SUV and then hit a line of traffic, passing a fatal accident. I stared at the battered vehicles as I gripped Jack and felt the terror race through my veins.

"Doesn't look good," I heard Jack note as I remained frozen and plastered to his back. His voice was distant, and I wanted nothing more than to beg him to pull over, but fear overtook me, and soon we were back on the dangerous stretch of highway. No amount of breath play or thought change could erase the budding panic inside me. I was in a full-fledged attack as we made it the last few miles to the center. Once parked, I quickly dismounted the bike, tore off my helmet, and threw it on the grass next to Jack's foot.

"I don't ever want you on this damned thing again," I declared with authority. "Ever!"

"Kind of hard to take you seriously when you look like Don King, baby." Jack chuckled as he pointed to my roof of frazzled hair. I pulled the ratted mess into a bun and went back in as he put the kickstand down and joined me on the sidewalk.

"Jack, I'm begging you," I said seriously. "You can have my car. Please don't ride that thing anymore, at least not on I-20 or I-35 or 635 or anywhere. God, I *hate* it."

"As I recall, that bike has been nothing but good to you," he joked.

Chest pounding, I didn't so much as blink until I was sure he could see just how serious I was.

"I'm asking you as your… whatever I am to you, not to ride that bike here anymore. And if you care about me, ever."

"You're really serious?" he asked, finally noting the panic on my face.

"I am. I won't ask for anything else from you, I promise. I can't handle it."

"You can ask me for anything you want," he assured me, looking back at his bike. "If that's the way you really feel—"

"It is," I said with finality. "I'm sorry. I know it's a lot to ask." I studied his face as my heart continued to pound out of control. Jack studied me right back with confusion, and I stepped forward again to plead my case, but he stopped me.

"Go on in," he said with slight irritation in his voice. "I'll come in. Just give me a few."

"Please don't be mad at me," I said, insecure for the first time that I might have crossed a line.

"Go on." He nudged me toward the door, and I went in reluctantly.

"Jack—"

"Baby, go!" he said with an impatience I'd never heard from him.

I felt completely crazy as I made my way in and crossed the lobby, looking for my family. They were all huddled around a large conference table and looked up to greet me with smiles. My mom was the only one to notice my ill ease.

"Rose, come walk with me. I want to show you something," my mom urged as she guided me back through the door I'd just entered.

"Mom, we have a thousand prep questions to write down," Dallas said with a squeak.

"Don't blow a gasket, Martin," she snapped in warning. "I'll have her back in five minutes."

My mom led me past the reception area and into the newly finished arboretum. I looked around in wonder at the large plants surrounding us, my gaze landing on the huge fountain Dallas had made sure was a part of our blueprints. It was her only actual request when it came to the building, and I knew why. Water was her calming element, and I looked at it, trying to allow its calming effect to work on me.

"Okay, your sister is officially losing her shit," my mom said with a laugh. "Dean and I are working on a plan to get her out of this building so she doesn't make a bad first impression on her new staff tomorrow. But before we execute 'project remove crazy Dallas' from the premises, tell me, baby, why are you panicked?"

"I had an incredibly bad day," I said as I looked at the entrance for Jack's return and came up empty.

"Okay, anything else?" My mom followed my eyes, and I was instantly thankful he hadn't come. I'd gone completely irrational again, and I didn't know if I'd just pushed Jack away by letting my emotions get the best of me. I recognized the behavior. I knew it wasn't healthy, and still, I couldn't keep from letting it take over. I began to break down in front of my mom.

"Rose?"

"What?"

"You're shaking," my mom said, pulling me to her. "What's going on?"

"Mom," I croaked as my whole body went numb. I kept looking at the entrance for Jack, who wasn't there. Fear covered me, and I broke out in a cold sweat, unable to answer her. She gripped me tightly to her as she yelled for my dad. Just as he raced through the door with panic covering his features, everything went black.

I heard my mom's tear-filled voice as she spoke to Dallas.

"Her vitals are fine, Mom. She's coming to now," she said, looking down at me with a worried smile. "Hey, sis, talk to me. What's your favorite song?"

"Jack?" I said in a whisper.

"He's in New Orleans," she whispered back. "What's your last name?"

"I want to go home," I insisted in an attempt to sit up.

"Lay down, little woman," my dad barked without apology. I stayed put. When my dad used that tone, there was no arguing with him.

"Okay, sis, answer the question, and I'll get you home."

I nodded, humiliated that I didn't have better control of myself.

"What caused the attack?"

I thought quickly, despite my reeling senses. I didn't want to have to explain myself further. "Highway accident."

Dallas nodded and shared a knowing look with my mom.

"Where are you?"

"The Grant Foster Cancer Treatment Center." The tears fell freely down my face as I croaked out the answer and the truth of what lay behind my fear. I didn't want to experience the same fate with Jack. I was terrified of losing him—and irrational about it. And the longer it took him to return, the more I was sure he was probably trying to think of a way to let me down and, more importantly, a way of saving face in front of my dad. I made the decision then to make it easy on him. For years after Grant's death, I'd managed to keep it together both professionally and, for the most part, personally. I'd fought months of similar panic attacks and come through it, but the way I felt as my family stared at me and I answered their questions was enough to make me realize I couldn't handle the feelings I had.

"It was just a bad day," I said as they sat me up. "Honestly, I felt it coming on, and I should have worked through it instead of pretending I was okay. I didn't mean to scare you."

"Don't worry about us," Dallas said as she gave me a disbelieving once over. Dallas had worked with me through a few attacks I'd had after Grant's death. As they helped me to my feet, I couldn't help but hug her a little longer. She held me tightly to her and dismissed my parents, who were not pleased.

"I'm just going to take her to a patient room and thoroughly check her out," Dallas said, walking me out of the arboretum. I mentally thanked her.

I looked back at my parents and gave them a reassuring smile. My mom returned it while my dad looked on with concern. The only way he would start to feel better is if I looked better. I knew that about him. His family was his life, and only when his children were at ease did he truly allow himself to function. I resented my inability to keep it together at that moment.

"We'll be here, little woman."

"I know, Daddy. I'm okay, really." Dallas walked me into an examination room and closed the door before sitting me on the table. Dean knocked on the door shortly after and inquired about me. I saw him peek over Dallas's shoulder, deep worry etched on his face.

"You okay?"

"I am, brother, thank you," I said as more guilt covered me.

"Can you get me a cold bottle of juice, any kind?" Dallas asked of her husband.

"Sure, baby," Dean said as he quickly moved out of sight.

Once the juice was delivered, Dallas again shut the door and handed me the bottle, forcing me to drink a good amount.

"What happened?"

"I'm falling for Jack," I said simply.

Dallas's shocked expression quickly turned into a warm smile, and I snubbed it out with my following statement. "It's not progress. I'm backsliding because of it." She waited while I came clean. "He gave me a ride home from work on the back of his bike, and we passed a fatal car crash. I got so damned scared that I freaked out on him and demanded he gets rid of his motorcycle. And it wasn't the first time. He probably thinks I'm crazy and is halfway home by now."

"Okay, so explain it to him."

"He doesn't know…about Grant."

A surprised look covered her features. "You haven't told him yet? Why?"

"I don't know."

"Yes, you do," she said, taking a seat next to me.

"Because I still love him, Dallas. I still love Grant," I argued.

She nodded as she grabbed my hand. "And you always will, baby, always."

"I just wanted Jack kept separate."

Dallas looked at me thoughtfully before she spoke. "You have the biggest and the most loyal heart of anyone I've ever known. It's what I love about you. But, Rose, you can't limit yourself anymore. You both need and deserve more."

"I think I scared him away, anyway," I said.

"I doubt that's true. He's probably confused. Your reactions are justified. Just tell him."

"And say what? Hey, Jack, I'm sorry I keep freaking out on you. My ex died in a car crash a week before our wedding, and I'm terrified you'll die too?"

"It's a start," Dallas said with conviction. "Anyone would be sympathetic to that reasoning."

"Exactly, I don't want that from him."

"What's so wrong with a little sympathy? It happened to you. It was horrible. Your life changed drastically. It's a part of who you are, and he deserves to know."

"There's nothing you can say right now that I haven't already thought of. But, Dallas, as easy as it is to dole out advice, you have no idea what this is like, and as much as I want to be strong and capable, it's not working out that way. It's just not. I'm handling it like shit, and as much as I want to, I can't just turn it around or *solve* this."

"So, you work through it with Jack. I can't believe he doesn't know," Dallas said, slightly exasperated. "Mom and Dad never told him?"

"Guess not." I shrugged.

"Well, you made it clear enough to everyone after he died that you didn't want to hear from anybody." I heard the slight resentment in her voice due to the space I put between us in the months that followed Grant's death. She was there for me at every turn, and after a few months of relying on her heavily, I'd pushed her away—along with the rest of my family—to find my footing. I refused to feel guilty about it even now because it was totally necessary, in my opinion. It was only now that I saw how much it bothered her.

I studied Dallas, who was already handling far more than her fair share of responsibility and shrugged off the last few hours. "I had a panic attack. It's not the end of the world."

"Look, I can handle tomorrow. Why don't you just—"

"Don't. I need sleep. I'll get a few hours, do some prep, and be here bright and early. Don't decide anything for me. I'm not an invalid," I said with aggression. "I don't want to be a stranger to my staff."

"I love you," Dallas said pointedly. "But just let me say something else, okay?"

I nodded and braced myself. Dallas was anything but subtle.

"He's a good man, and you aren't the only one in love with him. Your family is pretty smitten with him, too. And you know how Dad feels about him. We've all grown used to having him around. He's good people, Rose, and he's done nothing but help us. I will always side with you, always, but before you go and do something to break all of our hearts, really think about it."

"Okay," I said, defeated. "Don't tell them about Jack."

"You've been keeping a lot of secrets lately."

"And they are mine to keep," I snapped.

"Stop it," she snapped back. "I'm not your enemy. I'm just saying a bunch of shit you don't want to hear." She pulled me tightly to her and held me until I held her back.

"I love you, too."

Dallas pulled away. "You good?"

"Yeah, I'm just going to go sleep for a few hours."

"Good. I'll see you tomorrow."

Dallas opened the door, and I couldn't help but look around for Jack—who was still missing. I made my way home and glanced at my phone in hopes of word from him. My heart sank further as he remained silent. Feet heavy and completely drained, I paused when I saw a tow truck in my yard.

A short, balding man was looking through my window as he knocked on my back door.

"Can I help you?"

He turned around, slightly confused as he looked at me. He must have been sure someone was home with my SUV parked in the yard. "You live here?"

"Yes, sir, how can I help you?"

"I… uh," the man stalled in his words and slowly approached me from the porch. "I'm from Whitey's tow yard."

"Okay," I said, utterly confused. He seemed extremely uneasy as his eyes darted around me.

"We, uh, well, we've been clearing out our junk lot for the past few months, and I'm the one responsible for making sure the vehicles are clear of personal items, scraps, things of that nature, and, well, I found this a few days ago," he said, thrusting a bag toward me. I studied it, confused. It was a gift bag covered in candy canes. I looked at the man, still clueless, until I opened the bag and pulled out a stethoscope.

"It was stuffed under the seat of a Ford F-150."

Realization struck as I inhaled deeply and felt my heart crack in my chest as I looked at the inscription on the bottom of the metal.

Dr. Foster

Instant tears disbursed down my cheeks as the man rambled on, both apologetic and full of excuses. "It took a little digging to find this address, and I wasn't sure if it was the right thing to do, but I… well, ma'am, I was there that night, at the scene of the accident, and I'm sorry for your loss."

"Thank you," I said in a robotic answer.

"I just couldn't bring myself to throw it away, and I—"

"I understand, thank you," I said as I gripped the stethoscope in equal measure of shock and devastation.

The man started rambling again, and I made quick work of letting him out of the uncomfortable situation.

"Thank you. Really, you did the right thing," I said hoarsely.

"Again, ma'am, I'm sorry for your loss," he said as he excused himself and jumped into his truck. I watched him pull away and stood motionless as I willed myself to remain calm.

Stethoscope in hand, I walked into my room and fell into bed in a heap. Minutes later, I cleared the bag of tissue paper and searched for the note I'd seen sitting next to it before I discovered who it was from.

I opened the paper as I braced myself. I studied the first piece and recognized my own handwriting.

I didn't recall when I wrote it, but it was obvious I was practicing my signature for when I became a doctor. I studied it closely and realized I had been questioning whether or not I would be a single or a married doctor. I held the stethoscope to my chest as I opened the second piece of paper and gasped as I saw Grant's writing.

Bride,

The first time I saw you the heavens opened and that's no exaggeration. I swear, baby, the sky lit up and an arrow of sunshine pointed right to you. You were sitting under a tree, scribbling away in your notebook. With a hopeful heart, you were asking fate right at that moment whether or not you would belong to someone as I laid eyes on you.

And just as I started to convince myself something so beautiful wasn't meant for me, your question floated through the air and landed in my hands. How's that for a sign?

God made our hearts so similar that all it took was one bolt for us to recognize the other.

Your heart is the thing I love most about you, Rose, because it's where I live, where I feel safe, where I belong, and where I'll always be.

So if your tender heart grows weary beating for the burden of keeping us both, I'll keep my eye on the clouds and remind you of the lightning that brought us home.

I love you,
Grant

Dr. Foster

Darkness.

Dr. Foster

Darkness.

Dr. Foster

I stared at the stethoscope on the pillow next to me, continually alternating the flashlight button on and off my iPhone to illuminate the etched words on the metal.

Dr. Foster

Dr. Foster

Dr. Foster

My eyes burned with unshed tears as I continued to ignore the knock at my door.

"Rose," I heard Jack call out to me as he began to pound louder on the door. "I'm not leaving until I see you."

I pulled myself up to sit and stared at my door like the enemy it was. I could feel Jack's unease grow as his voice hit near hysterics.

"Open the goddamned door!"

I walked over to the door and, thinking better of it, quickly went back to the bed, stuffing the stethoscope inside the bag and shoving it in my dresser. I turned my bedroom light on as I walked over and unlocked it as Jack jerked it open. "I've been calling you nonstop for two fucking hours! I went back to the center, and Dallas told me you fainted. What the hell is going on?"

I'd never seen Jack so angry. I stared at him, at a loss for what to say. I knew he deserved the truth, and I was about to take the coward's way out. Looking at him now, I didn't have the strength to relive it. Not then, anyway.

"I'm sorry. I fell asleep."

"And it didn't occur to you to even wonder where I went?"

"I thought," I said as my voice grew weak, "I thought I scared you away."

Jack stood in my doorway as I made my way back to my bed, grabbed a pillow, and held it protectively in front of me. He sighed, scrubbing his face with his hand.

"I'm sorry I got a little irritated, but I didn't understand where it was coming from. Then it dawned on me. I know why you want me to stop riding."

"You do?" I said, slightly relieved. If he knew, then I was better off.

"The accident," he said with a little doubt. "You're a doctor. I'm sure you've seen all kinds of shit I couldn't imagine."

"Oh," I said as I looked down at my pillow. "Yeah."

"That's not it," Jack said as a statement. "Rose, I will do whatever you want me to, but you have to let me in. I'm afraid I can't keep up completely clueless. I've been in the dark long enough."

"Jack, look, I have about thirty interviews to conduct tomorrow," I stated as his jaw tightened.

"So, what? You're going to kick me out?" he asked incredulously. He gripped my arm, walked me to the door, and opened it. It took me a minute to realize what he wanted me to see. A brand-new Chevy graced the driveway, and I sank against him, feeling incredibly guilty.

"I don't ever want to see that look on your face again if I can help it."

"Jack," I said, turning to hold him tightly to me. Silent tears fell as he cradled me in his arms.

"Please, just talk to me."

"I'm sorry," I rasped out hoarsely as I looked up at him. I pulled out of his arms and saw his whole demeanor stiffen.

"Don't you dare."

"I've got too much going on right now. If you can, give me some time."

"No," he said in protest. "Tell me what the hell is going on."

"I don't want to be in a relationship right now!"

"Lie," he snapped as he took a step forward.

"I told you I wasn't capable."

"Lie," he said as his unforgiving eyes pierced me.

"I just need to be on my own for a while," I finished in an attempt to hold my ground.

"Another fucking lie!"

"You really don't handle rejection well," I snapped. "This is what I want. I'm asking you to respect that. I'm asking you to back the hell off!"

I saw the blows hit him with every word I spoke and wanted to do nothing short of cut out my tongue.

"Jack, I'm sorry. Please, just give me some space. Today completely wrecked me, okay. That's the truth."

He took a long, defeated look at me and walked out the door without a word.

chapter
sixteen

I WOKE UP AND TRIED TO MUSTER ENCOURAGING WORDS TO GET ME out of bed. I told Jack it was a ritual I did for motivation, but in truth, it was a ritual I'd started a few months after Grant died when I'd been forced into my new reality. The words had come to me naturally, and I'd made it a daily habit. That morning, nothing would come. I'd made a decision I regretted.

I searched my phone in vain for my usual morning greeting from Jack but knew better. I'd blindsided him. He deserved an explanation, and I knew I owed it to him. I would give him the answers he deserved and soon, but I had a day ahead of me I couldn't get out of, and I decided not to chance any more emotional upset until the day had concluded.

Reluctant but unwilling to let my sister down, I showered, dressed, and was the first to arrive at the center. Dallas walked in with an easy smile and the actress in me rose to the occasion as we spent a grueling day in interviews. Nothing about it was easy, though I made it seem so. And as the day wound down, I'd even had Dallas convinced that I was much better than the previous day when the truth was, I was splintered. I spent the short drive home thinking of my time with Jack and how happy he made me. My asking for space had been a knee-jerk reaction.

I pulled up to my house, all too eager to let him know as

much, when I saw Jack's truck. I didn't want to fight. I wanted to fall into rhythm with him again. I'd gotten myself to the point where I could admit he made me happy, and I was nowhere near ready to give that up. I got out of the car and expected to find him on the porch when I heard his voice sound behind me.

"You're in my head, my thoughts. You've completely invaded me, whether you wanted to or not."

I turned to see a disheveled Jack, a bottle of whiskey in his hand—*our* bottle. He looked over the water and waited.

"I don't understand what you want," I lied.

"What I want…" He grinned menacingly as a sinking feeling hit me.

"What do I want?" he asked as he took a step forward. I had pushed too hard, and now he was spoiling for a fight. "I want your breaths, your minutes, your movements, and to be included in your memories. I want to be the man you run to. I want to be significant. I want you. It's that simple.

"I fell in love with a beautiful woman. Looks aside, she makes me feel whole and happy. She can turn a shitty day into one worth remembering. She fills me up to the brink. She makes me laugh, and, well, looking at her… makes my chest ache. And when I kiss her, and she kisses me back—really kisses me—I'm convinced no woman will ever kiss me with as much behind it." He scrutinized me, and I felt my hesitance begin to break him piece by piece.

"Jack," I started, reeling from his words. He loved me. I felt the lump in my throat build and dissolve as I moved toward him, but he stepped away.

"Your hesitation tells me all I need to know. I don't want your half-assed love, and I sure as hell can't compete with whoever the hell it is I'm competing with."

A large piece of me cracked at the way his cruel words were delivered. "That's not fair…"

"To who? To me, to him, or to you?"

"Stop it!"

"I'm afraid I can't. I'm afraid I've pretty much cemented this idea of you and me in my head. But, hey, look, no hard feelings. I'm dedicating this bottle to you, and as soon as I take the last drink, I'll let you go. I've obviously misplaced my affection, and for that, I apologize." I watched him take a hearty drink and wipe his mouth with the back of his hand.

Without giving me a chance, he looked up at me with a sneer. "So let me guess…some guy did a number on you, promised the moon and stars but didn't deliver, and you're still holding out that he will."

He looked at me with wary eyes, and though my chest ached to tell him the truth, I couldn't get the words to pass my lips. Jack's mind was made up—that much was evident—and when his expression turned dark and expectant, I felt myself go livid with his attitude as truth and explanation died on my tongue.

"Yeah, Jack, you nailed it. I'm jilted and bitter." I crossed my arms over my chest for false protection.

"Hmph," he said, staring at the label on his bottle, "thought so."

"You're piss drunk. Let me call you a cab."

"No, baby, I'm pissed *and* drunk."

I had to tell him.

"Jack, look at me."

"I can't. Looking at you hurts," he said with a hoarse voice. "It always hurt. I just didn't know if it would be a good hurt or bad hurt—until now."

"I never meant to –"

"Well, you did!" Anger rolled off him as he finally faced me,

the *heart*

gray eyes blazing. Remorse and deep sadness crossed his features as he struggled with his pain. "And I asked for it."

The dire need to end his battle raced through me as I watched him. "Jack, what can I say?"

He tilted the bottle and finished the last of it before turning it over and emptying a few drops on the grass. It was a spiteful move on his part. His eyes penetrated mine as the one word he spoke ripped a piece of me in half. "Nothing."

Letting my emotions get the best of me, I took a step forward, tore the empty bottle from his hand, and threw it down hard, shattering it on the gravel between us.

"Real fucking mature, Jack. Your bottle is finished, and so are we? Just leave," I said as a tear rolled down my cheek.

I could feel the contempt rolling off him. "You *know* what I want."

"I explained this to you. Look, some things have happened, and I'm incapable right now. But it doesn't mean—"

"Of what exactly? I'm not asking you for anything but to acknowledge *me*, *us*, and this *relationship*. It's not much, Rose. Just tell me…I can see you're in love, but with *whom*? I mean, I don't see anyone else here. Exactly who am I competing with? He sure as hell hasn't been around the last three goddamn months!"

"Don't do this, Jack."

"You've never, not once, invited me into your home or your bed. Am I simply entertainment for you?"

"You know that's not true." I fisted my hands at my sides as he tore into me.

"I've played nice with you because I wanted to, because I wanted you, but just what in the hell are *you* playing at?"

"Nothing!"

"I just want to know what's in your heart, Rose. Jesus, just fucking tell me!"

"PAIN! OKAY! PAIN and… fear! The worst pain you can imagine and fear that I will never, ever, get over it no matter how hard I mask it." I looked down at the ground, afraid to meet his eyes. "And even with all these jagged pieces he left… you, you're here, too." I pounded my chest with my closed hand. "And you don't fit, or you weren't supposed to, but somehow, you're making all those pieces smoother and easier to carry around. I can't love you both and be fair to either of you. I have no idea how to do it."

A long silence followed as he studied me. I did my best to keep from looking at him, hurt coursing through my every limb.

"He's dead," Jack concluded as I snapped my head up to meet his gaze head-on with a slow, slight nod. Tears streamed down my face one by one, and I wiped them away quickly. Jack took a step back as shock-covered features studied me.

"Jesus, Rose… I'm sorry." He stayed where he was, looking at me like they all did when they found out. I hated that look. I never wanted to see it on Jack's face.

"When?"

"Almost three years ago." Tears I didn't bother to catch poured freely now that I'd confessed all. "He died a week before our wedding. This house—" I pointed behind me "—was supposed to be ours. We fell in love on this land, and it belonged to him." Jack stood motionless, watching me. "Every day, I live in what was *supposed* to be our life. So don't credit me for being a strong woman who moved on with her life because every night I'm cowering in that fucking house, afraid to let go, afraid if I move on too far, I'll forget him. And between the fear of forgetting him and wanting to give you the biggest part of me, I don't know what to do. I didn't want to fall in love again, Jack. Doing that somehow feels like I'm diminishing his memory or what we had, and I can't…do that to him." I braced myself as I told him the rest. "His name was Grant…" I watched him closely. "Foster." He physically flinched when he put it all together. "I didn't want you to know, Jack, and I wanted to keep it that way, just for a while longer."

"I thought he was a family friend," Jack said incredulously. "Jesus," he said, swiping his hand down his face, his jaw set. "Why?"

"Because," I said, taking a step forward as he took one back. I flinched as the pain spread throughout my chest. "For the first time since he died, I had a personal relationship that had nothing to do with him, and I wanted to keep it that way. I'm sorry."

"So, I was what? A way for you to test the waters?"

"More than that, damn you… Jack, stop it! You know how I feel. You've known. You're the only man I've been with since he died. We don't get a goddamn handbook, you know. I'm winging it here."

We stood facing each other, every piece of each other bared to the other, and though I felt a small amount of relief in Jack knowing, it was also tearing me apart. It was ruining what we had, and I could feel the imminent loss of us.

An endless and unbearable silence followed as he watched me. The stillness between us was a heavy weight in my chest as I waited with bated breath.

"You're afraid you'll love me less." He sighed, defeated.

"No," I said, pushing my shoulders back as I admitted my biggest fear. "I'm afraid I'll love you more." He took a step toward me, and I saw all the love in his eyes dim as I cowered away. "And that would mean I was wrong about Grant and the way we felt and what we had."

Jack watched me crumble as I tried my best to keep from shaking. It felt like years of bottled emotions were coming out at once—the anger of my loss, the fact that I had to hide my pain after the 'allotted' amount of time to grieve, and also the fact that I'd let myself get wrapped up in another man. I couldn't shake the fucking guilt that I knew was keeping me from moving on with him.

"Or maybe he just died, Rose, and there's no rhyme or good reason, and the man you're supposed to be with is standing right in front of you, losing his goddamned mind because he's competing with a ghost. You *don't* have to make a choice between us."

"That's not true," I said as I let out a small sob. "I've been holding on to him for so long, Jack. I have no idea how to let go." We stood and stared at each other, every part of me begging for the release of the guilt I'd inflicted upon myself, yet every bit of my words to Jack were the absolute truth. I was afraid to love him for so many more reasons other than just forgetting Grant. I was terrified of losing it all over again. And yet, as I stood watching him, I knew that fear was already becoming a reality. I was in love with him, totally, utterly, and completely, but I was losing him with every word I spoke. He looked behind me, studying the house, and I didn't have to ask to know what he was thinking. I had barricaded myself in my love for Grant, in my loss, and rebuilt my life *around* him, not without him. I made no room for anyone else. It had never seemed so damning for me until that very moment.

I saw Jack's decision before he spoke, but I spoke first. "No."

"I can't do this," he said as he turned toward his truck and looked back at me briefly. "I'm sorry, I can't. My chest can't take it, baby. You knocked the wind out of me again, and I'm not going to stand here and wait for you to rip the rest of me apart."

"Jack, please don't leave," I said weakly.

"I can't stay here and watch you throw us away. Tell your dad and the family I said goodbye."

"Jack, please don't leave like this." I was sobbing now as he looked me over, stepped toward me, cupped my face, and slid his thumbs along my cheeks. "My being here is tearing you apart, too, and as selfish as I feel right now, I hate seeing you cry. Don't cry, baby. I'm sorry. I'm sorry I was so fucking insensitive."

"Don't be sorry. I should have told you," I said as a fresh wound opened and my heart bled freely before him. "Don't leave, Jack."

"God, Rose, all I wanted to do was make you happy. I wanted in, but I had no idea what I was up against. I can't make you mine if you've already decided you belong to someone else. I can't stay, not like this, wondering if I ever had a real piece of you, fighting a battle you tell me I've already lost. You don't belong to me, and I can't handle it. I'm too far gone and I've made a goddamned fool of myself."

"I'm so sorry."

"What for?" He looked at me with unshed tears in his eyes. "I fell in love with a beautiful woman worthy of it. I'm not sorry." He leaned in and kissed me. Just as the kiss deepened, I gripped him to me desperately. He pulled away, making our separation unbearable.

Jack looked at me for a long moment before he kissed my tear-soaked lips one last time and climbed into his truck. I banged on his window as I begged. "Jack, please don't drive!"

Alarm covered his features as he rolled down his window.

"Please don't drive," I begged in near hysterics.

"I'm going to the center. I'll sleep it off there. I'll be fine. The bottle was almost empty when I started."

"You can stay here. You don't have to go. I want you to stay. I do!"

He cut me off when he looked at me again, the pain on his features unbearable. "Let's not fault each other, okay? There's too much here between us. I want you too much. Jesus, every time I look at you, it's like lightning to the chest." He missed my gasp at his words as he turned the ignition and took off, the gravel kicking up behind him.

"Jack!"

Sobs poured from me as I planted my ass on the grass, completely obliterated. He'd seen my baggage, and it had been too much for him. The gash in my chest openly bled as I curled up on my lawn, the foolish widow I was. After years of begging my heart—it finally stopped beating.

chapter
seventeen

Three Weeks Later...

I STOOD WITH MY SISTER BESIDE MY FAMILY AS I MOVED TO ADDRESS the crowd in front of me—a crowd filled with friends of the family, new employees of the center, media, and the building crew.

I hadn't thought about the words I would say as they looked at me expectantly, and for the first time in a very long time, I let my heart lead.

"My sister and I have known since we were young that we wanted to be doctors," I started, my voice surprisingly steady. "We made it our common goal to open a general practice and worked hard toward that goal." I looked over at Dallas and smiled as her eyes filled, and I rolled mine at her, trying to make her laugh—which she did. I couldn't afford to get choked up. With fresh breath, I faced the crowd.

"To say this is the most important day of our lives would be a lie. The two of us may look back on this day with fondness and pride. It may very well rank high as one of our best, but I can tell you with absolute certainty it won't be either of our favorite days."

I saw a mix of confusion on the faces of the onlookers.

"Because the two of us were raised to know what was truly important, and that's our time with people who shape our lives."

I saw my mom squeeze my dad's arm in approval before giving me a wink. "I can honestly tell you that for Dallas, a day that will top today was the day she married her husband, Dean. And me, well, I have one day in particular that stands out above most." My heart began to pound in my chest as inevitable tears built behind my steady demeanor. Dallas reached over and squeezed my hand, and I nodded at her in reassurance that I could do this.

"That day for me is the day I met Grant Foster." I sucked in a huge breath as I gathered every bit of strength inside me.

"Grant was an undeniable force of nature not to be ignored. And those he left in his wake were left better people for simply knowing him. I can tell you firsthand—as the woman who was most affected by him—that he was a free spirit with unyielding, unrelenting, unconditional love that is such a rarity that he shined among men. And though his life was cut far too short, he lived for a purpose, and that purpose paved the way for those of us involved in opening this center. He was a man to be cherished and honored.

"So today, we open the Grant Foster Cancer Treatment Center in hopes of doing just that. To keep a piece of his selfless legacy with us and to remind us all of what's truly important—to care for and protect the people who provide us with our favorite days because *they* are truly significant and irreplaceable. And that's how we plan to treat each patient who walks through our doors. Thank you."

I barely made it a step before Dallas pulled me to her in a ridiculously tight hug, which I returned.

"God, that was awesome," she said as she pulled away and beamed at me with tears in her eyes.

"We did it!" I beamed back.

"We have to cut the ribbon first," she said, taking the large scissors from Dean. I gripped them with her as we cut through the thick, woven ribbon my mom put together in every color to represent the many types of cancer.

Once cut, Dallas and I stood patiently as pictures were snapped and the crowd slowly disbursed.

"Jack," I heard Grant call out as he wiggled out of Dean's arms. I stood paralyzed as I saw the crowd part and followed Grant's movements as he flew into Jack's waiting arms.

"Easy, Rose," Dallas whispered.

"He saw the whole thing," I said, paling as my eyes met Jack's. He looked gorgeous as usual in dark denim jeans and a gray button-down shirt. He looked at me as if I was a mystery to him—as if we hadn't just spent the last three months inseparable and in each other's arms. A part of me tore in half as I felt the distance between us widen.

"He deserved to know what big shoes he had to fill," Dallas said before she stilled for another picture. "Smile, damn it. We don't get retakes," she snapped. I faked a smile, my eyes still focused on Jack as he listened to Grant tell him what was what. Forced to spend another ten minutes taking pictures, I lost Jack in the crowd as Dallas and I gave the eager reporters a short tour of the main building.

I'd spent every day of the past three weeks praying for any word from him and got nothing. I dialed his number twice and hung up the second time after he didn't return the first unanswered call. I spent very little time pretending our separation was for the best, and after the first week, I came close to losing my mind. The two Js had come to the rescue this past weekend, holding me hostage. Despite my heartbreak, I had finally come clean about everything, down to the smallest detail. I'd shown them the stethoscope and found myself comforting Jules, who had turned out to be a real softy and broke down into sobs on my behalf.

Both of them would be starting work at the center next week, and I was stuck at Memorial without them for the next year. I'd shot my foot off offering their jobs too soon. Neither of them wanted to wait. They now stood in front of me with wide eyes. I knew immediately that I was about to get a report.

"Where is he?"

"He left," they answered in unison.

"Shit," I muttered as tears sprang to my eyes.

Jules glared at Jamie briefly before she turned back to me. "Don't freak. He'll be at the party tonight. I heard your mom ask him if he would come."

"He said he would?"

"He told her he wouldn't miss it," Jules exclaimed proudly. "Let's get you home and Sandra Dee you up."

An hour into the party, and after staring at the doors from the arboretum, I began to lose hope. Jack was nowhere to be seen. I took my time making rounds, thanking my dad's crew, and chatting with the new staff as I attempted to keep from bursting into tears.

I loved him. I missed him. And now I belonged to him. It was that simple.

Champagne poured freely as everyone took to the dance floor next to the fountain. My dad grabbed my hand in passing and led me onto it with a smile.

"We haven't done this in a very long time," he said as he gripped my hand and began to lead.

"Remember when you first taught me and let me stand on your feet?"

He smiled at me with a nod. "I'm surprised you remember that. You were so little."

"It was one of my favorite days," I said fondly.

"Mine too, little woman," he said as he spun me around. "That was one hell of a speech you gave. Your mom and I couldn't be prouder."

"I had parents who molded me and gave a crap about my future. I'm the lucky one, Dad."

"You'll be the same way when you become a mom."

"Right," I said, being agreeable as I looked around. The party was in full swing, and I had to admit, it had been put together well in such a short time. I noticed the subtle touches. The finished floor-to-ceiling healing posts that Jack had spent hours on at the entrance were nothing short of spectacular. They were so intricately carved. I knew that on the nights we weren't together, that was what he was doing. Pink, white, and orange roses were arranged throughout the room in vases covered in ribbon similar to the one we cut today. I looked up at the lights strewn above us and froze. They'd been netted and woven together to cover the whole of the atrium. Soft green, blue, and streaks of white and light purple shone above us in alternating patterns as I stood in complete awe.

"Isn't it amazing?" my dad said, clearly impressed. "Jack set it up this morning before the ceremony. It's—"

"Northern lights," I pushed out as tears I could never hold fell down my cheeks. "They're beautiful."

I kept my head up, as did he, to appreciate them a little longer while he grabbed my hand and resumed our dancing. Once satisfied, my dad turned his attention back to me and noticed my freshly wet cheeks. His head reared back in surprise and question.

"I'm in love with Jack, Daddy."

My dad's eyes bulged slightly, and I quickly started damage control. "Please don't be mad at him. He treated me so well. He was nothing but honest, loving, and respectful."

"Was?" my dad said as he paused our dance and took a step back to look at me.

"I screwed up and wasn't honest with him about Grant."

"How long have you two been sneaking around?"

"Pretty much since he showed up at the center." My dad continued to dance with me as we shared a short silence before I begged him to end it. "Daddy, please say something."

"Jack," he said, looking down at me with a grin. "You love Jack."

"I do, Daddy. I do, more than anything. Lightning struck again," I croaked as I looked at him with a smile through tears. My dad stilled as he studied me, and unshed tears of his own surfaced.

"I didn't think it was possible," I said as I cried in his embrace. "I look at you and Mom and Dallas and Dean and think there isn't anyone else for you—could never be—and I thought the same for me. I was terrified to find out, but I got struck twice, Daddy. And I'm going to try to talk him into loving me back tonight if he bothers to show up. I need to know you'll be okay with it."

My dad smiled down at me with both shock and admiration. "I will say this again—like I've said a million times before—the only thing I care about is your happiness. And if Jack is the one who makes you happy, in my opinion, that's even better."

"He just didn't want to disappoint you," I said as our dance came to an end.

"Jack's good people, Rose. I have nothing but love for him."

"Thanks, Daddy," I said, giving him a hard hug before whispering in his ear. "You're my hero."

"And you are mine," he whispered back. After a few more minutes in my dad's arms, he gave me a knowing and hopeful smile. "I think I may have seen him walk through the doors a few minutes ago," he whispered to me in encouragement.

I nodded as he hugged me tightly and then reluctantly let me go.

I wandered through the bottom floor, noting all of the subtle changes in the last month, and I knew they had something to do with Jack, though he was nowhere to be found. He'd added so much charm to the lobby and adjacent rooms that there was no mistaking he was responsible. I walked into my office and stood at my desk as months of memories with him clouded me. With a sigh, I traced the wood with my fingertips, my lips trembling when I saw it. I picked up the book and felt my heart shatter as I flipped through the worn pages and whispered his name.

Jack

Some men do insane things for love.

Some never acknowledge it and deny themselves a life full of God's best gift in lieu of a career or a selfish bigger picture. They run from the notion of completion without a second thought to what they may miss.

Some men embrace love to the point of no return, let it fill their lives, their only motive, their reason for being.

Others, fueled by love's strength, pick up their sword to

fight selflessly and, without pride, lay it down for those they can't live without.

Some write songs or paint pictures to better express their appreciation or loss of life's most potent drug. They hide away in a world of their creation with a muse of love's past as their inspiration, never believing anything better than the world they've created could exist outside of it.

And some men can't handle the lethal dose of intensity that comes with loving another. These men are the most tragic, disillusioned, and helpless while staring it in the face.

I know these men because, without intention, somehow, at one point, I'd become all of them.

It took me years of soul searching, traveling the world, and collecting experiences to know I could outlast being all of them. I could, in fact, push away my selfish ambition, fight, lose, and escape the cloud of my past love. I was fighting and fighting hard because she was worth it. She was both my fuel and downfall, a double-edged sword that helped to decide which of these men I would become next.

Because, let's face it, when you give your heart away, you give the person you love the power to destroy you at will. Who you are at that moment defines who you will become next.

Those men capable of love, even the most confident, can crumble to its cruel fate.

But I'd trusted her, and that was the reason I was destroyed at that moment. I couldn't take a step in either direction. I was paralyzed by my need for her. I didn't want to be anything else than the man I was when I was with her. No matter how much strength I found, she weakened me in a way only she could validate. I belonged to her.

And her heart belonged to another.

I closed my eyes and took a deep, painful breath.

Beneath the pain, the waiting anger brewed as I studied her beautiful frame. Was I disillusioned? Or did I fight? Or had she asked me to put my sword down? Frustration rolled off me in waves as I tried to calm myself.

I hadn't been honest with her about my past, either. But I'd made peace with my past long before I met her.

Or maybe that was a lie I'd told myself, making me just as guilty.

My life had shifted just as drastically as hers. Was this the reason we crashed together in heat only to be frozen by our fears?

With Rose, my curiosity had turned into a dire need for her, her smile, her company, her body. Had we crashed together, or had I forced my way in?

There was no way I could escape her words, her truth. Even with what she didn't say when she'd confessed all, I knew I was defeated and had told her as much.

I had to remind myself again as my veins began to lace with anger that I'd asked to be cut. I'd asked for it. Now, I had no idea how to stop the bleeding.

My first instinct was to flee, to let the pain run its course and move on. I'd done it before. But my heart had other plans. It was rooted to her. Subtly and without me being truly aware, it had planted itself here—next to her. But I was unwanted, a weed growing wild in someone else's future.

And she wasn't alone.

Even as I watched her—knowing her thoughts were of me—I couldn't trust it. And I had a damn good reason not to.

I could turn and walk away—she would never know—and we would both heal with enough time.

And still, everything inside me wanted to hand her the rest of me so she could cut me deeper, even if it meant there would be nothing left.

She traced her fingers on her desk in thought, and I saw her posture stiffen and then slump as she saw the book. Picking it up, she studied it, and I knew I could no longer walk away the second she whispered my name.

Rose

"I wanted to congratulate you today, but you were busy."

Cajun

I took in a sharp breath to keep from bursting into tears.

I turned around, drank in Jack's tuxedo-clad body, and neatly combed hair as my nerve endings fired up in appreciation. My aching heart pounded in my chest.

"The lights," I said softly. "They're beautiful, thank you."

"I really wanted you to see them," he said as he kept his eyes low.

"I called you," I offered and then realized it was shit. I should have left a message begging him to call me back. I should have tried much harder, but my pride got in the way. I wouldn't make the same mistake again.

"I've been out of town working," he offered as an excuse, his hands in his pockets. I became jealous of those pockets, wanting to feel nothing more than his soothing touch. It was all I could do to keep from tearing into him. He looked better than any man in a tux had the right to. "Lubbock cell service is always horrible."

"You're lying."

He raised his brows but said nothing in his defense. Hands still in his pockets, I resisted the urge to go to him. Something about his demeanor screamed anger, and I wasn't sure I'd be received well.

"I wanted to apologize."

"You did that the last time I was here," he said absently, taking in my dress. I'd let the two Js doll me up in hopes Jack would find me irresistible, which seemed a moot point at that moment.

I was in a long black dress with a silk corset and a healthy slit down the front. It was 'elegant with just the right amount of sexy,' Jamie had declared, forcing me into heels. Jules had pinned half of my hair on top of my head and left the rest trailing down the V-shaped back. I'd felt confident and sexy when I left my house. That confidence was draining by the second as Jack stood in my office, openly glaring at me.

"Why are you so angry?"

"I don't know," he said, taking a step forward.

"Jack, give me a chance to—" He brushed past me, and I blew out a frustrated breath, ready to do whatever I had to make him a captive audience. Regardless of how angry he was, I had to tell him how I felt. I misjudged his move to leave when I turned to stop him and saw him lock the door. He was in front of me in a flash, his hands pushed through my hair, his mouth slamming down onto mine. I gave in instantly, opening wide and taking his punishing tongue. He lifted me off the floor and carried me to my desk as he sat me on the edge while his tongue coaxed mine.

Wet and eager, I reached for him and was forced on my back as he hovered above me.

"I missed you so much," I panted as he reached beneath my dress with caressing hands and shredded my panties. Without a word, he pinned me with one hand as he pulled out his hard length with the other and stroked himself as I writhed beneath him. His fingers found purchase in my ready sex, and seconds later, I was filled with him as he slammed into me. I gasped in surprise at his rough handling, and my back arched off the desk with each angry thrust.

Desperate for our connection, I looked up at him in a plea. "Jack, please."

"Please what, Rose? What do you want?" he pushed out with frustration.

"Just you," I promised as he stroked me harder and picked up his pace. "Please."

"Please," he said with menace. "Please what? Make you come? We both know I can do that."

"No," I said as my voice shook with hurt.

"No? You didn't have a problem with it while I was fucking your brains out the last three months."

"Please don't," I said, taking his punishing licks. Minutes later and dripping with sweat, he scooped me off the desk and took me with him to the chair. Still connected, I moaned on impact. He sat back, unmoving and expectant as I straddled him, his length buried deep inside of me.

"Jack," I prayed to him breathlessly. "I'm sorry."

"You keep knocking the wind out of me," he groaned, covered in hurt. "I can't even defend myself because anything I say right now will be cruel."

Unable to handle our connection, I began to move on top of him and cradled his head, staring into his eyes. "Say it anyway."

He wrapped his arms around me and began to move with me, the friction delicious and our rhythm slow. He looked on at me, lost and full of love.

"I wanted you to be mine even when you told me you couldn't be. I've never wanted anything so much." He kissed my neck and chest as I rode him slowly, memorizing him as a sinking feeling spread.

"I am yours."

"How can I believe that?" Jack murmured before he took my lips in a kiss and circled his hips. I detonated in his lap as he took my quick breaths and orgasm into his mouth. Seconds later, he came, filling me full with his hot release as he clutched me like he'd never let go—but he did. I knew he was leaving again.

"Don't," I begged him for the second time. "Don't go. Stay, and I'll prove it to you."

"I have to," he said, moving me from his lap to stand before him. I pulled down my skirt and leaned down to confront him as he tucked his shirt back into his pants. "I took a job," he said, unable to meet my eyes. "I'm going to give the traveling thing a rest for a while."

"Why?" I asked

He looked down at me, then pressed his lips to mine. When he pulled away, I could still see the same man I hurt. "I just want to be sure about us, Rose. You have a decision to make."

"Decide what? I've made my decision, and it's you."

"You weren't sure three weeks ago. You're still living in the past—with him. You said so yourself. I can't believe I'm saying this, but I'm jealous of a dead man." Jack scrubbed his face with his hands as I pulled at his arm, forcing him to acknowledge me and my words.

"You told me I didn't have to choose. You said—"

"And you don't, but I deserve a woman who can give me her future. I wanted to do it all with you, Rose, all of it. And right now, I can't see how that's possible."

Panic coursed through me as I thought of how hard the

last three weeks had been without him. "It is! I'm standing here telling you right now you're all I want! I love you, Jack."

His lips parted as he looked at me with soft eyes.

"You wanted me to acknowledge us. Well, I did. I told my dad I was in love with you." Jack gripped my shoulders and pulled me closer to him as frustration rolled off him.

"And now what? What would the next step be in our lives together? I move into the home you built with your ex-fiancé? I take his place in the life you were supposed to live with him?!"

"I hadn't thought about it," I said as I ripped my arms away from him. "It doesn't have to be that complicated."

"It is that fucking complicated? You buried yourself—" He pressed his lips into a thin line as he took a step away from me. "I'm sorry, I shouldn't have said that."

"I'm well aware of what I've done. And lying about it didn't help, but don't you dare criticize me for what I've done. I'm living in it!"

"And I can't!" Jack said, exasperated.

"No, you *won't*. If you can't let your jealousy go, that's on you, Jack," I said as I gathered what strength I had left. "I won't pretend I didn't make it hard on any man who eventually wanted to be a part of my life, but this right here is just you and your fucking pride. I'm not asking you to give anything up but that."

"Bullshit," he countered as he straightened his jacket. "You made it damn near impossible."

I moved closer to him and reached up on my toes to kiss him gently on the lips as I let him see my eyes, resolute. "Did I? Did he come between us in any way until you found out?" And even though I knew it was wrong to lie to him, I saw the realization of why I did it dawn on him.

"I can love you *anywhere*, Jack, even here, where I made

it *damned near impossible* to love or think of anyone but Grant. And I fell in love with you *here*. You resent this place now because you see it as a way for me to keep him close, and in a way, it will always be that place. But now more than ever, I'm in love with it because it's what brought you to me. It's a place filled with love and healing. It's my home. And I can love you *here*. And unless you can do the same, you're right—it won't work. *You* are the one with the decision to make, not me."

"And what if I can't make it work," Jack said uneasily.

"You have to try to fail," I said back, firm in my conviction. I would do whatever it took to make it work with Jack, but I would never give up my life's dream. I belonged at the center with my sister. I'd never been more certain of anything. Even if it meant losing a love I never thought I'd have again, I wouldn't sacrifice my life's work.

We stood studying each other for long moments, and I could feel Jack slip away from me. I wanted magic words, but there weren't any. I felt the last pieces of my heart break as he offered me nothing.

"I'm not a man who can play second fiddle."

"And if you weren't so damned blind right now, you would see that you aren't. I'm not her. And you aren't him. And we both have to let go of the past to be together."

Jack snapped back as if I'd just slapped him.

"I can't erase your past any more than you can erase mine. I'm not asking you to. I want to keep it. All of it, even the part that almost ended me. I'm not broken, and neither are you."

"How did you know?"

"You woke up one day and changed your entire life, your career path. I knew something must've happened to push you into it. We're see-through, you and me when we're together.

I've known you were keeping something from me, too. You were just better at hiding it."

Jack nodded.

"Tell me."

He remained quiet as I waited.

"Jack, just tell—"

"She was my first mate," he said in a whisper as he looked through me into his past. "The first person to really talk to me when my face was… the way it was," he said, circling his finger over his lip. "She just ignored it, like it didn't matter, and eventually it stopped mattering. I was eight."

I stood silently as he continued.

"She was the first hand I held, the first kiss. She was my first everything. She taught me how to dance, and we used to explore the swamps together. As we got older, we planned trips everywhere, all over the globe. She seemed to want it just as much as I did. She was passionate about it, about everything. She *was* my childhood in a way." He cleared his throat as emotion choked him.

"We grew up. I fell in love with her and remained devoted, but she pulled away and declared us life-long friends."

He shoved his hands in his pockets as he walked over to my window and peered through the blinds at the party. "And so, I waited for her to come back to me. But she didn't. She kept falling head first for asshole after asshole, and when they left her in pieces, I would pick them up."

I stood silent, scared, so much so that I was unable to go to him, my heart heavy as lead as his voice turned to gravel.

"One morning I woke up, drove to her apartment"—my stomach dropped—"but there were too many pieces."

"Oh my God," I said as I gripped my chest.

"I know exactly how you feel," he said as he turned to me

the heart 241

suddenly. "I've lived it, lived through it. I know that a brief explanation of what a person meant to you and how they died doesn't begin to cover it for the person who lost them." He took a fist and hit his chest. "I know this pain."

Words failed me completely as I stared at him in shock.

"I'm not a complete bastard, Rose. I'm dying a little each day without you. I just don't know how to handle this because I *have* lived it. I know what you're battling. I know how you feel… about him, how you will always feel. And now I know *why* you're so scared to love me. But mostly, I don't know if I'm the right man to walk in his shadow."

I nodded as the tear across my chest increased tenfold, and my throat stung unbearably.

"I have to go," he said as he looked at me with regret. There was absolutely nothing I could do for him. His insecurity and jealousy stemmed from a deep scar he'd suffered long ago, just as my paranoia and panic about his well-being had moved me to act irrationally and had pushed him away.

There was no quick remedy for our fears: my fear of losing and his fear of rejection.

I could tell him how amazing he was, how perfectly we fit. I could tell him how much I wanted him every day, how good he made me feel, but I knew it would be in vain. He'd been there right along with me. I couldn't force him to believe in what we had. He had to come to that conclusion on his own.

I couldn't stand to watch him leave me a second time, so I made my way to the door, my back to him, keeping my tears inside. I could fall apart all on my own. I'd perfected the art.

"I'm not sorry, not for any of it," I said softly. "No matter what decision you make, I'll never regret giving you my heart. You're the only man in the world I want to have it." I looked back at him, freely saying the words that felt so right. "I love you, Jack." I looked at him for another few seconds, both scared and beautiful, as he watched me, but no decision came. "Love doesn't have to hurt to be real. You reminded me of that."

I closed the door behind me and walked back to the party. Minutes later, as I reluctantly danced with the new lab tech underneath a blanket of Jack's stars, I watched him leave through the doors where I met him.

chapter
eighteen

"**I** FEELED IT MOVE, AUNT WOSE," GRANT REPORTED AS HE wiggled his fishing pole. "I have a fish?"

"No, buddy," I said, watching his bobber closely.

"I feeled it move!" Grant insisted as he pushed the pole toward me.

"Grant, look at your bobber, see it?"

"Wu huh," he said, watching the red and white plastic bobber as it sat perfectly still, afloat in the motionless pond.

"When that goes underwater, you know a fish has swallowed the worm. Then you jerk really hard, okay?"

"Otaaay," he said in a singsong voice, excitement evident in his features.

"Grandpa teached you how to fishing?"

"How to fish," I corrected. "And nope, it was Grandma," I said, thinking of the time my mom had taken Dallas and me out on the lake at her old house in Colorado. My dad had been busy with a project, and my mom had taken it upon herself to make us one with nature, though she refused to bait the hook and laid that burden entirely on me.

"Grandma!" Grant said, seemingly tickled at the idea of my mom fishing. He laughed heartily, and I looked down at him, his little, bare feet swinging off the dock. He was such a beautiful boy. I got just as tickled at his laughter and joined him as his bobber went under.

"Aunt Wose!" he said with big eyes.

"Okay, buddy, jerk hard," I said, setting my pole down and wrapping my arms around him to show him how to jerk at an angle. When it seemed we'd hooked the fish, I started reeling it in. Grant let go of the pole and stood in my arms, far too excited to do the rest of the busy work. When we'd pulled the fish in, and it began to struggle on the deck for air, Grant began to cry.

"No! No, I don't wanted it to died!" he insisted as I pulled the hook from the fish's mouth and held it out to him. "No, Aunt Wose!"

"Okay buddy, okay, look," I said as I gently set the fish in the water, and it thrashed wildly. "He's still alive." I looked at a clearly distraught Grant, who nervously watched the water. Was a two-year-old even capable of grasping the concept? After several moments of studying my nephew as he watched the water, I took him into my lap.

"Grant, what does it mean to die?"

"You go way up high," he said as he pushed his arms into the air, "to heaben."

My question seemed to upset him more, and I pulled him closer to me to console him. "Buddy, it's okay," I said, noting the time and wondering if he needed a nap.

"I don't want to kill the fishes," he started again, and I couldn't help the small amount of heartbreak I felt for him at the empathy he felt. Grant apparently didn't like needless suffering. I wondered where he'd gotten it from. His heart—though it had a lifetime of aches and pains to get through—was already so beautiful in that he cared so much.

"Baby, what in the world," I said as he sobbed into my chest.

"I don't want them to be died."

"You saw me put him back, baby blue. He's okay, I promise."

"Grant died. I don't want to be died, too."

And there it was—a full explanation of why my nephew was suddenly terrified of death.

"Who told you Grant died?"

"I heard Mommy say it to Daddy. Is Annabelle going to be died, too?"

Grant looked up at me with a quivering lip, and though I wanted to erase the worry from him, I felt I owed him the truth—even if in the smallest dose. It was apparent I had to do damage control for my sister, who I knew deep down hadn't meant for little ears to hear her conversation.

"Everyone dies, baby, every single thing dies, but you have a long, long, long, long, lonnnnnnng time before that happens, okay?"

"I don't want to," Grant protested. Realization struck me as I looked down at my fearful nephew and decided to break the cycle. I, too, had been afraid of death for far too long.

"Don't you want to go to heaven?" I said, kissing his sweet, full cheek and wiping his face.

"No," he protested.

"Oh, buddy, it's the best place to go. You know there are angels there that sing to you." Grant lay in my arms, sucking in shattered breaths as I soothed his back with my hands and explained what I thought heaven might be like. He was asleep in minutes as I looked over the pond and stroked his back.

My biggest fear was an inevitable fate we would all see. Death was the only absolute certainty in life, and I'd let my brush with it cripple me to the point of being afraid to fully live. It didn't matter how hard I'd try to escape it or to protect those around me from it. I would eventually lose them all. My parents, who meant more to me than anyone, would perish in my lifetime. The gravity of that alone had me slightly reeling. Who was I to think I could escape it? I was created to try to heal those preventable hurts, but it was only by design and not my own. Did I believe in God and heaven after death? I looked down at my sleeping nephew and decided then that I did. I didn't want to be a part of the bigger picture if it didn't include a sanctuary for those I loved the most after life. I had to believe Grant had a home elsewhere and lived in the tranquility of that home. That his gentle soul dwelled in a beautiful place I couldn't see, and it was full of joy. I had to believe that the beautiful baby in my arms truly had nothing to be afraid of. It was a decision to believe, just like it was a decision not to be scared of inevitable death.

And as the wind picked up and I held Grant closer to me than ever, the unthinkable happened. I completely embraced the idea and with renewed certainty.

"Grant, if you can hear me, I love you. I'll always miss you. I'll always wish you were here," I said as a few solid tears trickled down my cheeks. "I'm so thankful," I said as my chest burned. "I'm so thankful to have known you—to have loved you. God, you were awesome. I'll see you again."

I heard my wind chimes sound behind me as another strong gust kicked up and swept over the pond as thunder rolled in the distance. I grunted and stood with the baby in my arms and made it to the house just as the rain started to come down. My phone vibrated next to me as I sat in my recliner, watching the rain pound away on my deck. I looked over to see a message from Jack.

Jack: I love you.

Rose: Rap & R&B 101 Come Back to Me, Janet Jackson

In the six days he'd been gone, he'd texted me every day with the same words. I wanted to give him the time he needed to come to grips with our situation. I had no plans of giving up on him, and even though he'd been absent, I knew he wasn't going to let go of us, either. At least, I hoped he wouldn't.

Life had been cruel to us both. Even ten years after his devastation and loss, he was still giving in to his fear, but it was only through his love for me that he had to face it again. He'd lived through unrequited love and loss, and I'd put him in the position to feel the exact same hurt. I couldn't fault him for that. It made him human. It was hard to believe a man as beautiful as Jack could feel so insecure, but it made him even more real to me. He had a fragile heart—and it wasn't a flaw. It was a gift.

And I wanted that heart.

Laying Grant on my bed—a new decision made—I walked over to my desk drawer and grabbed an empty purple journal. I sat in my chair as I watched the rain fall outside and stared at the tree that had changed my world what seemed like a lifetime ago.

I picked up my pen and began to write.

We fell in love in a lightning strike, an anomaly in a sea of lost people.

"It's really coming down out there, folks," the broadcaster announced, along with flashflood warnings for the southern parishes of Louisiana. I pressed through the storm in my SUV, my wipers working overtime as renewed excitement raced through me.

I'd finished writing the story of me and Grant the previous day, and once I was done, I wrapped the journal in purple ribbon and tucked it away in a hope chest. But I knew deep inside, as Grant had professed in his last words to me, he'd always have a home in my heart.

Always.

Though I knew those memories and the time I spent with Grant would probably never truly fade in detail, I could no longer relive them the way I had been.

The same heart I swore could never hold another was now heavy and full of Jack and had been for some time. I'd just been afraid to admit it.

I missed him every minute of every day. That was how I was supposed to feel about the man I loved. I wanted to be surrounded by him constantly. I wanted that overwhelming need for him, a new and permanent part of my life. I was fully in love, totally invested in him, and determined to convince him of it.

The GPS informed me I had another twenty minutes, and I took the exit as instructed.

I spent that time remembering the rough patch my parents had gone through when I was twelve.

It had been far too obvious with the extended silences at the dinner table and my dad's long absences out of town for work. Though I'd never caught my mom crying, I could feel her heartbreak. It had lasted for what felt like an eternity. I remembered thinking—if they didn't make it, no one could. Even then, I knew how special their connection was.

But even the best, rarest kind of love had flaws and took work, patience, and dedication.

Feeling hopeless, I watched them disconnect. Those were some of my darkest days. I couldn't imagine them not being together. I couldn't imagine life with them separately, and apparently, neither could they because they'd put a stop to it. And I had witnessed it.

I was once again sneaking around for my usual midnight snack when I saw the living room light on. It was pouring outside, and I remember seeing lightning strike a few blocks away from the kitchen window. I heard the sound of the TV but knew my mom was simply staring at it without retaining anything. She'd been so quick to smile whenever Dallas and I walked into the room, but I'd wanted to—more than once—comfort her.

My dad had still managed to show up to every one of my soccer games, determined to save face, yet I felt their emptiness. Dallas ignored the tension in the house, lost in her own world, and refused to talk to me about it. I think she was just as scared as I was. I was just about to take residence next to my mom and pull a blanket around us when I heard my dad's truck brakes squeak in the drive. I dodged his headlights and jumped back into the kitchen to get a clear view of the front door. My mom lifted from the couch in confusion. When she saw his truck, she smoothed down her long hair and nightgown, then met him at the door.

My dad stood there, defeated and soaking wet, just feet away from her, as she looked at him with hopeful eyes.

"What happened?" he whispered, his voice hoarse with emotion.

"You stopped talking to me," my mom answered with the same shakiness in her voice.

"This life," my dad said with his eyes glued to her. "I can't do it without you. I can't, baby. I'm so fucking lost."

I heard my mom's soft sob as she wrapped her arms around him. "You can't shut me out, no matter what happens." I stood silently crying in the kitchen as my parents made promise after promise.

"This project just drove me insane. It's not worth it. Jesus, baby, what did I do? I'm so sorry. I'm so sorry. God, I love you. I'm so sorry," he whispered as my mom and I cried together in separate rooms.

"I should have listened, Seth," my mom said as he held her face in his hands.

"Never again, it's not worth it," he said as his mouth descended in a kiss. "You're all that matters. This family is everything."

"I know," she replied in a soft whisper and held him tightly to her. "Love me, Seth."

"I'll never stop," he whispered back as I made my way up the stairs, snack-less but with a huge smile on my face.

My parents would never truly know how much influence they had on me in the romantic sense. Maybe one day, I would confess to them just how much they'd moved me and shaped my heart. I had them to thank for the leap I was about to make. They had their timeless story, and I was ready to fight for mine.

I had no real plan but to show up in hopes that seeing me in the place he loved the most—in his world—would make a sort of difference in his outlook. I wasn't sure what it would take to convince him of my love, but I knew I had to try.

Because I was no longer the only one who needed him.

I was going to have his baby.

When the GPS told me I'd arrived, I parked quickly in the first available space and gave myself a good once over in the rearview. I'd spent the morning pampering myself at the spa and salon. It seemed I'd made a few permanent changes of my own. I looked over my carefully applied makeup, straightened my sweater dress, and noted that my Chucks were still tied. I'd never be the woman who suffered four-inch heels in lieu of comfort. I was comfortable in my shoes. The warm dress I'd bought was blue with gray flowers that reminded me of Jack's eyes.

I was six weeks pregnant, and neither of us had noticed, too involved, too busy trying to race back to each other. Even in his absence, I hadn't even blinked at my missed period or the new fullness of my breasts. It had only occurred to me when I began getting sick a few days ago to take a test, and when I did, I felt nothing but elated. Shocked but excited… and fearful. Jack and I had barely had the chance to get to know each other. I had no idea how he would react to the news or if he still wanted me.

Pushing my shoulders back with a deep breath, I ran my manicured hands through my blowout, thankful for the modern-day weapons to battle the ever-present frizz, especially on a day like today. I realized I hadn't looked at my surroundings once since I'd arrived downtown, but I ignored my disappointment. I had tunnel vision, and its name was Jack Sawyer. I scanned his building and jerked back slightly in surprise to see Jack on the balcony a few stories above me. He was staring into the distance, completely oblivious to me underneath him. I watched him for a few moments, admiring his rugged good looks as I sat there trying to come up with a good opening line and praying for some small reprieve from the relentless cold rain. The building was as old as New Orleans, that much I could tell, but it had been newly renovated. Jack had told me New Orleans was magical and that the city itself couldn't be explained but needed to be experienced. Even in the dreary setting, I believed him. Or maybe it was the optimism I felt from just looking at him.

"I love you," I whispered as I watched him, and a slow smile spread on my face. Seconds later, a beautiful woman appeared behind him. She had long auburn hair and a stunning figure and seemed way too intimately familiar with him. They said a few words, and I saw Jack's slow smile, *my* smile, light up his face.

"No," I whispered, then shouted as he looked back at her with… love in his eyes, and she folded him into her arms. I'd never been a jealous woman, not in all my years, but somehow that had changed with loving Jack. I would have to get a hold of it at some point, and bitch slap the hell out of it.

I moved quickly, unable to do anything else, and exited the SUV with a large lump of fear in my throat. I pounded up the steps, covered up to my ankles in the residual rain. I was soaked by the time I reached the doorstep and began to pound on it like a woman possessed.

I waited a full minute with no response and felt the vibration of music through the door. Minutes later, with my soul crushed and hope evading me, I was about to take my leave when a woman who looked like she'd just stepped out of Whoville greeted me.

"Hi," I said, taking in her bright green pants and purple… shirt, if you could call it that. "You must be Rory."

"Rose," she said, yanking me into the house and ripping my purse from my arm. "You should go upstairs."

I looked at her oddly.

"I saw a woman," I said as a lingering question. "He's with her up there?"

"My nephew is good-looking enough to make you crazy, I know," she said, grabbing my hand and lacing our fingers as she led me up the stairs. Holding hands with her like that was odd, but I couldn't say Jack hadn't warned me about her. She was an unusual person, as he'd described. We stopped at the doorway, and I instantly wanted to be anywhere else but froze when Rory announced my presence.

"LOOK!" she shouted at the top of her lungs as an entire table of people glanced our way. Jack's eyes met mine. He stood up slowly from the long, full dinner table.

"I'm so sorry," I said to Jack as heat spread throughout my face. "I should have called, but I wanted to surprise you." I looked venomously at the woman seated next to him and made my excuse. "Maybe you can call me when you're done here."

Jack walked over to me as if he couldn't believe what he was seeing, and the woman followed behind him while the rest of the table remained quiet. I didn't want to meet her. Why didn't Jack stop her?

"You just got here. Why would you leave?" Jack said as he gave me the same damned smile he gave her moments ago. I wanted to slap it off him.

Hormones, Rose.

"You're entertaining, apparently," I said, unable to keep the bite out of my voice. Jack laughed as he grabbed the hand of the woman who was ruining my life and squeezed it. "Told you she had a temper."

"You haven't a clue," I pushed out with pure contempt.

"Rose, this is my Aunt Nadine," he said with a chuckle as she stood in front of me with a humor-filled smile. She was much older than I'd initially deduced from afar. I wasn't sure how much older she was, but she was stunning. "And this," he said as he wrapped his arms around the next woman who approached and had his eyes, "is my mom, Amy. You've met my Aunt Rory. And over there," he said of the two men seated at the table, openly enjoying my display, "is my Uncle Spencer and my dad, Jack Sr."

I cleared my throat as water dripped from every porous surface of my body. "Nice to meet you all."

"Pleasure," his uncle said from the table, a drink in hand.

"Absolutely is," his dad said, giving me a once over and winking at his son.

"Easy, Dad," Jack scolded as his mom stood in front of me. "You're far prettier than he told us you were," his mom said before she pulled me into a tight hug. I hugged her back, afraid of soaking her, but gave as good as I got.

"All right, guys, she's soaked. Start on your dinner, and I'll bring her back in a minute." Wordless and stunned, Jack grabbed my hand and led me down the hallway—where I'd left a puddle of rainwater—then down a very long hall to his bedroom. I took a long look around at the high ceilings and the tasteful and strategically placed décor. There were masks of all kinds showcased on a shelf on his wall, along with tons of other objects I couldn't name to save my life. He had a four-poster bed that sat in the middle of the huge room, dressed in pure white. Stacks and stacks of books sat next to a newly built library case.

I was utterly floored. He'd been such a huge part of my world, and I hadn't so much as set foot in his. I pushed off the guilt as I thought of the way he'd left my world. Jack emerged from the adjoining bathroom with a towel and began to dry me off. When his attempt failed, and I was still shivering, he gripped the hem of my cotton dress, but I stopped him.

"You're soaked, beb. Take this off." Though unaware, Jack's endearment was a solid tear down in the deepest part of my chest. I shook slightly as his smell invaded me. His hands were warm, and I was suddenly freezing. Jack removed my shoes and towel-dried my hair and arms before he went in again for my dress.

"No, Jack, leave it. I'm fine." Even as I protested, my lips began to quiver. I wasn't sure if it was the rain or the man who held my heart captive.

"Lift your arms, damn it," he snapped as I looked at him with widened eyes.

When he lifted the dress and saw I had absolutely nothing underneath it, I heard his audible, "Fuck me."

"I gambled that you were alone," I said, slightly embarrassed.

"And right now, I wish I was—God, you're bare," he said as he made quick work of locking his door and pressed me up against it. "This is for me," he said as his eyes blazed with need. "We'll have to make this quick," he growled, pushing his tongue into my mouth as I gasped at the feel of his hand between my legs.

"Jack, no," I protested weakly as he spread my center, ran his fingers through it, and kissed my neck.

"You can't come to me naked underneath that fucking dress and ask me not to touch you," Jack said, pushing one finger, then two inside of me. I gasped at the feel of his warm hands as he assaulted my mouth.

"Oh God, I've missed you," he breathed into me as he worked his skilled fingers and my toes curled.

"Jack," I said as he pulled out his hard length at the same time he lifted my leg.

"Tell me to stop," he dared, his body still, eyes penetrating mine. I said nothing as he kept my eyes captive with his and pushed into me one delicious inch at a time. Vulnerable to the feel of him and seeing the man I fell in love with in front of me, without anger, I accepted him into me and wrapped my arms around his neck.

"Oh God," we moaned in unison as he buried himself to the hilt. It was so wrong. All five of his parents were only feet down the hall. Jack covered my mouth with his hand as he thrust into me, and I bit, licked, and sucked his fingers.

"More," he urged as he lifted me entirely around his waist and picked up his thrusts. I came minutes later as he sealed my mouth to his with a long moan and released into me, hot and heavy. He buried his head in my neck as we both gathered our wits. "I'll make it up to you later, I promise," he said as he kissed me slowly, the promise on his caressing tongue. "I had to have you."

"We need to talk."

"I know."

"Is this over for you?" I asked, hating myself for not waiting for the right moment or conversation.

"I'm still inside you, Rose. How could you think that?" He let my legs down as he pulled out of me and grabbed the towel to make quick work of cleaning us both up.

"Jack, I've got something that may fit her," I heard his mom call from right outside the door. I froze, butt naked, and then scrambled quickly to the bathroom, where I shut the door behind me.

"Thanks, Mom," I heard him say as the door opened and quickly closed. Had she heard us? Jesus, what were we thinking?!

I looked down at my stomach and felt a slight flutter, and I put my hand over it, willing it to calm down. The first-trimester sickness had just started, and the last thing I wanted to do was toss in front of him.

Jack knocked on the door once before he walked in with yoga pants and a sweatshirt. I took the clothes, thankfully. Jack stood in the corner of the bathroom with his arms crossed.

I pulled on the fresh clothes, took a towel off the rack, and attempted to straighten my hair.

"You look beautiful."

"You told them about me?"

"Of course, you were something good to report."

"I was?" I turned to look at him with slight defeat.

"You are," he said, taking a step forward.

"Don't do that. Just say what you really mean."

"Rose, I still love you," he said, taking another step forward.

"Well, it would be pretty shitty of you to love someone else so soon after," I countered, wanting to get to the heart of it.

"Let's go join them at the table, okay? We can talk after," Jack promised as I stood in front of the door.

"I don't have to be here. I can check into a hotel. I can wait for you there."

"Why the hell would I want that? I *want* you here," he said with slight irritation.

"Kind of hard to tell *what* you want," I said in an aggravated tone.

He was in front of me in an instant, cupping my face with his hands. "I want *us* back."

"Could've fooled me. I guess I didn't know quite how pissed off I was at you until now. Lucky you."

He chuckled as he caressed my skin. "We'll talk after dinner."

"I may not want to hear it," I said, letting my hormones talk. "Matter of fact, just shut up."

Jack laughed harder as he leaned down and took my lips. I whimpered as a tear slipped from me that told him exactly how hurt I was.

"I fucking hate to see this," he said as he wiped my tear away with his thumb. "Don't cry, baby."

"Then stop doing this to me," I said with a sigh.

"Come on," he said, opening the door for me. "I want them to know you."

"What the hell for?" Jack stopped in the middle of the room and turned back to me in all seriousness. I took in his blond halo, beautiful features, and stellar body, and my heart sighed as the flutter in my belly extended to my chest.

"Because you own me."

Well played, Jack, well played.

He reached back, took my hand, and yanked me to him. "I know we have a lot of hurt between us, but just give me dinner with my parents, and we'll sort it out, okay?"

"Okay."

We made our way back down the hall as I prayed that no one had heard us going at it. All five of his parents stopped their hushed conversations and greeted us with smiles. We took our seats at the table, and Jack piled food onto my plate. I had just shoved a heaping forkful of dirty rice into my mouth when his mom asked her first question.

"How is the center going, Rose? Have your doors opened yet?"

I nodded to give myself time to swallow as I turned to her with a smile. "We admitted our first six patients yesterday," I said with excitement. "Two of them are long-term care."

"Jack said you would be taking them in for the length of their whole treatment," Nadine said as she looked at me with admiration. "I just... we just think what you're doing is amazing, really."

"Thank you," I said, trying my best to keep from squirming under all the eyes trained on me.

"Such an accomplishment," his Uncle Spencer commented as he raised his glass toward me. I brought my glass to his and only took a small sip of the wine—I hadn't declined, so no suspicions were raised.

"So, you're in love with our Jack," Rory said without apology. The whole table went into complete mayhem when Jack's dad threw a potato pancake at her. "Couldn't let the woman have ten minutes, could you, weirdo?"

"RORY!" his Aunt Nadine scolded as Rory completely ignored their disapproval and met my eyes in challenge.

"I think you are. I think you're a woman severely in love."

Aware everyone—including an equally irritated Jack—was waiting for an answer, I stepped up to the plate.

Jack began to speak up this time as he put a hand on my thigh in reassurance, but I stopped him.

"Well, he's got an awful lot of confidence—almost to the point of being a flaw. He's outspoken and highly opinionated, and it can be overbearing. He speaks with a mouthful sometimes, which is just uncouth if you ask me. And he does that texting thing, you know, the one where he sends more than one to finish a complete thought. I hate it with a passion." His parents, all five of them, looked on at me with good humor. "He's got this whistling thing he does when he sleeps. It's not so much a snore but pushing air through his teeth—drives me insane. His clothes don't always match. He isn't a fan of base-ball, which *I* find sad and completely un-American. He's blind to any number of women vying for his attention and yet knows how to seduce them with a few select words."

Jack sat back in his chair with a chuckle and crossed his arms.

"He's not a fan of rap, which I find completely tragic since he listens to everything else."

"I love rap music," Rory said, urging me on.

"He's selfish with food, which is a major flaw as far as I'm concerned, and one of his best friends is my dad, to whom he will have no problem reporting my every indiscretion."

"Boo," Nadine said as the rest joined in chiding Jack, who turned to me with a smile.

"I mean, seriously, I have no idea what I see in him."

His Uncle Spencer raised his glass, and everyone followed. "Congrats, Jack."

Jack leaned in and kissed me solidly on the mouth with an added "Nice."

We all clinked glasses, and from there on out, conversation flowed much easier, and the whole table switched from interest in Jack and me to an apparent celebration the following night.

"Thirty-five years," his Uncle Spencer said to his aunt. "Can you believe it?"

"And I had to propose," Nadine said back to him with adoration.

"Not true, you beat me to it," he said, giving her a wink.

"Still liked my proposal better," she said as she gripped his hand and squeezed it over the table. He mouthed the words 'I love you,' and she did the same as I looked on. His Uncle Spencer was a handsome older man and had a solid head of silver hair. He was what the two Js would call a silver fox. And his wife defined the word beautiful. And it was more than obvious they were still in love.

I found it encouraging that his parents, Jack Sr. and Amy, had also been married for over thirty years. I hadn't believed him when he said our families were similar, but each minute I spent at that table made a believer out of me. Jack's mom was quiet and reserved but very well-spoken and had a sweet demeanor, while Jack's dad was just as outspoken or even more so than Rory.

"You should come tomorrow night. It's going to be one hell of a party," Jack's dad assured me. Jack looked like a mix of both his parents, getting his hair and eyes from his mom and his dad's strong features. I studied each of them as they spoke as I recalled the details Jack had told me of each of them.

"This party is thirty-five years overdue," Rory said, looking to fill me in. "They got married behind our backs at the justice of the peace. No wedding or reception. We got nothing," she bitched openly, full of contempt. Rory's current hair color was black on the top with blue and purple tips. I had compared her to a Who at first sight and stood by it now as I took in her wild, hot pink jewelry. She was overly animated, but it suited her.

I was smitten with the whole group and saw a little bit of each of them in Jack.

Rory talked a mile a minute, but I heard the last of her question, "… so will you come? They're finally going to have a wedding."

"Wouldn't miss it," I said, unsure if I would make good on my statement. Jack and I still had to talk, and for a brief second, I started to panic about whether or not he would be excited about the news of a baby. After a long meal filled with delicious food I devoured in abundance and wine that remained untouched only by me, the dinner party came to a close. One by one, Jack's parents retired to their rooms, giving us our privacy. I could see each of them smile as they hugged Jack. Nadine whispered in his ear as she left the room, and I saw a small smile play on Jack's lips. They were a highly unusual family but a beautiful one that worked. I was glad Jack had this mix of people to raise him.

They'd made him into the extraordinary man he was.

"You look tired," Jack said as he rubbed my shoulders before he began to clear the last of the wine glasses from the table.

"That's just a nice way of saying I look like shit," I said as I felt the day catch up with me.

"No." Jack paused as he looked me over in his expansive kitchen. "You look beautiful… and tired."

"I still want to talk," I said as he grabbed my hand and began to turn off the lights. "I didn't say I was staying."

"The hell you aren't," he said, looking back at me before he flipped the last light off and the room went dark.

Jack pulled me onto a large terrace adjacent to his massive living room, and I declined the tumbler full of fresh whiskey he poured us. I looked back into the house and noted a large stack of boxes in his living room but said nothing. It was time to ask the question and then really listen to the answer.

"I'm here because I miss you and no other reason. Well, there is a reason, but I'm here because—"

"I'm glad you're here. I *want* you here."

Suddenly nervous, I looked up at him as he finished his drink. I was sure I looked a mess considering my clothes, but from the way he was looking at me, none of it mattered. It never had. He'd always regarded me that way, and I loved that about him. Jack had the ability to make me feel needed and beautiful with just a simple look.

"You've pulled away from me." It wasn't a question, it was a statement, and he knew it was the truth.

"I did," he admitted. "I'm sorry, Rose. I got into my head."

"Well, are you done yet?" I said as I took a seat on one of his comfortable chairs. "You about done being selfish because I don't want to go another day wondering if you're still in this relationship with me." I stood again, my nerves getting the best of me as my stomach rolled.

Jack moved to stand in front of me, the soft light of the porch illuminating his perfect features. I didn't want to be the only one having the conversation, so I moved to touch the scar above his lip with my thumb. "Just tell me."

"I love you," he said gently. "I want you more than I've ever wanted any woman in my life. I got a little freaked out when I thought you couldn't feel the same for me. It felt like ten years ago all over again. But you were right. It was my pride. So, for the last week, I've done a little rearranging."

"You're moving."

"I hope so," he said, looking at the stack of boxes. "I thought it a little premature to fully pack for Dallas without talking to you first. I was coming to you after the wedding. I'd have already been there if it wasn't for that."

"Dallas?"

"Yes, I got on with your brother temporarily until I was sure you wanted me there."

My heart leaped in my throat as he put his arms around me. "I can love you anywhere, too."

I nodded as happy tears streamed from my eyes. "I don't

expect you to give up your life here. I know how much you love it."

"I love being with you more. I'll always call this home. I'll always keep my place here, but I want to be with you, Rose, whatever it takes."

"Why didn't you call me?" I asked, frustrated.

"Because I wanted to tell you in person," he said as he cradled my head. "I wanted to tell you I'm sorry. And I wanted to ask you if you could make room for me."

"I told you I would," I said as relief swept over me. "I want you with me."

"And I want to be there, but are you sure you can handle it?"

Guilt surfaced as I looked at him with certainty. "You don't have to worry about that, Jack, ever. Something happened to me yesterday. I can't really explain it, but I've never been more sure of anything. If neither of us had lost, we wouldn't have found each other. I can embrace that now. I'm so thankful."

He nodded as if he understood and pulled me tightly to him. "I don't work the same without you now, and I don't want to try. No amount of foolish pride could've kept me away. I hope you believe that."

"I do," I said as he rubbed a gentle hand down my back, and I gripped him closer. "I'm sorry about the way I've been acting. I don't pretend my behavior hasn't been borderline insane. I was terrified I'd scared you away."

"I just came to get my second wind," he said as he grinned down at me. "Nothing you could say or do can keep me away now."

"That's good to hear because I have to tell you something."

He looked down at me with furrowed brows, and I lifted my hand to erase them.

"I'm going to have your baby."

The smile I loved so much slowly spread over his face as he looked down at me with a mix of shock and pride.

"I confirmed it this morning. I'm due in June."

Jack leaned in and whispered, "You've just made my life."

He scooped me into his arms and walked me back down the hall to his bedroom, where he undressed me slowly and covered every inch of bare flesh he revealed. "I'm going to make love to you until the sun comes up."

"Jack," I gasped as he trailed his soft mouth all over my body, landing a wet, tongue-filled kiss between my legs. When he'd tasted me to the point of no return, he stood to undress. His eyes roamed my body and remained on my stomach. Fully revealed, I basked in his gaze.

"Tell me again," he said as he trailed kisses from my foot to my thigh and brushed his mouth over my abdomen.

"I'm going to have your baby," I said as he looked up at me with reverence, and a fresh tear fell silently down his cheek.

"There's nothing you could ever do from this moment on to make me love you more. I'm full."

"Well, you had a small hand in it," I said as I plucked at his wayward hair.

"A baby," he whispered.

"A baby that fought and won through layers and years of birth control," I said with wide eyes. "You're a potent man, Jack Sawyer."

He moved to hover above me as his lips brushed mine in temptation. "And I'm just about to drive that point home, beb."

"Jack… your parents!" I whisper-scolded. "No way. No

way," I said just as music started to blare from the adjoining room. It was rap.

"Rory?" I smiled as I looked up to Jack.

"Rory," he parroted back with conviction as he fisted my hair in his hand and captured my mouth.

"RORY!" I heard as I sat up in bed in alarm, Jack's sheet clutched to me. Jack sighed underneath his pillow as an argument began outside our door—or at least it sounded that way.

"You're damned near fifty-three years old! You can't walk around this house in a thong!"

"I'll have you know in some countries—" she started back defensively as other doors throughout the house started to open.

"What the hell is going on? It's 6 A.M., damn it!" I couldn't tell if that was Spencer or Jack Sr.

"Our nudist has decided to parade around in her underwear."

"Can you guys keep it down? Don't forget we have a guest here, and she can hear you. You're probably freaking her out." I recognized that voice. It belonged to Jack's mom, Amy.

"Look, freak show, can you just keep your damned clothes on for the weekend?" That was definitely Jack Sr.

"Who wants coffee?"

I pulled the pillow behind me to my face as I howled into it with laughter, and Jack remained where he was as another long sigh passed his lips. He smiled at me, and I sighed with relief upon seeing it. It was a smile that told me everything would be all right, that I wasn't alone in love.

It was a smile that held my future.

"Welcome, beb."

Hours later, after we'd witnessed one of the most romantic candlelit weddings imaginable, my dance partner and I swayed to Van Morrison's "Someone Like You" under the stars with the rest of the wedding guests. Jack held me closely, a new kind of protectiveness in his posture as his eyes wandered over me in love.

"Mind if I cut in," his Uncle Spencer said as Jack stilled us. He gave his uncle a solid smile as he handed me over with a kiss and a whisper that he would have the last one. I took his uncle's hand, slightly shy in my execution.

"No need to be shy. Didn't your man tell you *I* am an *excellent* dancer?" He chuckled as he twirled me underneath his arm and back again, and I damn near congratulated myself for pulling it off.

"Spencer tells me you're a judge," I said in an attempt to make small talk.

"Nah, you aren't getting off that easy," he said with a wink. "I just came to thank you for bringing our boy back. He's spent so much damned time away, I wasn't sure if he'd ever have a home."

"I can't take credit. He decided that on his own," I said as he moved me around the floor set up underneath a long, sloping oak covered in Spanish moss and twinkling lights.

"Oh, I believe you had a large part in it," he said with a twinkle in his eye.

"And now I feel guilty because he's practically moving to Texas."

"Trust me, it's much better than getting a damned new picture from Iceland."

"True," I said with a nod.

The song ended, and Ziggy Marley's version of "Drive" replaced it as my eyes widened. "I love this song," I said as Spencer kept our feet moving.

"Me too. I have a good feeling about you," he said with a wink as Jack approached to steal me away.

"Thank you for the dance," I said with a smile.

"No, thank you, Rose," he replied as he gripped his wife's hand as she approached. "Come on, baby, let's go give darkman some chores," he whispered to her as they drifted out of sight.

"Who is darkman?" I asked as I looked up at Jack, a sigh on my lips as he gave me a slow smile.

"For me, a bedtime ritual. For them, something else," he said as he looked in the direction they left. Crisp air surrounded us as fall made its presence known. "I'll tell our little man or woman all about him."

"Sounds scary."

"Anything but," he said as he looked down at me with soft eyes. "It's a wish for a long future."

After a brief grilling about what his uncle had asked, Jack swayed with me to the song we'd first danced to in my parent's living room.

My eyes on Jack's, I listened to the words as they asked the questions, and I danced with the answers.

Jack
Seven and A Half Months Later

I was stuck in a brightly lit room full of clocks that endlessly ticked. It was hell on earth. One by one, the alarms began to sound as I raced through the room to reset them. When I'd finally silenced them all, I felt a peace take over me and sat back against the whitewashed wall in relief. It was short-lived as another clock began to buzz repeatedly. Irritated and hungry for just one more minute of peace, I searched through the piles of clocks one by one and began smashing them with my fist to get the buzzing to stop.

"Jack?"

My eyes opened as I looked up to see Dallas peer down at me with concern. "You okay?"

I came to quickly, wiped the sleep from my face, and sat up in the bed. A bed I'd sought at the center what seemed like only minutes before to get some much-needed sleep.

"She's keeping you up again?"

Brushing off the last of my mid-day coma, I looked to Dallas with a plea. "She isn't getting any sleep, either. She spends the whole night tossing and turning. I'm fine."

"Jack, we really don't bullshit each other in this family," Dallas said in warning.

I bit my cheek and exhaled. "I'm exhausted and don't know how to help her."

"Only two more days and they will induce. Hang in there," she said as she left me to the single room and began to close the door behind her.

"Dallas?" I asked, still somewhere between delirious and guilty.

"Yeah, Jack?" she said as she looked on at me before a chuckle fell from her lips. "It's going to be fine."

"I was less afraid of a half-ton hungry lion in Africa," I said as I let out a harsh breath.

"She's been less than graceful with this pregnancy, I admit. But, Jack, you've been amazing. I promise you, she's just exhausted. She's almost two weeks overdue."

"I'm not complaining, I swear. I just want to help her."

"The only thing that is going to help her is getting your son out."

I looked down at my rattling phone with a sigh.

Rose: Babe, will you grab some cream cheese, salami, pickles, and horseradish?

Rose: Some tortillas and white fish.

Rose: Snickers ice cream bars. No fish.

"Grocery list?" she said with a chuckle.

"Yep," I said as I gathered my strength and gave her a weak smile. "Or a recipe for Voodoo."

"It's worth it," she said with encouragement.

"I know," I said as I grinned down at Annabelle, who gave me a shy smile from behind her mom's legs. I stared down at the little beauty until I saw her dad grab her with a, "There you are." Dean peeked over at me with a mile-wide grin and came to the conclusion his wife just had.

"It'll be over soon, man," he said as he kissed his wife's cheek and took off down the hall with his daughter in tow.

"Well," I said, gathering my wallet and keys off the table next to the bed. "Guess I better get to it."

"Jack?" Dallas said as she stood in the doorway and briefly pressed her lips together to suppress another laugh.

"Yeah?" I said, feeling slightly rejuvenated and ready to take on the night ahead.

"You might want to put your shoes on."

"This is an eviction, baby boy. I want my body back. I'm giving you notice," she said breathlessly as she lunged through the house, all baby up front and very little else. My son had completely taken over her small frame. I kept my laughter inside as I watched her from our bedroom doorway while she talked to our unborn son and frantically jumped around.

"Out! Come on! It's not so bad out here," she coaxed as she continued to do pregnant lunges across our living room.

"I'll make a deal with you," she pleaded as she wiggled and lunged in a pattern. I was about to lose my shit as I watched her tiny frame awkwardly bounce around. "You come out today, and I'll give you a brother," she said as she took deeper lunges and strained to get back up from them. After another minute of bargaining with our unborn baby, she stopped and then suddenly turned my way.

I was busted.

Her beautiful green eyes narrowed on me as I lifted her bag full of demands in front of my face as a peace offering.

"How long have you been there?" she demanded with her hands on her hips.

"Seconds," I lied as I discarded the bag on the counter, walked over to where she stood and placed a soft kiss on her lips. Her face was covered in moisture as she slumped into me with a heavy sigh.

"Did you get the chicken?"

"Chicken?" I asked as I looked down at her with confusion.

"Yes, I was specific. I need a whole chicken," she mouthed into my T-shirt. She looked up at me with wide eyes, and with a sigh, I turned back in the direction I came and started to walk out of the door with a new list flying at me.

"Make that two!"

Hours later, after she successfully dissected and repaired two whole chickens, we lay in bed, our new routine in full swing. She claimed she didn't want her surgical skills to get rusty, but I knew it was the restlessness in her that kept her moving. No matter what we tried, she couldn't get comfortable. After I'd finally talked her out of the kitchen and into a shower, she decided to attempt sleep.

"I'm so hot," she said in agony as she pushed the covers off with a huff. "Jack?"

"I'm on it, beb," I said, keeping my groan inside as I walked with my hands in front of me to avoid the wall I'd smacked into every night for the last week as I tried to maneuver in the pitch-black room to find the thermostat. Back in bed, I felt the first slap of a limb hit my chest as she tossed her small baby-filled body around without regard.

An hour after that, she curled up to me with freezing limbs. I jumped as her ice-cold hands wrapped around me. I pulled her to me tight as she looked up at me, eyes wide open.

"Cold now, huh?"

"I'm so sorry," she said as she pushed her head into my chest, and I wrapped my arms around her.

"It's okay, beb."

"No, it's not," she said hoarsely. "We haven't slept in weeks. I'm losing it, Jack. I know I'm acting a damned fool."

"Beb, you're a million weeks pregnant. I love you. I love the colorful asshole growing inside you."

"HEEEYYY," she said in offense as she smacked my chest.

"Just making sure you still love him," I said with a chuckle.

"I do," she said. "God, I can't wait to meet him," she murmured with a hiccup. "Now would be good."

I turned on the bedside lamp as I rubbed her back in an attempt to soothe her. "Let's read some."

"Now? You work tomorrow."

"I'm done," I said, giving her wide eyes. "I'm officially on leave until this kid comes out and then some. We can do lunges together."

"You ass," she said, smiling up at me. "You totally saw it all."

"Mais now, beb, jaw close," I said as I picked up our book. "One chapter left. Why don't you read it?"

"Me? You've read the whole thing," she said as she took it from me.

"Well, get on it," I said, placing my hands behind my head on the pillow as she burrowed into me further. I listened to the voice I loved to hear on the other end of the phone, the one that had turned my world upside down. The voice that would eventually shape and soothe my son, and smiled as she turned each page. I looked down at her light eyelashes and her slightly widened nose—a side effect of pregnancy—and had to press down the urge to push her beneath me.

God, I loved her. Everything about her—her spunk, her passion, her temper, her walk, the cluster of faint freckles just above the tip of her nose, the way her toes curled when she came, the way she looked at me across the dinner table. I'd started the most incredible journey of my life a year ago, and as she read the last page of the book and looked up at me in surprise, I vowed to make sure this one never ended.

"Jack?" she said as she pulled the ring from the adhesive I'd placed at the back of the book, then looked at me with tears in her eyes.

I took my cue and kneeled down in front of her as she struggled to get her emotions under control.

"The greatest adventure of my life has been loving you, Rose. This is one trip I don't ever want to come back from. Will you marry me?"

She leaped into my arms—well, as much as a severely

pregnant woman could—with an enthusiastic "Yes!" I spent the next hour thanking her for that answer until we both fell asleep.

Later that night, I woke to a new kind of alarm. This one was eleven pounds two ounces and twenty-inches long.

Rose
6 Years Later

"TUCKER!" I CALLED OUT AS I LOOKED AT MY WATCH. I had surgery in an hour and a full day ahead of me. Tucker came running across the open expanse of the park with his most prized possession in hand—a red Frisbee my mom insisted I'd loved as a child.

"Five more minutes, Mommy!"

"No, buddy, not this morning," I said as I grabbed his hand. I hated disappointing him, but I knew that once his daddy was off, he would take him fishing at our pond. It was their Friday routine.

Jack had merged his business in New Orleans with my brother Paul's. Together, they'd created a monster. The center had been recognized as one of the most effective in the U.S. within three years of opening, and Dallas and I had been running ever since. Jack refused to let our life's work overrun our time with our son or marriage, and I'd never been happier.

I looked back at my blond-haired son, who looked everything like his dad and nothing like me. I was sure it was karma for making fun of Dallas for the same thing. I pulled into the bustling parking lot of the center as Tucker told me all about the last fish he caught with his daddy. I listened carefully as we passed the house I used to occupy and honked as we saw Grant in the yard playing with Annabelle.

Jack and I had built a new house near our naked meadow. It hadn't been his decision—it had been mine. Dallas and Dean were thrilled to take up residence. Their commute had been their biggest issue when it came to the center.

I pulled up the drive to our two-story home and unbuckled Tucker just as Jack stepped outside.

"You're off early." I smiled at my husband as he greeted us at the door.

"I need my two minutes," he said as he pulled me into his arms and ravaged my mouth.

"I have surgery," I said as he let me go with a shrug.

"I'll take you, then," he said to Tucker, who squealed as Jack lifted him.

"So easily replaced," I said as I made my way back to my truck.

"Never," Jack said as he looked at me, his lips to his son's forehead.

"I love you," I said as I jumped into my truck.

They both waved as I backed out of the drive. I had a day full of surgeries, but deep down, I wanted nothing more than to go back to my house and give Jack that extra minute.

I arrived at the center and made my way inside, noting the bustle of employees. I noticed Dallas and greeted her with a brief hug.

"Surgery?" she asked.

"Four," I said as she gave me a nod and a pat on the back. "You've got this."

"Love you," I said as I made my way to scrub in. I looked into the room in front of me and noticed two extra bodies in scrubs. I walked in with my hands up as Jamie approached me with surgical gloves.

"Uh, Jamie," I said as I looked over at her with a question in my eyes.

"Dr. Whitaker," I heard from the table. "I didn't expect you today."

"Dr. McGuire?" I said in total confusion as Jules looked up at me. She simply shrugged as she glanced at Jamie with a smile.

"What's going on here?"

"Well," Dr. McGuire said in his usual no-bullshit tone, "I have a tumor to remove and all the staff I need, so from the looks of it, Whitaker, I'd say your presence isn't needed. You are dismissed."

"Pardon?" I said as I took another step into the room.

"I have three more surgeries after this, Whitaker, so if you don't mind… If you have an issue, I suggest you check with your administrator."

"I am the administrator," I said, feeling like I'd just entered the Twilight Zone.

"Dismissed, Whitaker. Go live a little." I looked to McGuire, whose wrinkled face suddenly twisted into an expression I'd never seen. The son of a bitch had just smiled at me. Completely baffled, I exited the operating room in search of my sister, who was waiting on the other side of the door with her arms crossed.

"You know he's capable, right? I mean, he *is* your mentor."

"What in the hell is going on?" I snapped as she hooked her arm into mine and led me to the entrance of the clinic. When we walked out of the double doors, Dean was waiting at his car with the passenger door open, Tucker, Grant, and Annabelle in tow.

"Dean?" I asked as Dallas shoved me into the front seat of his car and shut the doors.

"Big hug," Tucker said as I leaned down, and he squeezed

me hard and kissed my cheek. "Bye, Mommy," Tucker added as Dallas whisked them inside with a wink in my direction.

My eyes narrowed as I studied Dean, who wore an expression that told me he would be castrated if he spoke a word. I quickly texted my husband.

Rose: I'm being kidnapped!

Jack: Well, I'll miss you.

Rose: This isn't funny. What the hell is going on?

I got no response, and minutes later, Dean pulled up to Dallas Love Field Airport, where Jack waited with two suitcases in hand. Realization dawned as I looked over at Dean with wide eyes.

"Go on, Rose," he said with a chuckle as I exited the car and raced toward my husband.

"Jack, what is this?"

"Remember when you told me you would never be able to do this as a doctor? Just up and leave at the drop of a hat? I believe the words were 'Not in your lifetime.'"

"Yeah," I said with panic in my voice.

"Well, Doctor," he said as he leaned in and took my lips in a slow kiss. He pulled away as a smile crept over his face. "I just made a liar out of you."

"Jack, my patients—"

"You can save the world when you get back, Dr. Sawyer." Jack gave me a wink as he took a step toward the skycap and lifted our bags on the carousel. I followed behind him, completely stunned, as he pulled out our passports and guided me through the doors. I looked to Jack, who kissed my cheek and pulled me close to him—as close as two people could be.

"Two minutes, beb."

Moved beyond words, I let him lead as I studied him. Jack loved me beyond my career, beyond the family I had, and the home we made together. Jack loved me, heart and soul, and refused to let me forget it.

I looked down to see a text from each of the two Js. The first was a picture of Jack and Rose from *Titanic*, both at the bow of the ship, hands in the air. It had been the theme of my wedding shower, and they both thought it hilarious. I still hadn't forgiven them, but I couldn't help the smile that crept up on my face.

"Ready, babe?" Jack said as he guided us to the gate. I remained speechless.

This is your life, Rose. This is your husband. This is your reality.

As my husband guided me down the jetway, I realized people enter your life for a reason, a season, or a lifetime.

David, the first man to whom I'd given my heart, had thrown it carelessly away. For that reason, I knew our relationship was meant to be a learning experience and nothing more. Looking back, I knew I wasn't truly in love with him. I was in love with the idea, and he was far from deserving of my future. Thankfully, he knew better.

Grant had been in my life for only a season. He'd reawakened my romantic heart and renewed my faith in not only men but in humans in general. He was uniquely beautiful, and our season, though short, was perfect. I could never regret my time with him or the heartache loving him had left in his wake. It, too, had shaped me into the woman I'd become.

I looked at my lifetime as he guided me to my seat, amazed at how much life he'd given back to me. Baffled by the road I'd traveled to get to Jack, I remained thankful I'd kept my romantic heart because I knew, without a doubt, his had been waiting for mine.

Jack and I clasped hands as the plane began to speed down the runway. I looked over at him with clarity.

I knew who I was without a shadow of a doubt.

I was a wife, a mom, a daughter, a sister, an aunt, an accomplished surgeon, and as I looked down at my passport stamp and then to the lightning strike to my right, my list grew—world traveler.

THE END...*Well almost...*

FOUR YEARS AGO

Laura

I've lived a life that I would be jealous of. If someone would've told the twenty-one-year-old homeless me that I would meet, fall in love, and lose the man of my dreams and eventually reconnect and marry him fifteen years later as a wealthy business owner, have children, and remain happily married to him for over thirty years, I would have laughed in that someone's face.

That girl so lost in that park years ago, confused and completely alone, caught the eyes of the man who would spark that exact chain of events. A man both so loving and infuriating he could still bring me to my figurative knees. And still, I loved him like that lost girl did so many years ago... fiercely, unconditionally, and forever.

That man was now walking our youngest daughter down the aisle toward a man so similar in character that I wondered if she'd even thought of it.

The strawberry curls I'd dug my hands into endless times were now cropped short and tinted gray with age. His strong build remained, along with the jade-green eyes that had captured my heart and soul what seemed like several lifetimes ago.

And by his side, looking more beautiful than anything I'd ever seen, was a woman in love. A woman created from our love. A woman whom we'd cherished and raised and could never let go of. Rose, dressed in white satin, my finest and most carefully picked yellow roses in her hands, dark red hair cascading down her shoulders, looked for me and found my eyes. Her smile was breathtaking, and I hoped—with all my heart—she could see the elation and the pride in my eyes.

My baby.

Her dad gripped her tight, his smile just as filled with contentment as he led her to a man he had every confidence would make her happy. I followed them both as my heart overflowed and heard Seth's proud declaration that we together gave our daughter to Jack.

Jack overflowed as well. The only way to describe him would be beautiful. With my daughter by his side, he was absolutely gorgeous as he beamed at her, his eyes filled with wonder and enchantment.

I stayed glued as they took each other's hands and professed their love and promised to one another with tears in their eyes—their precious son asleep on my shoulder. I looked briefly at Tucker, whose perfect lips were parted, his breath sweet, eyelashes resting on his cheeks. He was a perfect mix of them both, but as he slept in my arms, I saw more of his mom than ever.

And he belonged to her in a way that she never saw coming. That's the thing with children. Upon their arrival, they surprise you by fully bringing out the amount of love you are truly capable of giving. Rose had barricaded herself in the idea that love only came to you once.

But even I knew different.

And Jack had taught her so, and her son… well, he had made her even more of a believer.

Seth sat next to me, our hands clasped tightly, fingers laced. I could feel the current of pride racing between us. As if we both thought of it at the same time, we faced each other and soaked in one another. I almost gasped as I sat next to the club kid I'd met all those years ago, his smug grin telling me he was so far past his twenty-two years and that I belonged to him. I inhaled as I saw the reflection of the dark-headed hell-raiser I'd once been. For one brief moment, we were back there. We were those kids who had fallen head first in love with so much life to live. Tears surfaced in our eyes as he gripped my hand tighter, and I nodded. He was with me, as he'd always been.

No one had a right to be this full, this happy. I could not have dreamed it better.

"By the power invested in me by the state of Louisiana, I now pronounce you husband and wife," Jack's Uncle Spencer announced with unshed tears in his eyes.

"Yay," Grant shouted as he clapped his hands and jumped up and down. The wedding guests laughed in unison as Rose leaned down and whispered, "I love you, baby blue." Grant smiled at her briefly before he ripped his sister's flower basket away and ran down the aisle, tossing them in huge clumps all over the floor. The laughter grew as Rose and Jack looked on, and Dallas quickly gathered a crying Annabelle.

And it was still perfect.

Jack took Rose's hand, and she beamed up at him with the glow of a bride. He stepped forward and enveloped his sleeping son from my arms and gave me a wink as they passed.

I know you've got them, Jack.

I looked on and soaked in every moment before I tucked it safely away in my memory.

"Thank you," Seth said at my side.

I turned to see a look I lived for. His eyes so intense, I had to brace myself.

"For?"

"Are you kidding?" He pulled me to him and held me tightly against his chest. "This life, baby. Our life."

Reveling in the moment, I broke in his arms the way I always did when Seth was concerned. "All the worthy memories of my life are with you," I whispered to him as he gripped me tighter.

"Mom, Dad," our son Paul said as he approached us.

"Walk away, Paul," I said with love and menace. "Walk away before I beat you like I never did when you were young."

Paul laughed, as did Seth, as he took immediate leave and left us standing in the park—our park—while the rest of the wedding party and guests scattered to their cars to get to the reception. Seth and I embraced as days of wedding-related stress fell away from me.

"How long do we have?" he asked as he looked down at me.

I raised a brow. "Not that kind of time."

"No, baby," he said with a sly grin. "I was thinking of a walk." He held me to his side as he led me to the far side of the park, straight to the place we met over forty-five years ago. Seth stood in front of me, his eyes filled with the same priceless memories as mine.

"What was your favorite part?" I asked in a hushed tone as the sun set beneath the trees.

Seth stood silent for several moments as he looked down at me. For a second, I thought he might not have heard me until he answered.

He cupped my face and leaned in close as his breath hit my lips. "You, you were my favorite part. It was always you, and it's not over yet."

I smiled as I thought of the years ahead of us. "I know." He leaned in and placed a soft, slow kiss on my lips. When he pulled away, the awareness was back.

"Can you feel that?" I asked in awe.

"It's amazing, isn't it? You always seemed so surprised, and I've been pointing this out for over thirty years."

"Remember when I told you we got back together for a reason? It was right here when I said it."

He nodded. "You said maybe we were supposed to be together for them—for Rose and Dallas." He looked down at me, his eyes wide. "Wow."

I nodded as the excitement raced through me. "I said maybe I gave birth to a future president or peace leader, and you said—"

"Which one?" he added. "I remember that. It's crystal clear."

"God, Seth, we sure got our answer."

"Both," he mused as he still held my face. "We did that."

"Yes, we did," I said, amazed.

I watched Dallas and Dean as they slow danced at the reception, eyes locked and full of love. My oldest daughter had taken a similar road to love as I had. She had also inherited my heart and stubborn will. I was completely enamored as Rose and her new husband danced a few feet away from them, locked in an embrace as they whispered to each other.

This night was special, and everyone could feel it, but for Seth and me, it was laced with the inner workings of fate and its confirmations. We had stumbled into love, screwed it up, fell back together, and at one time grew apart, and yet we remained.

As champagne glasses were passed out and toasts were

made, our secret celebration was further confirmed as our youngest daughter lifted her glass to Seth and me.

"When I was ten years old, I saw my parents kiss," Rose said wistfully as she stood beside her husband, who looked at her with adoration. "But this kiss wasn't just any kiss. It was filled with more love than any two people should be able to hold. It inspired me to want the same thing. So, I began to kiss everything," Rose said with a chuckle, and the room laughed. Rose stood silent for a moment, and her lips began to tremble as she looked at us. I heard Seth take in an audible breath.

"I can't tell you how beautiful it was to watch the two of you. I had no choice but to want the same for myself, and thank God I did." She looked over at Jack, who kissed her temple as she held her glass up higher to us. "You two were my guiding light, my hope, my wish for my own future. You were the foundation of the woman I've become and the heart I hold. I owe everything to you."

Silent tears fell down my cheeks as I felt Seth tremble beside me with just as much emotion.

"I am a romantic and owe this heart to my inspiration. So please, everyone, raise your glasses to my parents, Laura and Seth. To the romantics."

about the author

USA Today bestselling author and Texas native Kate Stewart lives in North Carolina with her husband, Nick. Nestled within the Blue Ridge Mountains, Kate pens messy, sexy, angst-filled contemporary romance, as well as romantic comedy and erotic suspense.

Kate's title, *Drive*, was named one of the best romances of 2017 by The New York Daily News and Huffington Post. *Drive* was also a finalist in the Goodreads Choice Awards for best contemporary romance of 2017. The Ravenhood Trilogy, consisting of *Flock, Exodus*, and *The Finish Line*, has become an international bestseller and reader favorite. Her holiday release, *The Plight Before Christmas*, ranked #6 on Amazon's Top 100. Kate's works have been featured in *USA TODAY, BuzzFeed, The New York Daily News, and Huffington Post* and translated into a dozen languages.

Kate is a lover of all things '80s and '90s, especially John Hughes films and rap. She dabbles a little in photography, can knit a simple stitch scarf for necessity, and, on occasion, does very well at whiskey.

Other titles available now by Kate

Romantic Suspense

The Ravenhood Series
Flock
Exodus
The Finish Line

Lust & Lies Series
Sexual Awakenings
Excess
Predator and Prey
The Lust & Lies Box set: Sexual Awakenings, Excess, Predator and Prey

Contemporary Romance

In Reading Order

Room 212
Never Me (Companion to Room 212 and The Reluctant Romantic Series)
The Reluctant Romantics Series
The Fall
The Mind
The Heart
The Reluctant Romantics Box Set: The Fall, The Heart, The Mind
Loving the White Liar

The Bittersweet Symphony
Drive
Reverse

The Real
Someone Else's Ocean
Heartbreak Warfare
Method

Romantic Dramedy

Balls in Play Series
Anything but Minor
Major Love
Sweeping the Series Novella
Balls in play Box Set: Anything but Minor, Major Love, Sweeping the
Series, The Golden Sombrero

The Underdogs Series
The Guy on the Right
The Guy on the Left
The Guy in the Middle
The Underdogs Box Set: The Guy on The Right, The Guy on the
Left, The Guy in the Middle

The Plight Before Christmas

Let's stay in touch!

Facebook
www.facebook.com/authorkatestewart

Newsletter
www.katestewartwrites.com/contact-me.html

Twitter
twitter.com/authorklstewart

Instagram
www.instagram.com/authorkatestewart/?hl=en

Book Group
www.facebook.com/groups/793483714004942

Spotify
open.spotify.com/user/authorkatestewart

Sign up for the newsletter now and get a free eBook from
Kate's Library!

Newsletter signup
www.katestewartwrites.com/contact-me.html

Made in the USA
Middletown, DE
17 March 2025

72805743R00176